TRACKING GAME

TRACKING GAME

A Timber Creek K-9 Mystery

Margaret Mizushima

CROOKED
LANE

NEW YORK

Published in the United States by Crooked Lane Books, an imprint of The Quick Brown Fox & Company LLC.

Crooked Lane Books and its logo are trademarks of The Quick Brown Fox & Company LLC.

Library of Congress Catalog-in-Publication data available upon request.

ISBN (hardcover): 978-1-64385-135-8
ISBN (ePub): 978-1-64385-136-5

Cover design by Melanie Sun
Book design by Jennifer Canzone

Printed in the United States.

www.crookedlanebooks.com

Crooked Lane Books
34 West 27th St., 10th Floor
New York, NY 10001

First Edition: November 2019

10 9 8 7 6 5 4 3 2 1

In memory of my parents,
Norman and Gwendolyn Minks

ONE

Tonight, the stage had been set for love. The ladies of the Saturday Evening Club had transformed the Timber Creek community building into a tropical island for the Celebration of Summer dance. Romance mingled in the air with the scent from huge flower bouquets that towered in each corner of the hardwood dance floor. Brilliant-orange bird of paradise and scarlet ginger plants spiked from vases above purple hibiscus and the draping spray of rosy bougainvillea. Smaller arrangements graced the bandstand, which framed a local group who specialized in country and pop hits.

Deputy Mattie Cobb stood by the refreshment table, watching the dancers, with her date Cole Walker. Though she'd set her law enforcement duties aside for the evening, she was finding it hard to relax and have fun. Her relationship with Cole had grown more serious during the past few weeks, which should have been fine, since it was what she wanted. But she felt like she was harboring a secret that she needed to get out in the open, and the right time had yet to arise.

"Let's dance," Cole said, slipping his arm around her. But before they could move to the dance floor, he stopped and reached for the cell phone in his shirt pocket. Frowning, he glanced at the screen. "Sorry, Mattie. I have to go outside to take this call."

"No problem." Mattie leaned against the wall while she waited. She'd learned that interruptions often accompanied a relationship with the only veterinarian in town, and she truly didn't mind. She loved her German shepherd partner, Robo, more than life itself, and she understood how Cole's clients must feel when they needed help for their animals.

Soft light from a hundred faux candles flickered throughout the room. Couples circled the floor, their feet gliding in various versions of the two-step, performing single and double turns and reversing direction, each pair executing their own signature moves while keeping up with the ceaseless counterclockwise flow.

Mattie's friend Rainbow danced past, resplendent in a flaring tie-dyed chiffon tunic over tight-fitting jeans. She snuggled close to an unfamiliar, rangy cowboy, her blond ponytail swinging as she leaned back to say something to him. The man, dressed in jeans and a turquoise western shirt with a black thunderbird on the back, bent to listen to what Rainbow was saying, his Stetson tipped low to cover their faces. He threw back his head and laughed, then stole a quick kiss before he twirled her away into the crowd.

Mattie sighed. Rainbow, dispatcher at the Timber Creek County Sheriff's Department and the daughter of two hippies, loved almost everyone. It was all so easy for this friend of hers—crossing over from friendship to love and then back again.

Not so for Mattie. Despite the festive atmosphere, she couldn't shake the ache in her chest that had been with her for weeks. It felt terrible to be so confused about something that should be so simple. Falling in love wasn't supposed to be this painful, was it?

The band ended a lively number and began to play the opening melody of a love song. Its melancholy strains touched her, making her yearn for an emotional lightness she'd never experienced. During her childhood, love and intimacy had meant secrecy and pain; in high school, rebellion and excitement; in junior college, escape and a numbing of bitterness.

What did love mean to her now? Cole had said the words *I love you* several times during the past weeks, but for the life of her, she hadn't been able to say them back. Why did it all have to be so complicated?

She wanted to move forward in her relationship with Cole, but her childhood loomed between them like the two-way mirror Sheriff McCoy had recently installed in one of their interrogation rooms at the station. She could see Cole clearly, but she and her baggage remained hidden from him.

Cole didn't seem to sense the barrier between them like she did. She needed to confess to him how Harold Cobb, a man she no longer considered her father, had abused her when she was only six years old, and she needed to do it tonight. She hoped it wouldn't change things between them.

Cole returned, taking her hand to lead her to the dance floor. She hesitated. "Do you have an emergency?"

"No, a client called to report. Everything sounds good."

Although part of her wished they had to leave, she followed him until he turned toward her to dance.

She suppressed a shiver of pleasure as she moved into his arms. Cole was a good dancer, and she swayed with him, his dark eyes holding her until he flattened her palm against his chest, covered her hand with his, and drew her closer. She rested her cheek against him, letting the music take over.

Even though they'd been building a relationship for months, tonight was their first official date in public, and he didn't seem to mind showing the world that they were a couple. Timber Creek would be abuzz with the news next week, because nothing escaped the small-town party line.

Quit thinking so much, she told herself. *Just feel.*

The band played their version of "Hello," a classic love song originally recorded by Lionel Richie. She concentrated on Cole's solid chest beneath her fingertips, the music's slow rhythm, his hand on her back—until the song's lyric lured her into thinking again.

The lead singer was begging his sweetheart to tell him how to win her love. Was she herself too damaged to return Cole's love in a way he deserved? Would he grow tired of dealing with her issues?

The walls moved closer; dancers pressed against her. Sweat popped on her brow, and her heart tripped a panicky tattoo as her claustrophobia kicked in. They were dancing near the entryway, so she seized Cole's hand to take him with her as she marched toward the open door.

When she reached the concrete porch, she slowed. "I need to catch my breath."

Cole slipped his arm around her waist. "It's stuffy in there."

She went down the few steps off the porch and skirted around the edge of the building, slipping between the cars in the parking lot. "I get a little claustrophobic sometimes."

"Yeah, I know what you mean."

Cole didn't know the extent of how bad it could be. She led him through the cars to the grassy park behind the building, choosing a towering cottonwood to lean against. The rough ridges from the old tree's bark grounded her as they pressed against her shoulders.

Cole rubbed her bare arm beneath her short-sleeved tee. "Are you warm enough? It's chilly out here."

"It feels good. It was too warm inside."

He faced her, moonlight filtering through the tree's canopy to cast shadows on the planes of his face. No doubt this man was handsome, with his dark chocolate eyes, close-cut brown hair, and easy smile. Last summer, they'd met through police business, and she'd thought he was married instead of recently divorced. Neither of them had sought a relationship, but they'd been drawn to each other from the start.

He turned to lean against the tree beside her, his arm brushing hers lightly.

She grasped at something to say and thought of his daughters, who were out of town visiting their mom. "When will the girls come home?"

"They'll be with Olivia until the middle of next week. After that they'll stay with Jessie a couple days. She'll bring them home a week from today and then stay to visit Mom and Dad."

Jessie was Cole's sister who lived in Denver. Generally, Mattie felt drawn to dogs more than people, but Jessie seemed direct and kind, someone who said what she meant so that you didn't have to guess. Cole's parents, whom she'd not met but could recognize by sight, owned a ranch outside Timber Creek. "I bet you miss the kids."

"Like crazy at first. The house was too quiet. Now I'm getting used to having some time to myself, although it's easy to fill it with work."

"I get that."

"I've noticed." She could sense the smile behind the words as he took her hand. "We share that tendency."

Someone opened the windows on the back side of the building, and the music drifted into the park. Another slow song.

Cole moved away from the tree, pulling her against him into dance position. He swayed with the beat. "You're a good dancer."

"You, too."

"Where did you learn to dance like that, Miss Mattie?"

He always could make her smile, despite the seriousness of a given moment. "In a bar over in Willow Springs when I was in college. And you?"

"I grew up dancing." He swayed with her in more of an embrace than a dance. "We move well together."

With his hand beneath her chin, he tipped her face up toward his. She closed her eyes as his lips touched hers.

The siren on top of the water tower began to blare, interrupting their kiss. They pulled away from each other a few inches to listen to the signal that called in the volunteers who made up the bulk of their small town's fire department.

Boom! An explosion from the west echoed off the building.

Mattie turned to search in that direction, seeing nothing but shadows and trees in the park. "What was that?"

Cole's hand lingered at her back. "I don't know."

Her mind jumped to Robo—she'd left him at home on the west side of town. "Let's go. I want to make sure that fire isn't at my house."

They rushed around the side of the building toward the front, where people spilled out onto the porch. Several headed off to their cars, while amid subdued laughter, others speculated on what was going on.

At his truck, Cole opened the passenger door for Mattie and handed her up into the seat before hurrying toward the driver's side. After starting the engine, he threw the truck into reverse, angled out of the narrow parking space, and steered toward the highway. "Let's beat the rush out of here."

Mattie pulled her cell phone from the hip pocket of her jeans and tapped the number for the sheriff's station. Sam Corns, the night dispatcher, answered.

"What's up, Sam?"

"Burning vehicle out on west County Road Seven. Fire department notified."

"How far out?"

"About a mile north of Highway Twelve."

It would take only a few minutes to get there. "I heard an explosion."

"Don't know what that was. Person who called in said it was a burning van before she disconnected."

"All right. I'm on my way."

"Fire trucks should be there soon. Garcia's on his way, too," Sam said.

Garcia kept night watch in Timber Creek, but in this small town all department employees were expected to be on call for emergencies. Mattie ended the call and turned to Cole. "It's not at my house. It's on County Road Seven."

Cole turned at the next intersection and reset his course. "What is it?"

"A burning van."

His eyebrows shot up. "Gas tank must've blown."

"Maybe. Although that's not as common as it's made out to be."

When they reached the highway, an orange halo glowed in the west, the blaze leaping up and taking shape as they turned onto the county road and drew near. Flames consumed a panel van that was parked on a pull-off at the side of the road. A pickup truck sat beyond the van, its driver's side door hanging open and its headlights backlighting three figures in the barrow ditch, one person lying near the van and another hovering over a prostrate form closer to the pickup.

Mattie opened her door as she spoke. "Pull over here, Cole. Don't park too close in case that van blows again. Leave your lights on."

Staying as far away as the fencing allowed, she skirted the burning vehicle, her shoes crunching on broken glass. Heat poured off the van in waves and fire curled around its body, creating a great whoosh as it gobbled oxygen. As she ran toward the people in the ditch, she raised her bare forearm to shield her face, and the intense heat stung her skin.

She stopped at the first person she came to, a man lying facedown, his clothing torn from shrapnel, a bloody wound on the back of his head. She knelt, curling her fingers against the front side of his neck, feeling for a pulse. Cole passed by, heading toward two other people about twenty feet beyond, where a woman was calling for help.

Cole evidently recognized the woman's voice. "Leslie!"

Leslie shouted to Cole. "It's Garrett. He's unconscious."

Mattie's gut wrenched as she realized that the man on the ground beside Leslie was Cole's best friend, Garrett Hartman, a man Mattie knew, respected, and yes—loved unconditionally. She'd met the Hartmans last summer after their daughter Grace had been murdered. Though her mind screamed to go see how badly Garrett was hurt, she had to let Cole tend to him while she focused on the man before her.

She couldn't find a pulse but noted a large bloodstain on his shirt. She strained to turn him faceup, bent to listen, and felt for a breath. Nothing.

She tore open the snaps on his western shirt. Blood covered his torso. There were two darkened wounds on his left upper chest. Bullet wounds? Though she believed it hopeless, she decided to try CPR.

Mattie positioned her hands over the lower part of his sternum, but when she pressed hard to deliver chest compressions, dark blood gushed from the wounds, streaming onto his chest and covering her hands. *Heart shot.* CPR would never bring this man back to life.

Fear that Garrett had suffered the same fate drove her to move on to see if she could help with him. She ran to Leslie as Cole bent over Garrett, touching his neck, apparently seeking a pulse. Waves of heat boiled off the blazing van. Shattered glass and debris littered the area around them.

Cole shouted above the noise from the fire, "What happened to Garrett?"

"He got knocked out when the van exploded!" Her eyes wild, Leslie pointed toward the man Mattie had just left. "That's Nate Fletcher! Garrett was carrying him on his back, but the blast knocked them down. I dragged Garrett over here."

Mattie needed to know what happened. "Did someone shoot Garrett?"

Leslie looked startled but shook her head. "No. He was fine until the van exploded. Why?"

Two bullets to the heart meant someone had shot Nate Fletcher at close range with the intent to kill. "Which vehicle is Nate's, Leslie?"

Leslie pointed at the blazing van. "The van! We were on our way to town and saw it sitting here, already on fire. Garrett tried to get Nate out to safety, but it exploded!"

Cole still knelt beside his friend, apparently assessing his condition, while Mattie's heart thudded at her throat. *Who in the world could've killed Nate Fletcher? And did the person who shot him torch his van to destroy some kind of evidence?*

Mattie turned her attention back to Garrett. "How is he?"

"Something hit him here." Cole indicated the back of Garrett's head. "He's unconscious, but respiration and pulse are steady. Lots of small cuts but no serious bleeding."

Mattie held Cole's gaze for a heartbeat while mutual fear passed between them. The Hartmans had lost their only child, and now this. This couldn't be happening to the couple.

Sirens warbled from town, signaling that help was on its way.

Cole's eyes flicked past her toward the dead man. "What about Nate?"

Mattie gave a subtle shake of her head, not wanting to frighten Leslie even more. Because there was a real chance the man Leslie loved would meet the same end.

TWO

Heartsick, Cole huddled beside Leslie as they watched two EMTs stabilize Garrett's neck and then lift him onto a stretcher. It felt unreal. His best friend, so strong and vital, lay limp and unconscious while they moved him into the back of the ambulance.

Leslie gripped Cole's hand. "I have to go with him."

Cole intercepted one of the EMTs, introduced Leslie as the patient's wife, and got permission for her to ride along. He helped her up into the ambulance, where the EMT guided her toward a short bench seat against the side panel.

"I'll follow and meet you at the hospital," Cole shouted as the door closed, leaving him with the image of an unresponsive Garrett lying on a stretcher, a sight that made his stomach clench.

He remained in shock over what had just happened. Garrett Hartman was a kind soul, his heart as big as his stature. *He has to be okay*, Cole thought. *He just has to be.*

Mattie appeared at his side and touched his arm. "Can I catch a ride to my place before you go to the hospital?"

Firemen were dousing the blaze with their hoses, but in the beams of the respondents' headlights, he could see reddened patches on Mattie's cheeks. He took her right hand and lifted her arm so that he could examine the blisters beading her forearm. Compared to his, her skin was soft and tender, and she lacked the protection of the long sleeves he'd worn. "Did you have someone treat your burns?"

"Garrett needed help more than I did. Come on, let's head back to town. I need to get Robo to help us with this crime scene. Stella's here to take over, so I can go."

Stella LoSasso, the detective who worked with Mattie at the Timber Creek County Sheriff's Department, would be in charge if there had been foul play. Cole hadn't had a chance to talk with Mattie privately yet, but he suspected that foul play was exactly what they were dealing with here. Nate's van hadn't turned into a fireball through spontaneous combustion; someone had to have burned that van on purpose.

He followed Mattie to his truck. After starting the engine and pulling onto the highway, he voiced the question. "How did Nate die?"

"He was shot, Cole. The scene is a mess now, so Robo probably won't be able to find evidence, but Stella and I thought we should try."

Though he thought he'd taken all the hits he could for the night, the news came as another shock. "Who in the world would shoot Nate Fletcher?"

Mattie peered at him from her side of the truck. "Do you know Nate?"

"He's married to Kasey Redman. She's Lillian and Doyle Redman's daughter. They own most of the valley to the north of the highway out there."

"I'm familiar with the ranch; it's a Timber Creek landmark. I vaguely remember Kasey from grade school, but she's several years younger than me."

They'd hit the edge of town, and he turned onto her street. "Nate Fletcher makes a living as an outfitter. He has a string of horses with a ready-made way to take care of them on the ranch."

"So Nate and Kasey live on the ranch?" A glance told him that Mattie looked worried, a feeling he shared. What a terrible way to end their date: another killing in Timber Creek.

"Yeah, they have their own house, but they live there, and so does Tyler, Kasey's younger brother. The ranch is huge, and part of it borders my parents' place. I grew up knowing the family. They've had some tough times this past year."

"How so?"

"Kasey's dad had a major stroke last fall. Spent some time in rehab, but he's home now. I heard it affected his ability to talk and use his right arm."

"And now we're going to have to tell Kasey that her husband is dead."

Cole parked in front of Mattie's house and turned off the engine. He didn't want to leave her like this. Not yet. "Let me look at that arm before I go."

"You need to get to the hospital for Leslie. I can take care of it." She reached for her door handle, giving him a thin smile tinged with regret.

He stepped out of his truck. "It'll only take a few minutes. I'll get supplies from the back and meet you inside."

While she hurried to unlock her house, he searched for gauze and ointment in the mobile vet unit that filled the bed of his pickup. Robo barked from inside, but as soon as he cleared the doorway, he leaped off the porch and charged out to the truck, white teeth flashing in the moonlight. Thank goodness, the dog was grinning.

Cole gathered supplies in one hand in order to free the other long enough to ruffle the fur on Robo's neck. At one hundred pounds, the black-and-tan German shepherd could tackle a man twice his weight and bring him down. Cole knew, because he'd seen him do it. But unless Mattie told the dog to attack, he was a friendly guy, and although Cole was Robo's vet, the dog visited him and his family often enough to think they were best buddies. Cole hoped to keep it that way.

"Robo, take a break." Mattie's way of telling him to do his business.

Cole closed the back of the mobile unit and headed toward the porch while Mattie held open the front door. He stepped inside, glancing around her small living room. Though he and Mattie spent most of their time at his house with the kids, he'd been here before and knew the general floor plan—bedroom off to the left down a short hall, kitchen off to the right through a doorway. He pushed aside his hope that he could spend time with her here tonight and took a right. "I'll set up in the kitchen."

Energized from an evening nap, Robo barreled in behind him. Cole placed his supplies on the counter, and Mattie came up beside him while Robo settled at her feet, head tilted up to watch. Cole reminded himself to move slowly and carefully when touching Mattie, because he had no doubts about how seriously Robo took his duty to protect his girl.

He held out a hand toward Mattie and waited for her to place her wrist in his palm. "Let me take a look."

She'd worn a snug, black T-shirt over jeans to the dance. She looked great—more than great, actually—but her bare arms had suffered from lack of protection when she'd sprinted past the van.

It scared him the way she always rushed to the front line, no matter what she was doing. While he loved that about her, it caused him no end of worry in light of the danger associated with her job. A cop—a K-9 cop, no less. Always out front, searching for the bad guys.

The reddened skin on her forearm bore a cluster of small blisters, running from the fine bones of her wrist almost to her elbow.

Cole drew her toward the sink. "Let me wash my hands, and then we'll run some cool water over this."

"It doesn't look too bad."

"I bet it hurts."

She shrugged. "Some."

His tough girl. He washed his hands, set the water to a cooler temperature, and placed her arm under the drizzle. She sucked in a breath.

"You can take whatever you have for the pain, but I'll put on some cream that contains lidocaine, some aloe, and an antibiotic. That should soothe it. Then we'll dress it with sterile gauze. Let me check it again tomorrow, but if it starts looking like it's infected, we should get you to Dr. McGinnis."

"I'll wear a uniform with long sleeves to protect it."

Cole held her gaze, her brown eyes serious and intent. He could tell she was already planning what she needed to do next to start this investigation. He'd hoped he could show her exactly what she meant to him tonight—if she felt the same way, that is. Sometimes it was hard to tell exactly how Mattie felt, and he remained fearful that she would withdraw again like she had last spring.

Gently, he applied the cream and then wrapped her arm. This way of showing his love would have to do for now. He could tell she was anxious to get back to the job, and he needed to get to the hospital to support Leslie.

As he finished securing the gauze bandage, she surprised him by placing her hand against his cheek. He turned his face into her palm to press his lips against it.

"Thank you for taking care of me, Cole. No one's ever done that like you do. I appreciate it."

He knew she'd had a tough childhood, and she'd built a wall between herself and others, a wall he was trying to climb over. "I like doing things for you. I'm grateful when you let me."

He tipped her face toward the light to inspect the reddened skin on her cheeks. "This isn't as bad as your arm, more like a sunburn. I'll leave this cream for you to put on to help decrease the sting. Promise me you'll do that before you go back out."

She gave him a small smile. "Call me when you know something about Garrett, okay?"

"Sure. I'll need to hear your voice."

"This isn't how I thought this evening would end," she said, frowning. "Not that I should be thinking of us, in light of what's happened to Garrett and Nate Fletcher."

Cole took her in his arms and held her close. "I love that you're thinking of us. Kiss me now before I have to go."

The way she slid her arms up to hold him, cupping his neck with her hand, sent a shiver of pleasure across his shoulders. Her lips were soft and responded to his when he deepened the kiss, until Robo squeezed between them, forcing them to pull away from each other reluctantly. The dog pranced around the floor at their feet, trying to get their attention.

"Our chaperone," Cole said. "Let's remember to leave him home on our next date."

Mattie's already reddened cheeks flushed, and she bent over the shepherd, ruffling his fur. "You're incorrigible."

Cole hoped she was talking to her dog. "I'll leave these supplies here, so that if your dressing gets wet or soiled, you can change it."

She turned to go with him toward her front door. "Be safe. Don't drive home if you're too sleepy."

"Yes, ma'am. Call me."

"You do the same."

He hurried to his truck, turning his thoughts back to Garrett and Leslie Hartman and his fears about their well-being. He knew of no one else who'd suffered the terrible loss of a child and survived as gracefully as they. While a child's death could sometimes drive parents apart, it seemed like it had only drawn the Hartmans closer together. Leslie was a strong woman, but a person could only take so much.

He turned toward home so he could put his own dogs, Bruno and Belle, into their outdoor run, in case he couldn't make it home to let them out in the morning. His resident housekeeper, Mrs. Gibbs, had taken advantage of his kids' vacation to go visit her daughter, so she wouldn't be around to help.

This was nasty business with Nate. Poor Kasey. What in the world was going on? Nate was just a rancher, a man who'd married into a family that was tied to the land, and he'd seemed happy to join them in their livelihood.

He thrust these thoughts aside and focused on driving. Mattie was right; he needed to stay safe on the road, because terrible things could happen and life could change in a heartbeat.

THREE

In a hurry to get back to the crime scene, Mattie splashed cool water on her face before applying the cream to her reddened skin. When she glimpsed herself in the mirror, she wondered if there was someone out there in the world who resembled her. A few weeks ago, she'd submitted her DNA to an ancestry database, and she watched her email daily, hoping for a match. She loved her Mama T—no one could ask for a better foster mom—and she'd recently connected with a foster sister named Doreen, but she still wanted to know if her biological mother or any other relatives were out there looking for.

When she thought of family, memories of her brother Willie surfaced, as they often had since his death the month before. His loss and the way he died still haunted her. It hurt to think that she'd missed the opportunity to reconnect with him, and she supposed it always would. She'd let emotional scars from her past delay their reunion, a mistake she wouldn't make again if given another chance to unite with relatives.

Robo followed her into her bedroom to watch her strap on her Kevlar vest and put on her uniform. He darted back and forth to the front door, revved up and ready to go to work.

That was Robo. No matter if it was day or night, he found his job exciting.

"Let's go." Her words set off his usual scurry toward the doorway, toenails skittering across the hardwood floor. Mattie lagged behind to retrieve her service weapon from her gun safe. She racked the slide, checked the cartridge, and jammed it back home.

"Okay, buddy. Out to the car."

Her uniform's long sleeves felt good, because the velvety evening had turned chilly. Robo loaded into the back of the K-9 unit, a converted Ford Explorer, and she paused to check her supplies before leaving. All was in order, so she jumped into the front and headed toward the crime scene.

She thought of Cole while she drove. Remembering his tenderness when he'd treated her burn made her teary. If she was being completely honest with herself, she had to admit she was glad she'd been unable to share details from her past with him tonight. What if doing so drove him away? She didn't think she could handle losing Cole now. Not after how close they'd become since Willie's death.

When she reached the outside of town, she could see flashing lights from emergency vehicles in the distance, but the orange glow of the fire appeared to be extinguished. Gravel on the county road peppered the bottom of her car, and as she drew near, smoke thickened the air. The flames had been doused, leaving the blackened body of the van's hull a sodden mess. Firefighters remained on the scene, aiming spray from the fire truck's tank at the van's undercarriage.

As she parked, her headlights illuminated Stella. The detective had pulled her auburn hair into a ponytail, and she wore a brown Carhartt jacket with a Timber Creek County Sheriff's insignia on the sleeve. She'd elected to stay home instead of going to the dance, saying she preferred not to have to deal with cowboys and their wandering paws. Stella had once shared that she'd divorced a cop not all that long ago, and the bitter tone of her story led Mattie to believe that she didn't hold any fondness for most men in general, at least not for the time being.

Stella came to the passenger side and climbed in. "Gotta warm up a minute. With all that water, it feels like hell frozen over out there."

Mattie restarted the engine and turned up the heater.

Stella leaned forward and rubbed her hands together near the vent. "I released the body and the coroner took him away. I wanted to preserve whatever I could on him for the medical examiner. I marked his position, and we'll need to take measurements of the crime scene layout as soon as we can get in there to work."

"Some kind of accelerant must have been used to create that kind of a blaze. Probably to cover up evidence, but it'll be hard to sort that out now."

"I've called CBI," Stella said, referring to the Colorado Bureau of Investigation, "to request a crime scene unit and fire investigation team. I'm not sure how soon they can get here."

Mattie recalled the two bullet entry wounds she'd seen on Nate's chest in a tight pattern over his heart. The person who'd pulled the trigger had been close. "I think Nate Fletcher might have known his killer."

Stella stared out the windshield at the blackened van. "Shot at close range. Sitting in his van at the side of the road. He could've stopped to talk to a stranger, but the familiar shooter plays out better. Did you know Mr. Fletcher?"

"No, but Cole did." Mattie summarized what she'd learned from Cole. "I'm a little familiar with his wife. She was a few years behind me in school."

"What do you think about her as a suspect?"

"I don't know her well enough to have an opinion, but we'll have to look at her." In a case like this, and especially with suspicion of a familiar shooter, you always had to look at the spouse.

"With Sheriff McCoy away on vacation," Stella said, "I'll need to notify her. I want you to go with me to help observe reactions. After you let Robo do what he can with this scene, we'll go on out to the ranch."

Upon hearing his name, Robo came to the front of his cage, and Stella turned to thrust her hand through the heavy-gauge steel mesh grill that separated his cage from the rest of the unit. She buried her hand in the fur at his neck. "You're warm, you big lug. Mattie, your partner comes in handy for more than just his nose."

Stella knew only part of it. Robo had become Mattie's best friend and protector. He'd saved her life in more ways than one, and he was about the only fellow being she could whole-heartedly trust.

The firemen were rolling up hoses, evidently having drained the fire truck's reservoir.

"Looks like they're finishing up out there." Stella tousled the fur behind Robo's ears as he leaned into her hand, looking like a big teddy bear. "Game on, Robo."

Mattie turned off the SUV's engine, slipped on a jacket similar to Stella's, and stepped out into the damp breeze. The acrid stench of burned rubber and plastics hung in the air. What with the washed-out soil from around the truck and the smoky residue of scent that surrounded the area, she wondered how Robo could find anything at all. But dogs had the special ability to sort through layers of scent and home in on whatever they were searching for, and she had confidence in Robo's nose.

Stella joined her at the back of the Explorer just as Chief Deputy Brody drove up in his cruiser. "Here's Brody. I wondered if they'd be able to reach him."

Mattie opened the hatch and leaned in to pet Robo. She'd spied Brody early at the dance, circling the floor with various partners until he'd settled on a tall blonde with an athletic build who looked like she knew how to handle herself on a dance floor. Brody, built like a wedge with seriously broad shoulders and the energy of a jackhammer, had appeared to be in his element, twirling his partner in a series of gymnastic moves. Thinking back on it, she realized they'd disappeared and he hadn't returned.

Stella headed to meet him, and Mattie heard her start to brief him on what they knew so far. Brody was in charge of the department in the sheriff's absence, while Stella would head up the investigation, but they would all work on the case together.

Robo snuggled against her, wagging his tail as she patted him down—part of her method to rev up his prey drive, his cue that it was time for the hunt. "Are you thirsty, Robo? Let's get you a drink."

Because moisture enhanced a dog's olfactory ability, she splashed fresh water into his collapsible bowl from a jug she kept stored in his compartment. He lapped at the water while she debated which equipment to use. His blue nylon collar was used for evidence detection, while his search harness was typically used for tracking a human. She needed to use both tonight.

As a police patrol dog, Robo was trained in search and rescue, search and apprehension, and detection of narcotics and gunpowder, so he could find spent shell casings, dope, and people. With this dog, the specific equipment wasn't as important as it might be with others; he often seemed to take on whatever task lay before him, whether she'd planned it or not.

She looked toward the hay meadow beyond the burned van and wondered if Nate Fletcher's killer could still be out there in the darkness, observing the theatrics of the firestorm he had created. She decided on Robo's harness and stuffed the collar into her utility belt, thinking they would look for the shooter's scent first. She strapped on Robo's Kevlar vest, and because of the amount of shattered glass in the area, she decided to put on his leather booties to protect his feet.

With a hand gesture, she signaled Robo to jump down from the vehicle. The booties made him high-step around for a few seconds before gliding around her legs and attaching himself to her left heel. He gazed into her eyes with expectancy. On the job.

Brody sauntered over, his thumbs hooked into his utility belt, resembling a well-sated feline. Or maybe that was just her read on him, knowing what she did. Stella followed and they huddled together.

"CBI called," Stella said. "They'll have a crime scene unit here in about thirty minutes."

Mattie scanned the litter in the area. "The spray from the hose has probably washed anything useful out of the van, but I can have Robo search for evidence as soon as things cool down. First, I want to see if there's anything he can tell us about the shooter."

Brody cocked an eyebrow. "Ask him to give us a description?"

Mattie gave him a thin smile. "Seriously, I wonder if the shooter stayed around out there."

They all turned, trying to search beyond the headlights into the meadow. The moon cast enough light to reveal a stretch of rolling grass dotted with haystacks, but that was about it. The base of the foothills defined the farthest edge of the field over a mile away.

"If anyone's out there, you and Robo would be sitting ducks," Brody said.

"Not sitting. We'll be on the move." Mattie waved her hand toward the road. "And maybe the shooter jumped into a vehicle and took off. Let's see if we can find out."

"Okay. Go to it. There's very little traffic on this county road, but let me tell Garcia and Johnson to stop anyone that might come." Brody left to get things set up.

"Don't leave this area without someone with you, Mattie," Stella said.

"I won't. I'll wait for Brody." Brody covered her back whenever possible, and she'd come to rely on him. "First I plan to search a circle around the periphery of the scene to see if Robo hits on fresh scent."

Mattie led Robo toward the edge of the road, where she could pat his sides and begin the high-pitched chatter that told him it was time to start. He bent around her legs before backing off to wag his tail and watch her face, prancing on his front paws.

A fugitive often exuded a scent tainted by stress that some officers called endocrine sweat. As part of his patrol education, Robo had been trained to track people leaving the scene of a crime on foot, and he could do it without a scent article.

Mattie unclipped his leash, and he circled her feet, a bundle of energy in anticipation of a command that would release it. She raised her arm and waved it outward. "Let's find the bad guy, Robo. Search!"

Robo ran along the edge of the road, sniffing the ground, searching for scent. Mattie kept a keen eye on him while he worked. It was up to her to read his body language, to interpret his movement, each tiny communication between dog and handler.

When he didn't hit on anything near the road, she called him back and asked him to start working a circle around the van. Robo quartered the area, his head moving back and forth, and her heartbeat quickened as she realized he was narrowing in on fresh scent.

He led her into the grassy barrow ditch beyond the debris field, where he stopped and stood with one front paw raised for a second before stretching his neck forward to touch something with his mouth, something hidden from view by the foliage. Then he sat and stared at her, his signal that he'd found some-thing left behind by the person he'd been tracking.

With a buzz of excitement, Mattie praised him as she pulled her flashlight from its loop on her utility belt. The polished steel barrel of a deadly-looking revolver glittered in its beam. She recognized this handgun and didn't need Brody to identify it—a Smith and Wesson .38 Special.

"We've got a gun," she called to Brody as she marked the spot with a short spike topped with a strip of orange flagging tape. "I'll leave it for the crime scene techs to process."

Carrying his AR-15 Colt rifle, Brody came up behind her. "That's one strategy. Leave the murder weapon so it won't be found on your own property. I'll bet the gun will be untraceable."

Stella had followed Brody. "We'll see. I'll check it for prints, and if it hasn't had its registration number tampered with, I'll run it through the ATF National Tracing Center for ownership. Maybe we can get a quick turnaround."

Mattie doubted it would be that easy, or the shooter wouldn't have left the gun at the crime scene. "I'll see where the track goes from here."

After being told to go ahead and search, Robo took her across the barrow ditch to a barbed wire fence that separated the ditch from the meadow. Beyond that, slight indentations in the tall grass beckoned.

"Robo, wait." Her intuition had paid off. She'd believed it possible that the shooter had left the scene on foot, especially if Nate had known him. Maybe the guy had even sat in the van with Nate before he killed him.

Brody joined her to look out into the meadow.

"He's got a hit," she told him. "We need to let him follow it."

"I'll get backup." Brody keyed on his radio mic. "Garcia, pull back in. We're going into the meadow to search."

Stella joined them. "How do you two want to work this? You know the shooter could still be out there."

Reading Robo's body language would be more important than ever. He could tell her "someone *is* here" versus "someone *was* here." "I'll follow Robo on the scent track. Can you and Garcia flank me?" she asked Brody.

"Sounds like a plan. LoSasso, you stay here and control this area. Make sure the public stays out. Shut off the headlights on the vehicles around here. I don't want us backlit like targets at a shooting range."

Garcia jogged up, his tactical rifle held ready. A force veteran, he was built like a fireplug and he looked eager to go.

Brody took a few seconds to brief him, and then they stamped down the bottom two strands of the sharp barbed wire so that Mattie and Robo could pass through.

She clipped on Robo's leash, wanting to keep him close as her eyes adjusted to the darkness. A breeze rippled the knee-high alfalfa and grass mix as Robo tugged on his leash, wanting to follow the hot scent. Mattie's chest tightened as she felt the responsibility of leading the others into the field, where she could barely see Robo's shadow, much less interpret the nuance of his movements.

She took a breath. "Ready?" she murmured.

"Go ahead," Brody said.

She bent, ruffled Robo's fur, and used an excited voice to direct him. "Robo, let's go find the bad guy. Search!"

Robo surged forward, forcing Mattie to trot a few steps until she could slow his momentum. She didn't want him going out too fast through the tall grass. She pinned her eyes on his shadow and spoke to him quietly, asking him to take it easy whenever he pulled against her too hard. She strained to listen, locating the quiet rustle made by Brody and Garcia, slightly behind and off to each side.

Moonlight glinted off Robo's back. He kept his nose to the ground, and soon enough it became apparent that he was leading them toward a large stack of baled hay, a perfect spot for someone to hide.

She kept her voice down while she spoke to Brody over her shoulder. "We've got to clear that haystack. That's where Robo's headed."

Brody called a halt. "Garcia, you hold a point here and watch the front and left side. I'll circle to the right and clear the backside. Cobb, you stay on the track."

Mattie raised her face and tested the breeze against it. Northerly, coming from the haystack. If the shooter remained hidden behind the stack, Robo would probably catch his scent on the wind. But no guarantees.

She let Robo pull her forward through the deep grass while she watched his every move, looking for his head to go up and his hackles to rise, his way of telling her that *someone is here, someone is out to get us.*

Robo raised his face into the wind, and her heart did a double-step. She drew a breath to shout a warning to the others, her eyes glued to Robo's back. But his hackles remained down. No change.

"Clear!" Brody shouted from ahead and off to the right. Static crackled the air as he used his radio to check in with Garcia, who reported an all clear from his side.

Robo's head went back down, nose to the ground, as he led Mattie up to the stack and around its right side, where she could see for herself that it was clear. But as her dog swept around the corner, he came to a sudden stop, sniffed the area, and backtracked. He stuck his nose in a depression between bales to sniff, then turned to sit and stare at her. His signal that he'd found something.

Already adrenalized, she felt a new high surge through her. "Robo's got a hit on the stack."

Brody moved forward. "What is it?"

"I don't know. He's trained to indicate anything outside the environmental norm when we're on a track like this."

Brody turned on his flashlight and aimed its beam into the stack. A pint jar filled with liquid and topped with a strip of white cloth under its cap was nestled in the crease between the bales. "Molotov cocktail," Brody said, moving closer to take a whiff. "Smells like kerosene or some type of fuel."

This was probably the reason Robo had raised his head to sniff the wind out in the field. Brody had to move close to smell it, but her dog had picked up the scent at about thirty yards.

"After pouring accelerant inside the van, this is probably what our guy used to ignite it," Brody said. "He evidently didn't need this one. Garcia, keep a watch out here until we can get the crime scene unit to process this. Maybe we'll get prints."

"You got it, Chief."

Brody turned to Mattie. "Can Robo pick up where the guy went from here?"

"I'd bet on it." She patted Robo's sides and told him again to search. He lowered his head to whiff the base of the grass around him with a soft snuffling sound before setting a course on a diagonal toward the road.

Now that Mattie knew the stack was clear, she shrugged away the tightness that had gathered between her shoulder blades. She and Robo took the lead while Brody fell in behind. Robo took them to a fence about three-quarters of a mile from the crime scene and lowered his head, making it clear he intended to slip under it.

"Robo, wait." Mattie made him pause so they could safely cross through the barbed wire before allowing him to sniff his way through the tall grass into the barrow ditch. He touched a hidden object with his mouth and then sat, his eyes finding hers.

Mattie grabbed his ruff and hugged him close, praising his find. She signaled to Brody, who came forward with his flashlight. He parted the grass to reveal a tan leather, work glove, large enough to fit a man.

Brody's grin looked grisly in the light's glow. "Our shooter must have dropped this after climbing through the fence."

Mattie smiled, sharing a moment of satisfaction with him. "It's probably loaded with gunshot residue on the outside and DNA inside."

"We'll flag it for the investigators to process. What's the likelihood of some defense attorney saying a glove by the side of the road could belong to anyone?"

"They can say what they want, but when a K-9 with Robo's credentials leads us right to it on the shooter's scent track, that's powerful evidence." While she spoke, Mattie stroked the top of her dog's head as he leaned against her leg. All their training and all her documentation in her training journal paid off at a time like this. She couldn't have been prouder of her partner.

But Robo wasn't finished. He put his nose back on the ground and tugged Mattie toward the road. Up on the road base, he pinned his ears and circled, sniffing in all directions. Within seconds, he sat and stared at her.

"The scent ends here." Mattie hugged Robo against her leg as she patted his side and told him what a good boy he was. "We need to be careful. There could be prints."

Brody lit up the area with the beam of his flashlight, and she spotted sharp ridges and valleys in the dirt. "Right here. Tire prints."

Robo was beginning his happy dance, signaling the end of the track, so Mattie quickly moved him down into the ditch before he could destroy the evidence he'd just found.

"Good job, Robo!" Brody apparently couldn't resist celebrating either, and he leaned down to deliver a few victory thumps on her dog's side.

Robo fawned against the chief deputy's legs for a split second before coming back to press against Mattie. She knelt and grabbed him in a bear hug.

Brody got down to business. "Okay, let's get this area taped off and preserve it for the crime scene techs. We're on our way to catching this guy."

FOUR

Mattie had deemed the panel van at the crime scene too hot to send Robo in to search, so she and Stella were driving toward the Redman Ranch to notify the family of Nate Fletcher's death. Evidently still excited from his search, Robo sat at the front of his compartment, panting slightly and staring out the windshield.

"Two o'clock in the morning," Stella said. "What are the chances that someone will be up and awake?"

"Slim to none."

Her headlights pierced the darkness, revealing tall telephone poles with a wooden sign posted between, REDMAN RANCH burned into it below their brand—quarter circle, backward *R*. Mattie turned off the road and crossed a cattle guard, her tires thumping against the metal rails. From there she followed a private dirt road that twisted and turned through grassland pasture and then crossed a sturdy bridge over Timber Creek, which flowed down from the northern mountains and ran through the Redman property.

The ranch headquarters buildings were visible from the highway during daylight, and Mattie remembered them as a cluster of white stucco houses of various sizes with green metal rooftops. A large barn made from weathered planks and surrounded by pole corrals sat at the edge of the buildings.

It wasn't unusual for a ranch of this magnitude to have more than one house. Employees typically required housing, and it would take several hands to keep a business of this size running. If Cole was right, Kasey Redman lived here on the property, but in which house was anyone's guess.

As they approached, she could see that light glowed from the windows of the first house they would come to.

Stella pointed at it. "That's a surprise. I guess we should start there."

"I wonder why someone would be awake at this hour."

"Maybe Kasey is waiting up for her husband to come home."

A sinking sensation tugged at Mattie's heart. "I hadn't thought of that."

Mattie pulled up in front of a long, ranch-style home with a flower bed that ran along the entire front wall. The lower part of the wall was stained by mud that had been splashed up during watering.

The home had probably been built decades earlier, and she would guess that this outer layer of stucco covered thick adobe walls, a method of building used by the original Spanish settlers that had carried over into the area's architecture during the early part of the twentieth century. Though well maintained, the central structure of this house could be over one hundred years old.

Mattie turned off the engine. "How do you want to do this?"

"Let's find out who lives here and play it by ear. I'll take the lead."

Mattie told Robo he was going to wait in the car and then followed Stella up a graveled pathway that led through the grassy yard toward a screened-in front porch. Light from the house filtered into the enclosed area, revealing a wicker table and a daybed set up in the corner.

Stella knocked on the door to the porch. They waited. When no one answered, she glanced at Mattie, shrugged, and knocked louder. After a long minute, a dim light over the wicker table switched on, illuminating the pleasant outdoor space with its faint glow. Soon the door leading into the main house opened, and a figure backlit by indoor lighting came through. A woman dressed in a blue sateen bathrobe walked across the porch. Not Kasey.

Stella spoke up. "Mrs. Redman?"

The woman, tall and lithe with graying red hair, stopped on the other side of the screen, one hand clutching her robe's collar. "Yes, I'm Lillian. Who's calling at this time of night?"

Stella held her badge up to the screen. "I'm Detective Stella LoSasso from the Timber Creek County Sheriff's Department, and this is Deputy Mattie Cobb. May we come in?"

Lillian squinted through the screen, looking at the badge. "Oh my. What's happened?"

"Could we come inside, Mrs. Redman?"

Lillian opened the screen door. "Of course." She backed away and stood beside the table while Stella and Mattie filed inside. Her fingers fluttered as they went back to her collar. "Do we have cattle out on the highway?"

It was a common problem in ranching country. The grass was always greener on the other side of the fence, and livestock loved to escape through even well-built fences. At night, cattle on the highway and speeding cars with visibility limited to the depth of headlight penetration didn't mix. Mattie wished that was the bad news they were here to deliver.

"No, ma'am, your cattle aren't out that we know of." Stella motioned toward the inner door. "Could we come inside your house? I'm sure it's chilly for you outside here."

Lillian turned and led the way into the house. Warm air washed over Mattie as she stepped inside a large kitchen, its floor covered in dark-gray linoleum with tan and white flecks. Serviceable white cabinets with lighter-gray countertops lined two walls, meeting at a stainless-steel sink in the middle.

Small appliances—toaster, mixer, and coffeepot—sat at the back of the counters, as did various medical items such as stacked cans of a liquid nutritional supplement, a wrist brace, utensils with built-up handles, and rolls of stretchy Ace bandages.

Lillian turned to face Stella, and with the bright overhead kitchen light, Mattie could see that the darkened skin beneath her eyes sagged. In fact, the downward tilt to the lines around her mouth and eyes represented a weariness that didn't happen overnight. She remembered what Cole had said about Doyle Redman's recent stroke.

"Mrs. Redman, does your daughter Kasey live here with you?" Stella asked.

A frown of concern etched her brow. "She lives here on the ranch, but not in this house. Why? What is it?"

"Could you call her and have her come meet us here?"

"You're scaring me, Detective . . . Was it LoSasso?"

"Yes, ma'am. We do have bad news."

Alarm consumed Lillian's face. "Is this about my son Tyler? He's not hurt, is he?"

"No, ma'am. Tyler is fine as far as we know." Stella threw a troubled look at Mattie. "This is rather unorthodox. Typically I'd speak with your daughter first, but I don't mean to make things worse for you. This is about your son-in-law."

"Nate? Has he been hurt? A car wreck?"

"I'm sorry, but he's been found dead."

Lillian's eyes darted to Mattie and then back to Stella. "Dead? That can't be."

Stella held the woman's gaze. "I'm sorry for your loss."

Mattie spoke up. "My sympathies, Mrs. Redman. Would it be easier on Kasey if we spoke to her here at your house, or would it be better to go over to hers?"

Shock still registering on her features, Lillian gave Mattie a sharp look. "It's not going to be easier on her either way."

Mattie nodded, feeling chastened. "You're right. But we'd like to do what's best for Kasey."

Lillian pressed trembling fingers against her cheek. "I'm sorry, I shouldn't lash out at you. Should I wait until morning to tell her?"

"It's best for us to notify her as soon as possible," Stella said.

A crash in the next room startled Mattie. She whirled to face the doorway, placing her hand on her Glock.

"*No, no, no, no, no!*" A man's voice, deep and rough, followed by a few expletives, came from the other room.

Lillian was already hurrying through the doorway. "Oh, Doyle!"

Mattie followed at her heels. A tall man dressed in pajamas stood behind a small metal folding table that lay on the floor, dirty dishes spread out on the carpet in front of it. With his left arm, he was reaching for a cane that leaned against a chair at his back.

Lillian rushed forward to retrieve his cane for him. "You need to call me to help you get up from your chair, dear heart."

Mattie knelt to gather the dishes while glancing up to observe the man whom she assumed to be Doyle Redman. He took the cane with his left hand, his right arm hanging by his side, the hand slightly curled. She recalled Cole saying that Mr. Redman had lost the use of his speech and his arm.

Lillian took the dishes from Mattie, thanking her and moving off with them toward the kitchen. "I'll put these in the sink and come right back."

Mattie picked up the metal tray and sat it on its feet, while Doyle Redman stared at her with gray-blue eyes that were startling in their fierceness. He was a large man, big-boned but gaunt, perhaps from his illness. She held his gaze for a beat until Lillian reentered the room and he turned his eyes toward his wife.

"This is my husband, Doyle. Doyle, this is Mattie Cobb and Detective LoSasso." Lillian's eyes were reddened, her features tense and strained, holding it together as she completed what probably felt like a bizarre social ritual, given the circumstances of having just learned of her son-in-law's death. "Doyle had a stroke that left him with expressive aphasia. He can't say what he wants to, but he understands everything. You can speak to him like you would anyone."

Mattie met Doyle's gaze again. "It's nice to meet you, Mr. Redman."

He rested his cane against his leg to free up his hand and then poked his forefinger at her. "You . . ." He leaned back and beat the air with his finger as if thinking. Then he twiddled two fingers in a walking gesture, moving them through the air.

She thought she knew what he meant. "I run?"

He nodded, the left side of his mouth tipping upward in a half smile.

"Yes sir, I used to run track when I was in high school."

He waved his forefinger close to his temple, as if to say he remembered.

"That's why you look familiar," Lillian said. "We used to watch you."

"I remember Kasey from school, but I don't remember your son."

"Tyler. He's two years younger than Kasey." Lillian's eyes filled, and she looked down at the floor. "I suppose I should call her now."

"Yes, please do that, Mrs. Redman." Though Stella's features remained bland, Mattie could tell from her abrupt movement that the detective was getting antsy to move on to the reason they were here.

"Doyle, please sit back down, sweetheart." Lillian pressed him into the recliner behind him. "I'll just step into the kitchen to use the phone and be right back."

Stella followed Lillian into the kitchen, leaving Mattie alone with Doyle. She stood awkwardly in front of him for a few seconds while he examined her with those gray-blue eyes that were almost iridescent in their intensity.

She cleared her throat, breaking eye contact to look around the room until her gaze lit on an armchair upholstered in navy velour fabric. "Is it all right if I sit?"

He waved his hand in the chair's direction.

Once seated, Mattie didn't know what to say. What conversation could she strike up with a man, speechless from the effects of a stroke, whose son-in-law had just been shot and killed? Her mind drew a blank.

She arranged her features into her neutral cop's face as she settled in to wait, but movement on the far side of the room caught her eye. A young woman paused at the entry from a hallway. When she spotted Mattie, she looked startled, her sleepy gray-blue eyes—so much like Doyle's—opening wide. Tall and slender, she was dressed in a blue cotton tee and silk boxer shorts that looked like pajamas, her short blond hair tousled as if she'd risen from bed.

"What happened, Dad?" she said. "I heard a crash."

Doyle waved his hand in dismissal and then beckoned for her to come, patting the arm of his chair in an invitation to sit.

Mattie gestured toward the tray. "The tray fell over. That's what you heard."

The young woman—Mattie would guess in her late teens or early twenties—approached her father and stood by his chair, her brow furrowed with concern as she looked at Mattie. "What's up?"

Mattie introduced herself. "And you are?"

"I'm Eve. Why are you here in the middle of the night?"

Lillian and Stella reentered the room. "Oh, Eve, you're awake," Lillian said before turning to Stella. "Eve is our youngest. She's home from college for the summer."

Eve directed her concern toward her mother. "What's going on, Mom?"

Lillian looked like she might be yielding to the stress. A tear slipped down her cheek as she took a seat on the sofa. "They've brought bad news, dear. Here, come sit."

Looking apprehensive, Eve settled onto the arm of her father's chair. "What news?"

"It's Nate, dear. He's . . ." Looking confused, Lillian turned toward Stella. "I don't know the details, but the detective said he's been found dead."

With her duty to observe family members in mind as they were each notified, Mattie thought the surprise that registered on both Doyle and Eve's faces appeared genuine. Eve lifted her hand to her throat. "How?"

"Let's wait until Kasey gets here," Stella said. "Then I can tell you all at once."

Sorrowful, Lillian looked at Mattie. "Kasey was here helping me until about an hour before you arrived. She said she'd just fallen asleep, but it will take her only a few minutes to get here."

"How long had Kasey been with you this evening?" Stella asked.

"She helps me most afternoons. She usually comes around five to help with dinner and stays as long as I need her. Tonight Doyle has been particularly restless, so she didn't get away until late."

It appeared that Stella had just obtained an alibi for the victim's wife.

"She was with you since five o'clock today?" Stella evidently wanted clear confirmation that the typical schedule applied to today as well.

"She was."

The screen door on the porch slammed, then the door into the kitchen. Lillian rose from her chair, crossing the room to meet her daughter. When Kasey appeared at the living room threshold, Mattie remembered her flowing mass of red hair from their youth. But the lines of fatigue on her face and dark circles under her green eyes, much like her mother's, were new. And the carefree expression of her youth had been replaced by one filled with concern.

"What's going on, Mom?" Kasey's eyes went to her father as she took her mother's outstretched hand. "You okay, Dad?"

"No, no." He waved his left hand, shaking his head.

Kasey studied him hard, then turned her gaze on Mattie. "I know you."

"I'm Mattie Cobb from the Sheriff's Department, Kasey. We went to school together."

Mattie introduced her to Stella, but even as Kasey shook hands with the detective, her eyes went back to Mattie. "What's this about? Something's happened, hasn't it?"

Stella nodded at Mattie, her signal that she was relinquishing the lead. Probably best, since Kasey evidently remembered their connection.

There was no way to soft-pedal a death notification. "I'm sorry, but we do have bad news. Earlier tonight, your husband was found dead. I'm so very sorry for your loss."

Kasey's eyes registered shock, while her hands flew to cover her mouth. Her mother released a pent-up sob as she placed her arm around her daughter's shoulders. Kasey spoke through parted fingers. "Dead? He's out of town this weekend. What happened?"

Unsure how much information the detective wanted to share with the family at this point, Mattie glanced at Stella.

"This is a tough thing to have to tell a family," Stella said slowly. "Nate was shot. The medical examiner will have to confirm, but it appeared that his wounds were immediately fatal."

"Shot?" Kasey's response came out in a shriek. "No. That can't be."

Her face ashen, Kasey's knees buckled, and Mattie jumped to help Lillian settle her onto the sofa. Lillian sank down beside

Kasey, taking her into her arms while Eve rushed to her sister and knelt in front. Mattie stepped back to allow the women some space.

Glancing away from the threesome, Mattie's eyes met Doyle's for a brief moment. His lids were reddened, and he swiped at the tears that threatened to brim. Stretching his good hand out toward Kasey, he shook his head.

"Damn," he muttered.

And Mattie had to agree.

FIVE

Mattie and Stella sat and waited while the three women sobbed in each other's arms, their initial shock giving way to grief. After several long minutes, the sound of weeping subsided and Stella spoke. "Kasey, I don't want to press you while your emotions are raw, but it would help our investigation if you could answer a few questions. Do you feel like you could do that now?"

Lillian tried to reach for a box of tissues that was just outside her grasp. Mattie jumped to retrieve it and handed it to her. As Lillian took the box, their gaze met, and Mattie read an endless depth of sorrow in the woman's red-rimmed eyes. She could understand why. Even though not connected by blood, Lillian's son-in-law must have meant a lot to her. And certainly she would share in her daughter's grief.

Kasey took the tissue that her mother gave her, then used it to wipe the tears from her cheeks and dab at her eyes. She appeared to be fighting to contain her sobs, though tears continued to flow. "I want to help. What happened? You said he was shot?"

"Yes. We found him outside Timber Creek in a white panel van. The van has been burned."

"That can't be."

Stella nodded affirmation. "You thought he was out of town?"

"I thought he was in Sidney."

"Sidney, Nebraska?"

Kasey nodded, looking stunned.

Mattie wondered why Nate Fletcher wasn't where he was supposed to be. If his plans changed, why hadn't he notified his wife? She probed gently. "Were you expecting him home tonight?"

"No. Not till tomorrow."

"Why do you think his plans changed?"

Kasey shook her head. "I don't know."

"Why did he go to Sidney?" Stella asked.

"To pick up supplies at Cabela's. Nate's an outfitter, you know."

"Tell me about that," Stella said. "I'm not familiar with the term."

Kasey was staring off in the distance as if lost, so Eve answered while she rubbed her sister's shoulder in a repetitive circular motion. "Nate organizes hunts, trail rides, and camping trips for tourists. He provides horses, pack saddles, and all of the equipment for overnight stays in the mountains."

"Where is his territory?" Mattie asked, wondering how far the business ranged from Timber Creek.

"We have about ten thousand acres here on the ranch in addition to private-access BLM land up into the mountains."

"Huh!" Doyle said. Mattie thought she could interpret a look of pride on his face as he and his youngest met each other's gaze.

"So he uses your land exclusively?" Mattie asked.

Lillian placed her arm around Kasey's shoulders again. "And stables his horses here. Has for about three years now, right, honey?"

"That's right, Mom," Kasey answered vaguely as she bent to hug her knees, eyes focused on the floor in the middle of the room.

Mattie wanted enough information so that she could do the research later. "What's the name of his company?"

"Mustang Outfitters."

"How does he get his customers?"

"Word of mouth and his website, for the most part."

Which means that anyone could come from anywhere, Mattie thought.

Stella leaned forward. "Can you think of anyone who might have wanted to hurt Nate?"

Lillian looked startled. "Absolutely not. Everyone loves Nate. He's always the life of the party. People flock to him."

Stella prodded. "Kasey, how about you? Anyone who might have been angry with your husband? Someone he might have argued with?"

Once again, Kasey's eyes brimmed, and a tear rolled down her cheek. "He got along with everyone."

"What about his company? Any employees?"

"Flint. He helps out during hunting season."

"Flint?"

"Flint Thornton. He lives up the creek."

Mattie knew the name. "Oxbow Ranch?"

Kasey swiped tears from her face with the tissue. "That's the one. But Flint would never hurt my husband."

Flint Thornton had attended high school in Timber Creek and must be in his early twenties by now. He might not be violent, but off the record, Mattie knew he'd been charged a few times as a juvenile. Underage drinking, possession of mar-ijuana—teenage crimes, but his parents had taken them seri-ously and put the smack down. As far as she knew, he'd never been charged as an adult.

Kasey looked at Stella. "Where is Nate now?"

"He's been taken to Byers County for the medical exam-iner. It's standard procedure for suspicious deaths. The ME will confirm cause of death and estimate time. He'll also give us information on anything else he might be able to discover."

Kasey frowned. "Does that mean they'll cut him? Run all kinds of tests?"

"Lab tests are typically standard. The examination involves incisions, but they'll be as noninvasive as possible."

Mattie cringed inside at Stella's stretching of the truth; Nate's entire chest would be opened up and probed.

Stella continued. "Once Nate is dressed, you won't be able to see the incisions."

Lillian straightened, concern creasing her face. "Wait a minute. How do you know this person is Nate? Are you sure it's him?"

"Leslie Hartman and Cole Walker identified him. And there was a wallet and driver's license in his pocket." Stella's tone was laced with sympathy. "We'll need a family member to go as soon as possible to confirm identity."

Lillian slumped in defeat. Kasey leaned her head against her mother's shoulder and patted her knee. "Oh, Mom," she moaned, as if in sympathy that her mother had tried to fix things for her but failed.

Stella cleared her throat quietly. "Getting back to the panel van, Kasey. Is that your vehicle?"

"It is. That's what he took to Sidney. You said it was burned?"

"Yes."

Kasey shook her head. "I can't imagine that. Why?"

"That's what we're going to find out," Stella said. "Just a couple more questions, Kasey. Where do you work?"

"Here on the ranch."

"I see. And I understand that you help your mom here at the house some evenings."

Kasey directed a sad look toward her dad. "I eat dinner with my folks and stay here until we're ready for bed every evening. Dad and I like to watch TV together, right, Dad?"

Mattie found it heartwarming to see how the Redman women tried to include the family patriarch in the conversation. They must love him very much to be so dedicated. Was there hope in her life to achieve a lasting kind of love like that?

"So were you here tonight?" Stella asked.

Lillian continued to hug her daughter close as she nodded, though Kasey was the one who answered. "Every night. Tonight included."

"What time did you go to your own home?"

Kasey gazed at the floor again. "I don't know for sure, but I stayed late. Dad didn't want to go to bed. I'd only been home about a half hour or so and had just gone to sleep when Mom called."

That matched what her mother had said earlier.

The double door slam reverberated from the kitchen, and a young man wearing jeans, a red plaid western shirt, and a billed cap walked into the room. "What's going on, Mom?" he said, urgency in his voice. "Is it Dad?"

This must be Tyler Redman, Mattie thought.

Lillian spoke, rising from the sofa to greet her son. "Dad's fine."

Tyler looked around the room. "Why are the police here? What's going on?"

The cap that Tyler wore said BEEF BUILDS BETTER BODIES. SEE BELOW. The body below might have once been hard and lean, but the years had gathered around Tyler's middle to turn it soft and pudgy. He glanced at his mother and removed his cap, revealing a blond crew cut and a receding hairline. Still holding his cap, he stepped forward when his mother introduced him and offered a firm handshake.

Stella cut right to the chase. "We're here to notify your family that your brother-in-law, Nate Fletcher, was shot and killed earlier this evening."

Tyler frowned. "In Sidney?"

"No, right outside Timber Creek."

"But Nate went to Nebraska, didn't he?" He looked at Kasey for confirmation, but she was staring at the floor. He turned to his mother. "Didn't he?"

Mattie thought Lillian looked like she was getting close to the end of her rope.

"That's what we thought," Lillian said as she sank back down on the sofa beside Kasey.

"Well, why wasn't he where he said he'd be?" Tyler said, his frown deepening.

"That's what we'd all like to know," Eve said, rubbing Kasey's knee. "Don't make this any harder on Kasey than it has to be."

Tyler's expression appeared more confused than grief-stricken, which made Mattie wonder where he'd been earlier in the evening.

Evidently Stella did, too. "Tyler, we're investigating Mr. Fletcher's death and the circumstances around it to determine what happened, and right now, I need to establish where everyone was earlier tonight around eleven o'clock. Could you give me that information?"

Tyler raised a brow. "No problem. I was at the dance in Timber Creek with Jasmine Pierce until around ten thirty, and then I took her home to her place. I was there with her until I left to come here."

"Which was what time?" Stella asked.

"Thirty minutes ago. I drove straight here."

Mattie couldn't recall seeing Tyler at the dance, but she hadn't known him then and might not have noticed. She'd have to ask Cole if he'd seen him. "And where does Jasmine live, Tyler?"

"South of town on the trout farm."

Mattie knew the place he was talking about, where the Pierce family had raised trout for stocking lakes and streams for years. "I'll want to get her phone number from you before we leave."

Tyler didn't look too happy about it, but he read Jasmine's phone number to her from his phone.

"And where do you live?"

Tyler raised a brow, as if surprised she didn't know. "Here on the ranch, in the log cabin on the other side of Kasey's house."

Mattie made a quick decision to swab Tyler for gunshot residue. Odds were good that his alibi would hold up, but just in case, she didn't want to neglect getting valuable information now that could be showered away by morning.

"In the interest of being thorough," she said, "I need to run a quick test for gunshot residue. This is standard routine with cases like this, and all it involves is a swab like they do in airports. It helps us eliminate family so we can move on." Mattie scanned the family's faces but focused most of her attention on Tyler. "Is that all right with everyone?"

His frown had turned into a scowl. "I took a shot at a coyote yesterday. Is that going to show up as a positive?"

"We'll keep that in mind." Mattie stood to go retrieve the kits from the car.

"All of us handle guns now and then," Eve said. "Except Mom and Dad. But go ahead, do your job."

"Yes, sir," Doyle said, adding his agreement.

Mattie glanced at Stella, who nodded, and then made her way out through the kitchen and porch to her Explorer. When she opened the door, Robo lurched to his feet, blinking his eyes. She put her hand through the mesh to stroke his fur. "We'll be ready to go soon. You can go back to sleep."

She grabbed several of the packaged swabs from the console and went back inside. It took mere seconds to determine that

Tyler's clothing and hands were negative for GSR, and so were all the women's. Though Mattie didn't intend to swab Doyle's hands, he reached his left out to be tested, and she swiped it quickly so that he would feel included.

"Thank you," Mattie told them. "These results will be logged as part of the investigatory record. That way, if someone questions it in the future, we can clearly state that the results were negative for all of you. Your cooperation is much appreciated."

Stella spoke up. "Eve, we've established a time frame for everyone else this evening, but what about you? Could you share where you were earlier tonight?"

Lillian was quick to answer. "Eve went to bed around eight o'clock."

"I can speak for myself, Mom. I'm not a child," Eve said.

Lillian bowed her head in acquiescence. "I know you're not. I just knew when you went to bed by what was on television at the time."

"I've got a summer job at Clucken House," Eve said to Stella. "I worked until close at midnight on Friday and then opened at five on Saturday morning to work breakfast and lunch. Tyler and I branded calves in the afternoon, so I was beat and went to bed early . . . evidently at eight o'clock." This last bit was said with a glance at her mother.

Lillian gave her youngest a thin smile tinged with sadness.

"All right," Stella said, rising from her chair. "Does Nate have other family, Kasey? Someone we can contact for you?"

"His parents live in Montana."

"I can call them," Lillian said.

"No, I'll do it," Stella replied. "I need to talk to them anyway. If I could just get their phone number from you."

"I have it pinned to the bulletin board in the kitchen," Lillian said, rising from the sofa to go and Stella followed.

Mattie scanned the sorrowful family faces, her gaze linger-ing on Tyler. He had yet to shed a tear. Maybe he was a stoic guy, but his lack of emotion made her wonder if he'd had any-thing to do with his brother-in-law's death.

She stood. "I want to tell you again how sorry we are. We plan to track down what happened to Nate and arrest the per-son who killed him."

As Kasey looked up at Mattie, tears brimmed in her eyes. "I hope you can. I don't want whoever did this to get away with it."

Stella handed them each a business card before leaving. "Call me anytime if you think of something that might help us with our investigation."

Lillian escorted them into the porch, pausing as she closed the door behind her. "Mattie, Stella . . . You've been very kind. You're in a hard profession, and I appreciate what you're doing to try to make things right for our family. It's, it's . . ."

Emotion interfered with Lillian's ability to finish, and she covered her face with her hands. Sympathy made Mattie reach out to touch her arm. "We'll do the best we can, Mrs. Redman."

Lillian drew a deep breath as she withdrew her hands from her face. "I know you will. Thank you."

Mattie said goodbye, following Stella through the porch, while Lillian returned inside her house.

Glad that the hardest task in her job was now over, Mattie drew a sigh of relief. As they approached her unit, Robo popped his head up in the window to greet them. His eager face never failed to make her feel better. Realizing how tired she was, she drew a breath.

What a night. And still much to do.

Stella climbed into the passenger seat and reached for her seat belt. "That was a tough one."

Mattie turned the key to start the engine. "I'll say."

"I'm typically not convinced when a family member provides an alibi, but I think it's safe to say that both Kasey and Eve were here when Nate was killed. I think we can clear Kasey as the shooter, but whether or not she's involved with the planning still remains to be determined."

"That's true, but she seemed genuinely shocked by the news. I'd place my money on her innocence."

"Agreed." Stella used both hands to massage the sides of her neck. "Poor family. They've had it rough, and hard times still lie ahead. Lillian Redman looks tired. I wonder how she copes."

Mattie had been struck by the same impression. "Love. It's obvious how much she loves her husband. She loves her family, too."

"Dedication. Can't say I've ever experienced that for anything but the job."

Mattie nodded, but remained silent. She had to admit that sometimes she wondered if it might not be easier to remain a loner rather than to get tangled up in the messy affinity of love and family. But then, she really wasn't willing to go back to her life before falling in love with Cole.

"So what do you think about Tyler?" Stella asked.

"I think we still need to look at him. He could've changed his clothes and showered to pass the GSR test. We'll have to check his alibi with Jasmine Pierce."

"Didn't seem too torn up about his brother-in-law's death."

"I noticed."

"If the lab finds DNA inside that glove Robo found, we'll need to get a sample from Tyler to compare it to."

In total agreement, Mattie nodded.

"What do you think about this guy, Flint Thornton? Do you know him?" Stella asked.

Mattie told her what she knew while she drove out onto the highway.

Stella took in the information. "We need to talk to him. Does he know you?"

"He probably knows Brody better than me. I think he was the one who arrested him on the drunk and disorderly."

"That's all for the better. Before we go talk to him, I'll do an online search to get to know our victim. I'm wondering about past customers. If Flint Thornton doesn't appear to be involved with the shooting, maybe he can shed some light on other suspects."

Mattie thought of something else that bothered her. "Why did Nate Fletcher return home tonight? And why didn't Kasey know about it?"

Stella nodded and leaned back against the headrest. "I wonder if he was hiding something from her."

It was a beautiful night, and Mattie stared out at the landscape while she thought about it. The moon lit the area beyond their headlights to reveal grassy meadows that stretched north to meet the first layer of foothills, rounded and rocky, their native vegetation reflecting silver in the moonlight. Above the foothills, towering peaks white-capped with glaciers provided a jagged skyline below a multitude of stars.

"Imagine owning all this land," Stella mused. "And private access into BLM land? Do you know what that means?"

"Not precisely, but it has something to do with grazing rights that a rancher can obtain from the Bureau of Land Management. It's government land that goes up into the mountains."

"Is it legal for outfitters to take groups on hunting trips up into that country? Sounds like double-dipping into government land."

"It's entirely legal. I think ranchers pay for the permits, so it's like a lease. They can use the land however they want. The government makes money off the program."

"So Nate wasn't breaking the law that we know of."

"Right, but we don't know much yet."

"True. Well, let's get back to the crime scene and see if Robo can tell us anything about that van. He's given us a lot of evidence already, but let's see if he's got any more tricks up his sleeve."

SIX

Sunday morning

By five thirty, the sunrise painted an orange glow on the eastern horizon, giving off enough light to provide visibility beyond the halo of lamps set up by the crime scene investigators. Brody and Stella had waited outside the perimeter while Mattie prepared Robo to work.

Ready to go, he stood beside Mattie outside the debris field that circled the van. Except for his short stints at work, he'd slept the night away in his compartment. Hovering at her heel with a waving tail, he looked much more refreshed than she felt.

"Let's go to work, Robo." Mattie had put leather booties on his feet again, and he high-stepped his way beside her. An evidence search was serious business, but still, Mattie had to suppress a smile.

Torching the van had transformed it into a twisted and blackened metal sculpture. Ash and sooty grime covered everything. The driver's side door hung ajar, left open since Garrett had pulled out Nate's body. Upholstery on the two front seats had burned away, leaving a metal framework with bits of scorched cushion.

After leading Robo to the open door at the back of the van, Mattie unclipped his leash and told him to search. He hopped inside and skirted the back of the van, sniffing at two plastic toolboxes that had melted around metal tools inside and a steel cage that looked like a large dog crate, torqued and distorted by the fire. He rounded the back area, giving the side panels a sniff before leaping outside. Nothing in back seemed to have captured his attention.

Planning to perform a typical vehicle search for narcotics, Mattie clipped Robo's leash back on his collar and directed him in a counterclockwise sweep around the van's exterior. He sniffed the vehicle's undercarriage and headed toward the driver's side. At the open door, he sniffed the inside panel and then whiffed it again as if checking his work. He turned, sat, and stared at Mattie.

Mattie's pulse quickened, and she praised Robo while he beat his tail in a happy cadence. Since it had remained open, this door panel had been relatively spared from the fire. She spoke over her shoulder to Brody. "He's got a hit here. Let's take off the panel."

Stella called to one of the lab techs, a young woman named Karissa, and asked her to help. First Karissa photographed the door from several angles, and then with a tool she removed from a kit she wore at her belt, she pried loose the inner door upholstery.

Mattie leaned in for a closer look. Nothing. "I don't see anything, but can we swab that to see if we can get a sample for testing?"

"I have a NIK kit here," Karissa said, referring to a presumptive test kit that could detect and identify narcotics in the field. "Let's use it."

While Karissa retrieved the kit and set to work, Brody came close to watch. Mattie and Robo finished sweeping the van without any other alerts.

"I swabbed out a few grains of something," Karissa told Mattie when she returned to the driver's side. "I hope it's large enough to react."

The lab tech held the small fluid-filled test pouch and carefully broke ampoules of reacting agents over it. As she worked through the ampoules, the fluid turned a faint shade of blue. "That's positive for cocaine," Karissa said, grinning at Mattie.

She couldn't help but return the smile. "Thanks, Karissa. That's a huge find."

"I'll swab it out and see what we can identify in the lab, but it's safe to say this van was used to transport cocaine inside the door panel." Karissa started to leave but turned back toward Mattie. "And could you get a sample of your dog's hair for me, so we can have it on record? You have to pluck it to include the follicle, and I'm afraid of him."

"As you should be," Brody said, with an expression of pride on his face. "This dog can take your hand off."

Mattie thought Brody might be going a bit overboard, but who was she to argue?

★ ★ ★

Morning light filtered through the hospital room window where Cole sat with Leslie. Garrett lay unconscious in the bed, looking older than his years, small cuts and bruises marring the stark whiteness of his face.

Garrett's CT scan had revealed a hematoma in a place in his brain that made the doctors nervous. The neurosurgeon didn't recommend operating unless internal vessels in the brain bled further and the hematoma enlarged overnight. So far, his vital signs had been stable, so there was nothing else to do but wait and watch, which had occupied both Cole and Leslie.

Leslie's forehead was creased with worry, her eyes reddened by unshed tears, and Cole knew there was no way he could leave her to stand vigil on her own. He'd tried to keep his game face on and project an air of confidence that Garrett would be fine, but the strain seemed to be getting to them both.

Since their daughter Grace's murder, Garrett had made an attempt to heal by volunteering for the sheriff's posse, a group of horseback riders that responded to search-and-rescue calls or routine events such as crowd control at rodeos. He'd thrown himself into community service, while Leslie had isolated herself in their home.

A few times each month, Mrs. Gibbs and Cole's two daughters, Angela and Sophie, had driven out to the Hartman ranch house to visit Leslie. Mrs. Gibbs was a rock with a solid knowledge of human nature, and the two women seemed to enjoy each other's company. Grace and Angela had been best of friends, and Cole had been relieved that her visits with Leslie didn't seem to be painful for either of them. Garrett often commented how much Leslie loved seeing the kids and how young Sophie made her laugh.

Coming into town together to enjoy the community dance had been a big step for the Hartmans. It had been almost a year since Grace, and as far as Cole knew, this was the first time they'd planned to attend a fun event. It made his heart ache that they hadn't made it, and now Garrett lay unconscious on this bed, his life suspended in the blink of an eye.

Cole arose from his chair to stretch his legs and open the blinds a crack. The sun had risen well above the horizon, and it slanted in, hurting his eyes. He closed the blind. "Do you want some breakfast, Leslie?"

She looked away from her husband's face for a brief moment. "I don't think so, Cole."

He fought to keep himself from yawning. "A cup of coffee?"

She gazed at Garrett as if willing him to awaken. "That would be nice."

Cole thought he knew the answer but decided to ask anyway. "Do you want to take a walk, go get it yourself? I'll stay with him."

"No. You go."

Just thinking about food made his belly rumble. It had been a long, hard night. "I'll be right back."

Cole found the alcove where the nurse had said they could get coffee and snacks. He poured two cups of the dark brew, grabbed a couple packets of sugar and creamer, and placed them on a tray. He decided to check the refrigerator, found containers of yogurt and Jell-O, and selected two of each. He snagged bananas from a fruit bowl, some packets of crackers and cookies, topped off his tray with utensils and napkins, and then headed back toward the room.

When he entered, he was startled to find Leslie on her feet hovering over Garrett, gripping his hand, shoulders bent and heaving. Cole set the tray on the bedside table as he rushed toward her. When he followed her gaze to his friend's face, his breath caught.

Garrett's eyes were open, and he was staring up at his wife.

Cole placed his arm around Leslie, her shoulders still twitching with sobs that she held inside, silently crying. "Hi, Garrett," he said softly.

Garrett's lips twisted in a quirky half smile. "Hey. What are we doin' here?"

"You're in the hospital." Cole pushed the button to call for the nurse. "You remember getting hurt?"

Garrett frowned and winced as if the movement alone pained him. "How?"

Unsure how much he should say, Cole dropped his arm from Leslie's shoulders and leaned against the bed rail. "You got hit on the head."

"That explains the headache." Garrett's eyes went back to Leslie, and he raised the hand she still clung to so that he could touch the tears on her face. "Don't cry, sweetheart. I'm okay."

She moved his hand to her lips and pressed them against it. She choked on her first attempt to speak, cleared her throat, and tried again, this time managing a shaky voice. "We'll see if they can give you something for the pain."

The nurse came in, took one look, and bustled over to the other side of the bed where she could read Garrett's vitals on the monitor. "Nice to see you're awake, Garrett. How do you feel?"

He squinted at her, then closed one eye. "Head hurts like a son of a gun."

"We'll get you something for that." She asked him to squeeze her hands, checked his pupils, and asked him to say his full name, all of which he responded to like a champ. But when she asked him what year it was, he hesitated.

Garrett checked in with Leslie. "Nineteen ninety?"

Leslie grimaced. The nurse didn't even bat an eye. She corrected him and told him to repeat the date aloud. "Try to remember that, okay? We'll be asking you what year it is every time we come to check on you. Let's see if you can remember it next time, but don't worry if you can't. Things will clear up in time. I'll be right back with that pain medication."

After the nurse left, Garrett reached for Leslie's hand and looked at Cole. "Didn't know there would be a quiz. Embarrassing."

Cole took a stab at levity. "Hell, doesn't she know that you go around not knowing what year it is half the time anyway?"

Garrett tried to smile before turning sober. "There was an explosion."

"That's right." Cole turned serious as well. "Do you remember anything more about it?"

"Doyle." Garrett met Leslie's eyes. "Did I get him out in time?"

Cole worried when Garrett said the wrong name, but Leslie touched her husband's cheek. "It was Nate, dear," she said. "And you got him out before the van caught on fire."

"I meant Nate." He looked at Cole, appeared to try to focus, and then closed one eye. "He had blood on his shirt."

Cole nodded, wanting to confirm that his friend had remembered it right this time, but afraid to mention Nate's death.

"He was shot, wasn't he?"

Cole hesitated before replying. "Apparently so."

"Dead?"

"Uh . . . yeah." Cole hated being the bearer of such bad news. "But you got him out of the van before it burned. He was dead when Mattie and I arrived, and it looked like the gunshot killed him."

Garrett closed his eyes. "I thought he was dead when I tried to lift him."

Cole touched his shoulder. "You did all you could and then some."

Garrett opened his eyes, squinted, and closed one eye again to focus in on Leslie. "Are you all right? You weren't hurt, were you?"

"No, sweetheart. I was far enough away when the van blew."

Cole had grown concerned about the squinting and eye closing. "What's wrong with your eyes, Garrett? Why do you keep closing that one?"

"Sometimes there's two of you, bud. You're ugly enough when there's only one."

The nurse came back with a glass of ice water and medicine in a little cup. She pressed the button to elevate the head of the bed while Cole told her Garrett was seeing double. She nodded as she placed a small pill in Garrett's mouth with a gloved hand and held the straw so he could reach it. "Let's see if you can swallow this. That's good. No problem, eh?"

Garrett licked his upper lip. "No, ma'am."

She set down the water and then held up two fingers on both hands, asking him to count.

"There's four," he said with his quirky half smile. "But that's easy . . . count and divide by two."

"Fair to say that you've got some double vision going on?" she asked.

"Comes and goes."

"We'll let the doctor know. She's already ordered another scan for this morning to make sure everything's stable inside your head." She smiled as she said it and straightened the covers.

"What's going on inside my head?"

Her attention was on the monitor beside his bed. "Your doc-tor will be in to see you soon. She can answer your questions."

Good way to pass the buck, Cole thought.

After the nurse left, Garrett turned to Cole again and gave him that squinty-eyed look. "I saw fire boiling out the back end of that van, and I knew I needed to move fast to get Nate out before the gas tank blew."

His friend's vision might not be right, but his memory seemed to be coming back strong.

Leslie was nodding. "Garrett told me to back the truck away, and I called 911. When the van exploded, I dropped the phone and ran to him." She looked at Cole. "I dragged him as far away as I could, and then you came."

Garrett had rested his head on his pillow and closed his eyes. "And did someone say that Mattie was there?"

"Yes," Leslie said, "she came with Cole."

Garrett pinned him with one eye. "You two were together?"

"We were at the dance when we heard the explosion."

"You were at the dance with Mattie?" Garrett closed the one eye he'd been using on Cole, relaxing as the pain medicine did its job, his face peaceful. "You'd better grab her if she'll have you, bud. Only one woman in the world better than that one, and I've already got her."

Garrett smiled as Leslie touched his shoulder, and then he drifted off to sleep.

★　★　★

The doctor came and went. Garrett slept through her visit, but she said she would be back after he'd had his brain scan and she'd seen the results. She told Leslie that the hematoma they'd found the night before was in a place in his brain that might affect his vision, but all things considered, his medical status looked good. She stressed that it was early yet, and if the scan showed that the bleeding in Garrett's brain had stopped, they would keep him for observation and have the therapy department assess his functional abilities. Sounded like a good plan to Cole, and he set his hopes on the scan showing the right results.

Focusing on Garrett's pale face, his every breath, and his heart monitor were all beginning to drive Cole crazy. "I need to make a phone call, Leslie. I'll be right down the hall by the elevator, okay?"

"Go get some breakfast if you want to."

He'd already eaten everything on the tray that he'd brought for Leslie. "I'll grab some more snacks before I come back."

As he walked, he pulled his cell phone from his pocket and dialed Mattie. She answered on the first ring, and it gave his achy heart a lift to hear her voice. He drifted over toward a window where he could at least *see* the world outside the hospital. "How are you doing?"

"I'm fine. Stella and I are about to leave the van to do one more interview before we head home to get a few hours' sleep. How are you?"

Cole thought she sounded tired. "Doing better," he said. "Garrett's awake. Well, he's sleeping at the moment, but he woke up and talked to us for a few minutes."

He heard her release a breath. "That's good news."

Cole summarized Garrett's condition. "We'll know for sure about the hemorrhage here in a bit. Still waiting for him to go downstairs for the scan."

"Will you call me when you know more?"

"Will do." He paused, wondering if he should ask about the case. "How's everything going?"

"Stella and I spoke with Kasey and her parents. That was hard." She paused, and he wondered if she was reliving the moment. "Cole, you mentioned you knew the Redman family. That includes Tyler, right?"

"I do know Tyler."

"Did you see him at the dance last night?"

"I did. He was there with Jasmine Pierce. Her parents own the trout farm out south of town. Why?"

"We met him at the Redman house last night, and that's what he told us. He said he left the dance early to go back to her place."

Cole tried to think of when he'd seen him, because he knew without asking that Mattie was trying to confirm an alibi. "I can't recall exactly when I saw him, but it was earlier in the evening. I can't tell you when they left."

"Stella tried to call Jasmine, but no answer." She paused again, and Cole waited to see if she had anything more to say about the case. "Have you heard any rumors about Nate Fletcher and drug use?"

That was a surprise. He wondered why the case had headed in that direction. "No, nothing."

"Do you do his vet work?"

"I do all the Redman Ranch horse work. They have about thirty head most of the time."

"Have you ever suspected drug use?"

"Not at all. Nate Fletcher is a good ol' boy. You know what I mean? Pure country. Likes to fish and hunt and probably pounds down his share of beer, but he's always sober when I go out to their place. I've never suspected he was under the influence of anything."

"Okay."

"Uh, why do you ask?"

"I don't trust these cell phone connections, so I'd rather talk about it in person. When do you plan to come home?"

"I'll stay with Leslie until after we talk to the doctor about Garrett's brain scan. Then I'll decide if I can leave her alone or not." He wished he could see Mattie in person, be with her face-to-face. There was more he wanted to say to her, and as usual, he felt like this case was pulling her away from him. "What are your plans?"

"We've wrapped up at the crime scene and turned it over to the techs. After we get a few hours' sleep, we'll meet back at the office at ten."

"I hope you can get some rest."

There was a long pause before she spoke. "Have you been able to sleep?"

"No, but I'm doing all right. Had some coffee." He realized they'd digressed to chitchat, but the circumstances didn't feel right for sweet talk.

"Here comes Stella. I guess I'd better go." He heard her speak quietly to Robo to load up.

"Take care of yourself and call me when you can. I won't call you back for a few hours since I know you'll be sleeping, but I'll text you an update when we know more."

"You can call me anytime. I doubt if I can sleep."

"Love you, Mattie."

A short silence before she responded. "You too. Drive carefully when you come home. Don't fall asleep on the road."

"I won't."

After Cole disconnected the call, he paused for a moment. The call was no substitute for being with her in person, but that was as close as Mattie had ever come to confessing any love for him. He sighed as he put his phone back into his pocket and braced himself to go back into Garrett's room.

SEVEN

After finding trace cocaine in Nate Fletcher's van, Stella had decided it was important to talk to Flint Thornton as soon as possible. As Nate's sole employee, Flint should know the most about Nate's business, excluding Kasey and others in the Redman family, of course. But Stella and Mattie wanted to gather as much information as they could before talking about the evidence of drug possession with the family.

Mattie turned off the highway at a huge wrought-iron sign that said OXBOW RANCH. She rattled over a cattle guard and steered onto a long winding dirt road that would take them through grass pastures toward a tree-shrouded ranch house off in the distance.

"So this is where Flint Thornton lives?" Stella said. "Pretty big spread."

"He lives here with his parents. Nice folks who had to deal with a wild child when he was growing up. They were pretty involved, from what I could tell."

"It happens." Stella shrugged as if dismissing the ways of the world. "How old is Flint now?"

Mattie thought about it but couldn't come up with the answer. "I can't tell you, but I know he's no longer a minor. Haven't seen him in years. His offenses were all committed as a juvenile and his record is closed."

"We'll see what he has to tell us. If drugs were a part of those hunting trips, he would know about it."

"I think so, too." Mattie breached the copse of cottonwoods around the ranch house and pulled to a stop in front of it.

The house was a sprawling log one-story with a porch swing hanging under the eaves. Instead of lawn, the space had been left natural, with a row of pine planted out front. Flower beds were scattered here and there in patches of sunlight, and a hose stretched from a house spigot sprinkled some young pansies. No sooner had Mattie put on her parking brake than a man stepped out the front door.

Tall and rugged, he had graying brown hair and a mustache that was more salt than pepper. He wore denims, a western shirt, and a frown of concern. Mattie recognized him as Flint's dad, John David Thornton, also known as JD.

Stella and Mattie exited the Explorer and met him at its front. After exchanging greetings and introductions, he peered at Mattie with amber eyes under bushy eyebrows threaded with wild gray hairs. "I know you," he said.

"Yes, sir. We've met before."

"You've taken over the police dog work for the sheriff."

"I have." Mattie gestured toward the back of the SUV, where Robo watched from the window, ears pricked. "That's Robo."

When drug traffic had threatened the peaceful town of Timber Creek, local merchants and ranchers had gathered together to raise money to purchase a narcotics detection dog. Thus Robo had a certain star quality within the community. Though Mattie didn't know each donor personally and the donor list wasn't for public consumption, she suspected this man might have been part of the fund-raising effort.

He studied Robo for a few beats while Robo gazed back at him. "Looks like a fine dog."

"He is, sir. I'm grateful to have him for a partner."

JD quirked a corner of his lips and set his attention back on her. "What can I do for you?"

Since Mattie seemed to have the rapport, she took the lead. "We're hoping to speak with Flint. Is he home?"

The line between JD's bushy brows deepened. "He is. I suppose you want to talk to him about Nate Fletcher."

This last bit came as a surprise. "Yes, sir. How did you learn about Nate?"

"Tyler called early this morning, needing Flint's help. Nate had a trip scheduled for tomorrow that Tyler plans to go ahead with, so he wanted Flint to help him get ready."

"I see." Mattie glanced at the house. "Could we speak with Flint, please?"

JD gave an abrupt nod and went to the front door. He opened it and shouted inside to Flint, telling him to come out because someone wanted to talk to him. Mattie thought it odd that he didn't clarify that the "someone" was the police, but maybe it was this dad's way of letting his adult son stand on his own two feet.

"He said he'd be out in a minute," JD said, coming back to join them.

Stella took a step forward. "Did you know Nate well, Mr. Thornton?"

"Well enough. Flint has worked for him over a year now. Most of us ranchers know each other up and down the valley."

Mattie couldn't help but wonder if Flint had fallen back into his old habits and Nate had become his supplier. She hoped she could get a feel for that sometime during this interview.

Stella continued. "We're out doing sort of a canvass of the neighborhood. Asking folks if they've seen or heard anything that might help us with our investigation."

"Tyler said Nate was shot."

"That's right."

Hard lines of judgment creased JD's face. "That's a terrible thing. I have no idea who might do something like that."

"Speaking to Flint is also routine. He should be able to tell us about Nate and his customers." Stella seemed to be trying to reassure the father.

"You think one of his customers did it, then?"

"Hard to say. We're exploring every possibility." Stella wore a pleasant expression as she posed her next question. "Do you happen to know if Flint was with Nate yesterday? Helping get ready for the trip, I mean."

JD tucked his thumbs into the front pockets of his jeans, and Mattie sensed that he knew exactly what Stella was doing—trying to get information about his son's whereabouts at the time of the murder. "From what I was told, Nate was out of town yesterday on a trip to Nebraska for supplies. Flint worked at the Redman place until about four and then came home to get ready for the dance."

"So he was at the dance last evening?"

"As far as I know."

From JD's frown of concern, Mattie could tell he was worried that Flint might have strayed from the straight and narrow, too, but then Flint himself came out of the house. The years hadn't changed him much; he looked older, but he was as tall and lean as he'd ever been. He had dark hair and eyes like JD, but unlike his father's, his handshake was hesitant and soft. He looked nervous, and his eyes bounced from his dad to Mattie and Stella during the introductions, then settled on the K-9 unit and Robo for a few seconds as he apparently took in the situation.

JD Thornton leaned against the front of the Explorer, arms crossed over his chest, and Mattie worried that he planned to stay for their interview with his son. No one liked to confess or share critical information in front of an audience, and as an adult, Flint had the right to privacy. But she needn't have worried, because she and Stella were evidently on the same wavelength.

"Mr. Thornton, we appreciate your time and help this morning, but we need to talk to Flint privately," Stella said. "Would you please give us a moment?"

JD squinted, his gazing moving from Stella to Flint, who stood with his head lowered as he studied the ground.

"All right," JD said, dropping his arms from his chest and stepping away from the Explorer. And then to his son: "I'll be in the house if you need me."

"Thank you, sir," Stella said. "This is just routine, and I have only a few questions."

After JD went inside, Mattie wondered if he would linger at the door to try to listen.

Stella opened the interview. "Flint, your dad said that Tyler called this morning to tell you Nate was shot last night. How much do you know about it?"

Flint looked up from the ground to meet Stella's gaze. "Tyler said Nate was killed and his van was burned. That's all I know."

Mattie watched as Stella nodded encouragement, working at getting him to open up. "We heard that Nate went to Nebraska for the weekend. Is that true?" Stella asked.

"Yeah, as far as I know."

"When did you expect him back?"

"I thought he was coming home today. We have a fishing trip scheduled for tomorrow."

"Why do you think he came home early?"

"I have no idea." He crossed his arms over his chest.

Mattie thought he looked defensive, and evidently Stella did too, because she changed the subject.

"I'm unfamiliar with the outfitting business," Stella said, her body language open and friendly. "What do you do as Nate's employee?"

"I'm mostly just a gofer. I handle supplies, take care of the horses and the tack, help set up camp and cook meals."

"Sounds like a lot."

Flint nodded, releasing his crossed arms to let them hang at his sides. "Between trips, I repair equipment, trim the horses' hooves, and replace shoes if they've lost them."

Since he appeared more relaxed, Mattie decided it was safe to interject with a question, as long as it was about Nate's business. "How does Nate get his customers?"

Flint shifted his gaze to Mattie. "From his website. He also advertises in hunting and outdoor magazines, and there's a certain amount of referral from satisfied customers."

This led perfectly into what Mattie had been wondering about—she hoped it would give them a lead. "Were there any dissatisfied customers that you're aware of? Someone who might've wanted to hurt Nate?"

Flint appeared to give the question some thought before he answered. "Nothing like that. Sometimes people get cranky because they didn't get a deer or didn't catch the number of fish they wanted, but Nate can usually talk them out of it, and he shows them a good time."

Mattie thought of the cocaine in the van. A party drug. "How does he do that?"

Flint's attention seemed to turn inward before he responded with a sad smile, the first real emotion he'd shown other than apprehension. "Nate was a great guy. He liked to party, and we always had plenty of booze to cheer up the customers. People had a great time when they were with him."

"Just booze? Any marijuana?"

Flint shook his head. "Nah. Nate said pot was illegal on federal land. He didn't want anything to do with drugs. We provided beer, wine, tequila, and whiskey—enough to fill one pannier."

Mattie thought he looked sincere. "Did Nate use drugs himself?"

Flint frowned, meeting her gaze as he shook his head. "Not whenever we were together. He drank only beer, not even the hard stuff. That was for the clients."

Mattie nodded. His answer might have given her a dead end, but she would pursue the lead elsewhere.

Stella spoke up. "Flint, do you have any idea who might have wanted to shoot Nate?"

Flint looked down at his feet. "I've been wondering about that since I heard about it. I haven't come up with anybody."

"If you do think of someone or something, it's important that you call us. We need to know anything at all, even if it seems minor," Stella said, handing Flint her card. "Will you do that?"

"Yeah." Flint took the card and studied it.

Mattie figured that Stella would ask Flint about his own alibi before they left, but she wanted to know more about Nate's business first. "Tyler plans to carry on with the fishing trip Nate had scheduled for tomorrow. Does he usually participate in the outfitting business?"

"No, this is a first." Flint's chest puffed slightly. "That's why he called to make sure I could be in charge."

"Does Kasey go on the trips?"

"She used to. She used to be a lot of fun at the campfire, too." Flint shook his head slowly, and his face took on sadness again. "She hasn't been able to help out since Mr. Doyle's stroke."

Even though Flint's irregular eye contact appeared deceptive, the respectful way he said *Mr. Doyle* made Mattie think maybe they were dealing with a big kid who hadn't yet grown out of the awkward stage. She couldn't think of any other questions, so she glanced at Stella to see if she wanted to wrap up.

"Flint, I have one more routine bit of information that we're getting from everyone," Stella said. "Tell us where you were last night around eleven o'clock."

"I went to the dance last night."

Mattie noticed a flush was beginning to color the skin at his neck. "Were you there when the siren went off to signal the volunteer firefighters?" she asked.

"Uh-uh." He blushed as he shook his head. "I left before then."

Mattie wondered what had caused the flushing. "Where did you go?"

He shook his head, avoiding eye contact. "Just for a drive."

"By yourself?"

"I went with a girl, someone I met at the dance."

Maybe he was embarrassed. Or maybe he was lying. "We'll need her name, Flint."

He glanced at Mattie before looking away. "Sadie. I don't know her last name."

"Did she give you a phone number?" Stella asked.

"Nah." He was shaking his head as his arms crossed over his chest again.

Stella evidently decided that was all they were going to get. "It's important that we identify where you were last night, Flint, so we can cross you off our list and move on to other people. If you get back in touch with Sadie, please get her name and number so we can follow up and confirm your alibi."

Flint looked toward his house as if searching for escape, or maybe to see if his dad was listening, and he mumbled that he would call if he talked to Sadie. Stella's hint that he was a suspect had hit home.

Mattie had one more question before they left. "The kind of work you do requires a good pair of work gloves. Can you show us yours?"

Looking puzzled, Flint reached for his back pocket. "You mean these?"

He pulled out a pair of light leather gloves, typical of those worn by ranchers for outdoor work. Although they looked similar to the one left in the ditch, they were smaller and of a different style. "What size are these?" Mattie asked, rolling back the open ends of each glove to see if there was a tag.

"Medium."

"Thanks for your time, Flint," Mattie said as she handed him back his gloves. Wanting to offer another line of communication, she gave him one of her own cards before saying goodbye.

While she drove away, she checked the rearview mirror, having to look over Robo as he stood staring out the back window. Sure enough, JD came out of the house to stand beside his son, indicating he'd been keeping tabs on what was going on outside his front door.

Stella pulled her seat belt across herself and fastened it. "Was everyone at that dance last night except me?"

"Just about."

"Did you see Flint there?"

"I can't say I did. But the place was packed, and we were dancing most of the time before the explosion. I wasn't really looking for him."

Stella shot her a sideways glance, eyebrows raised. "So the handsome Dr. Walker was taking up most of your attention, huh?"

Mattie felt her own face begin to flush, like Flint's. "I was off duty, Detective."

"Right." Stella took out a small notebook she carried with her and started recording notes. "What did you think of Flint?"

"I'm not sure. I was about to give him the benefit of the doubt until he lit up when you asked him for an alibi. But that blush could've been embarrassment over hooking up with a girl he barely knew."

"Possibly." Stella paused her writing and looked out the window. "But we can't eliminate him yet."

Mattie thought they shouldn't underestimate the influence this kid's dad had on him. "I saw JD step outside to join him when we left. Let's let him have some time with Flint. Maybe he can get him to come forward with more information before we need to give it another go."

"In the meantime, it's good to know that the gloves Flint wears are a smaller size than the one we found. Did you think it was odd that he had them in his pocket?"

Mattie remembered seeing gloves shoved into the back pockets of many a rancher as they went about their business. "Not really. He was getting ready to leave for work, and it's common enough to keep work gloves handy."

"Okay." Stella yawned, making Mattie suppress one, too. "Let's head for home and try to get some sleep before that ten o'clock meeting at the station."

Sorry they hadn't turned up any new leads, Mattie set a course for Timber Creek. She wished they'd come up with something more solid, but she consoled herself that it had been less than twelve hours since Nate's death.

Her mind jumped to Cole as she drove in silence, and she hoped she could find a way to see him before this day ended. She still felt pressed to share the most traumatic part of her childhood with him and she wanted to get it over with, but not on the phone. It would have to wait till later.

EIGHT

Mattie pulled into the parking lot at the station shortly before ten, noticing that Brody and Stella hadn't yet arrived. She'd slept hard for three hours and without dreams, a welcome change from her usual pattern of insomnia. Total exhaustion might be the key.

The burn on her arm still tingled when she changed the dressing, but the lidocaine in the ointment had soothed it. Many of the blisters had broken or resorbed with the treatment, and there was no sign of infection. She'd worn another long-sleeved uniform shirt to protect it.

Robo hopped down from the back of the Explorer, and with a waving tail, he trotted ahead to the front door. Ever conscious of alpha training, Mattie made him wait for her to enter first and then gave him permission to cross the threshold after her. It was a small thing, but Robo was the type of high-drive dog who would decide to take charge if you let him, and it was always good to remind him who was boss.

Once inside she told him he was free to go, and he hustled over to the dispatcher's desk to greet Rainbow, who received him with open arms. Literally. After Mattie clocked in, she joined them.

Her dog was having a love fest, leaning against Rainbow as she scratched his ears, his mouth open in a toothy grin.

"You spoil him," Mattie said, giving her friend a smile behind the words.

"He's just a big baby, that's what he is." Rainbow ruffled the fur at his neck as he stretched upward to lick her face.

Mattie had to correct him, even though he was fresh from a nap and hadn't had a run yet to dispense all that energy. "That's enough, Robo. You know better. Come. Sit."

He obeyed, though he eyed Rainbow lovingly.

"Sorry, Mattie. I'll try not to get him so riled up. He's just so cute, I can't help myself."

Mattie knew Rainbow would get her dog worked up again another time—that's the way the two of them rolled. But she had to look at it as a good training opportunity; Robo needed to learn to behave himself when he was at work, even when he was tempted not to. "Am I the first one here?"

"You are. This is an awful situation about Nate Fletcher. Poor Kasey."

"Do you know her?"

"Some. She was a few years ahead of me in school, but I remember she was a cheerleader. She seemed to be active in all the sports, too."

Since Rainbow had been born and raised in Timber Creek, Mattie considered her a good source of information about the community. "Did you know Nate?"

"Not really. I mean, I know who he was and all that. Called himself Mustang Fletcher. Liked to flirt with all the girls at the Watering Hole."

This was the first she'd heard about Nate flirting at the local bar. "Before or after he was married?"

"Well, he moved here after they married, but it didn't seem to slow him down with women. I tended bar before I started working here, and I remember he loved to party."

"Huh. Do you think he could've been cheating on Kasey?"

"I have no idea, but his flirting in those days seemed harmless and directed at everyone. He often brought groups in from out of town for hunting. They would all stop at the bar, and the drinks flowed."

Nate must have been quite the party animal. "Drugs?"

"Gosh, no. You know I'd let you know if I ever suspected anyone of drug use."

Rainbow might be a good source of information, but Mattie would never want the community to associate her with being a narc for the department. "Don't let anyone else hear you say that."

"Why not? Folks know we take a hard stand against drugs here."

"I guess you're right." Mattie remembered the man she'd seen Rainbow with at the dance. "By the way, who was that cowboy you were dancing with last night?"

Rainbow giggled. "Ben Underwood from California."

Mattie's brother Willie had come from California. Even mention of the state brought the events surrounding his death back to her, and she had to push them out of her mind. "What brought him to town?"

"Fishing trip. With Nate Fletcher, actually."

Mattie frowned in surprise. So Rainbow's cowboy was one of Nate's customers.

Rainbow continued to chat. "I haven't talked to him today, so I don't know what he's going to do now. They might have to go home."

"They?"

"He's with a friend, I guess, although Ben's the only one who came to the dance."

Mattie couldn't help but wonder if they were involved somehow in Nate's death. "When did they come into town?"

"They got here yesterday."

Mattie put the pieces together, and they fell into place easily. She needed to find out more about these out-of-town visitors. "Do you happen to know his buddy's name?"

"No, but I could call Ben."

Just in case these fishermen from California were involved with a homicide, Mattie didn't want Rainbow drawn into it. "No, don't mention it to him, okay? Since they're hooked in with Nate's business, Stella and I need to interview them. Let us take care of it. I don't even want them to know that you and I had this conversation. And I want you to stay away from Ben until we can clear him."

Rainbow frowned. "I'm sure they had nothing to do with Nate."

"Probably not, but I don't want them to connect you with the investigation, okay?"

"So serious, Mattie." Rainbow shrugged as if dismissing her concern. "Ben is just a normal guy, but I don't really know his friend, so I'll let you handle it your way. Police business and all that."

"Good."

Stella entered the front door, and Mattie lifted her hand in greeting. After checking in, the detective headed for her office. "Meet you in the briefing room in five minutes, Mattie. Let me grab a cup of coffee and my laptop."

Mattie wrapped up her conversation with Rainbow and went to the staff office, a large room with four desks lining the walls. Hers sat in the corner with a bright-red dog cushion beside it, which Robo leapt on before going shoulders-down in a play pose, his way of saying he wanted a treat.

She couldn't resist his request, although she decided to make him work for it. She called him over to her and told him to sit and then lie down. She asked him to do the more difficult task of standing up from a down, which he performed within a split second. She gave him two treats.

"You're pretty smart, aren't you?" She stroked his head and gave him a kiss on the broad place between his ears. "Go lie down and wait."

Robo pounced on the cushion, looking at her expectantly as if hoping the work-and-reward game had not yet ended. When she didn't respond, he circled and lay down.

She signed on to the Internet and Googled Nate's business, Mustang Outfitters. It popped up immediately, the screen displaying a full spread of beautiful photos of the Rocky Mountains around Timber Creek. There was a posed shot of Nate dressed in fringed chaps and a leather vest, sitting astride a black horse as he casually leaned toward the camera, his arms crossed over the saddle horn. He'd been a handsome guy, dark eyes, cocky smile, and he looked about her age—around thirty.

Mustang Outfitters advertised a ten-thousand-acre ranch with private access to BLM land, which matched the family's information and was what Mattie expected. The site's photos gave her a clearer picture of the ranch headquarters than what she'd glimpsed in the dark last night. Pictures of a string of saddled horses tied in front of a picturesque old wooden barn and campsites set in gorgeous forested high country suggested a dream vacation for those who wanted to see the Rockies from the back of a horse.

She shut down the site and got up to fill her coffee mug with dark brew that sat on the burner in a half-full pot. Giving Robo a training challenge, she told him, "Let's go find Stella."

Robo had been watching her every move, and he scrambled from his cushion and trotted out of the staff office. Carrying her cup of coffee and a notebook, Mattie trailed behind and observed him. He put his nose to the floor outside Stella's office and then followed her scent trail to the briefing room. He scratched at the closed door, and confirmation that her dog had now learned the detective's name left her shaking her head in admiration as she opened the briefing room door for him.

"Come in, Robo," Stella called from inside. She was setting up the whiteboard to record evidence for the case and had posted Nate's photo at the top, after evidently grabbing the one Mattie had just seen from his website and printing it.

Brody came into the room carrying his own mug of coffee—fuel for a long day after only a few hours of sleep. He looked bleary-eyed and grumpy, and his voice sounded raspy. "What do we have so far?"

Mattie took a seat at the table nearest the whiteboard, and Robo settled in beside her. The briefing room was set up to be functional. Photos of the Timber Creek County courthouse and the Colorado state capitol building on the walls, the Colorado state flag standing in a corner of the room, and five long tables with aluminum-framed plastic chairs were the room's only appointments.

Stella replied to Brody's prompt. "I'm going to drive over to the Byers County morgue to observe the autopsy later this afternoon, and I'd like to get as much done as we can before I go. We've got information we need to share with you, Brody, and then we need to coordinate and lay out a plan."

Stella went on to summarize the results of the family notification and the interview with Flint Thornton for Brody while she recorded salient bits on the whiteboard. "We have to look at wife and family when we ask who killed Nate Fletcher, but GSR swabs were negative for all of them. I think we can clear Lillian and Doyle, and we can accept the alibis for wife Kasey and sister-in-law Eve. Agreed, Mattie?"

Mattie thought the reasoning was sound. "Agreed, but we have to talk to Kasey about finding trace cocaine in Nate's van. I'm willing to bet she knows something about that."

"Okay, we'll keep her on the Persons of Interest list." Stella started a new heading on the board. "And brother-in-law Tyler. He needs to be on this list."

Mattie recalled Tyler's lack of emotion about Nate's death and wondered if he wouldn't eventually turn into a full-blown suspect. But there were more people to consider. "Let's add Flint Thornton to the list, too."

Stella added Flint and then wrote Jasmine Pierce. "I haven't been able to reach Jasmine to confirm Tyler's alibi. I'll keep trying and hope to pin down that detail."

Mattie decided now was a good time to share the information she'd learned from Rainbow about the fishermen from California. After explaining the details, she added, "All I have at the moment is the name Ben Underwood and a friend. Ben was at the dance, but the unknown is unaccounted for. They're staying at the Big Sky Motel."

"That's good," Brody said. "We need to get to them today before they leave on that fishing trip tomorrow with Tyler."

Mattie wasn't sure it was the best idea to stand by and let most of their persons of interest leave town to go into the mountains for days. "Should we try to abort this fishing trip?"

Brody's brow creased as he thought about it. "I imagine they want to go forward with the trip for financial reasons, but you could try to find that out from Kasey when you talk to her. Unless we have a warrant for someone's arrest, we can't stop it."

"We'll talk to this guy, Ben Underwood, and his friend about it, too," Stella said, stepping up to the table to tap the keys of her laptop. "Let's move on to review the evidence we've got. I received a report here from CBI lab. They were unable to determine a brand name from the tire prints, but they're typical of those found on smaller sedans and lightweight trucks rather than SUVs or heavy-duty vehicles. They won't be much help unless we can find a car that has an exact match."

Mattie found that news disappointing. "Any word on the glove?"

"Yes," Stella said, scanning the laptop screen. "They found gunshot residue on the exterior, and they've swabbed the interior for DNA. I've asked them to fast-track those results, but we're looking at Thursday at the earliest."

That sounded more positive to Mattie. "We can still collect DNA samples from people of interest and get them into the lab for comparison as soon as possible. All we have to do is ask."

"And of course refusal always raises a red flag," Stella said before turning back to the computer screen. "The glove is a Wells Lamont cowhide work glove with adjustable wrist, men's size large, and I've got some photos of it that I'll email to you for your phones."

Mattie's phone beeped as the email came through, followed by an echo from Brody's. She opened hers to download the photo. "What's the status on that .38 Special Robo found?"

"The registration number on it was clear as a bell, and I submitted it to the Tracing Center," Stella said. "I hope to know its ownership within forty-eight hours."

That was better news than she thought they'd get. "Have we heard anything from the fire investigators yet?"

"I talked to the lead investigator," Brody said as he swiped and tapped his phone. "He'll get a report to us when they're done, but he shared some preliminary information. The gas cap was removed from the gas tank, making it more likely for it to ignite."

And showing intent to cause as much damage as possible, Mattie thought.

"The Molotov cocktail contained diesel and cotton fabric similar to that found in a white cotton bed sheet," Brody continued. "They'll pin down the exact fabric in the lab, but this will at least give us something to look for. The accelerant used inside the van was also diesel. It's common for an arsonist to burn a vehicle from the inside out, since the interior materials are flammable."

Mattie wanted to bring the conversation back to the cocaine inside the van's door panel. "Cole, Flint, and Rainbow have all indicated that Nate Fletcher wasn't the type to use drugs, and according to Flint, he wasn't supplying narcotics to clients for parties in the mountains. But trace amounts of cocaine in the door panel begs the question—was Nate into drug running? Is that what got him killed?"

Brody rolled his head, making his neck pop. "He's got clients coming in from all over. Perfect setup for trafficking."

Mattie felt her excitement start to build. This was something she and Robo could sort through, which might lead them to Nate's killer. "That could open up a whole new group of suspects. A drug ring? These two men from out of town? We need to find out what Kasey knows about this."

Stella frowned as she nodded. "This is important, Mattie. We're going to have to see if we can search Nate and Kasey's house for narcotics. I hate to put her through it, but we need to determine if she's somehow involved in this as well."

Mattie agreed with Stella. So far, everything indicated that Kasey was a victim here as well as Nate, but maybe they would turn up something to indicate differently. "Right. It's important to see what she has to say, and we can tread lightly. First, I'll ask her permission to search."

"And if she refuses, we have enough that I can get a warrant," Brody said. "It's a shame for the family, but in this case, we've got to dig into Nate's past. That's probably where we'll find the person who killed him."

NINE

Stella decided they should stop at the Big Sky Motel to meet the out-of-towners before driving out to the Redman Ranch. Mattie pulled into the motel and parked outside the office, marked clearly by a sign located on the outer left wing of the U-shaped building. The walls were painted turquoise with white trim, and boxes of newly planted petunias and geraniums adorned the sidewalk that ran along the front of the rooms. Two white metal lounge chairs sat outside each door.

"I'll find out what room they're in," Stella said as she opened her door and stepped out.

The place had only about twelve rooms and there were no cars to be seen in the lot, making Mattie worry that the fishermen had already checked out. It took only a few minutes for Stella to return from the office.

"Ben Underwood is in room eight," Stella said. "He's still checked in, but he and his friend drove away early this morning. Maid cleaned and their baggage is still there, so I expect they'll be back and we can catch them later. We might as well go out to the ranch."

"All right. Did you get the vehicle info and license plate?"

"I did."

"Let me call it in to Rainbow and let her run a registration check."

As Mattie pulled out onto the highway and headed west, she radioed dispatch. After giving Rainbow the information, she drove in silence while Stella gazed out the passenger window and brooded about the case, one of her habits that Mattie had grown used to over the past months.

Within minutes, Rainbow called back. "The vehicle is a silver Cadillac Escalade, Luxury model SUV, registered to Zach Irving of Los Angeles, California. I ran a background on him: no priors, no warrants."

"Thanks, Rainbow."

When Mattie glanced at Stella, she nodded acknowledgment that she'd heard and was taking notes in her notebook.

At about six miles outside town, Mattie turned into the entryway of the Redman Ranch and scanned the layout by the light of day. The headquarters for the place had been built near the actual stream called Timber Creek, and the buildings were surrounded by a leafy canopy of trees: cottonwoods, elms, even maples. Off to the left, a stand of flowering trees, some with rose-colored blossoms and some with white, suggested some kind of orchard.

The white-painted homes were readily apparent, and it looked like there were two of them separated by an ancient barn. The barn was huge, its open door a darkened maw. It had been built of rough-cut lumber and log, weathered by decades of standing resolute out in the elements and the sun. A rusted tin roof covered the top.

A log cabin sat off to the far right, which must be Tyler's home, leaving the second white house as Kasey's.

Mattie took a narrow right fork in the road and followed the gravel path to the front of a boxy white stucco house that looked much smaller than that of her parents. There were two cars parked in front—a silver Honda Civic and a cherry-red Kia sedan—so she assumed Kasey might be at home.

After parking, she told Robo to stay in the car, and she and Stella exited to walk a stone pathway. This home wasn't graced with a cozy outdoor room like Lillian's. Instead its porch consisted of a square slab of concrete with an awning.

They went up onto the porch. Mattie opened the screen door and knocked on a solid wooden one that had been painted green to match the trim on the windows. When no one answered, she knocked harder, thinking she would try one more time before going to look for Kasey at her parents' house.

Kasey's voice came from inside. "Just a minute." A moment later, she opened the door, her eyes reddened and swollen from crying. She wore cotton pajamas beneath a knitted shawl that she clutched tightly around her shoulders with both hands.

A brunette with long, curly hair, fully dressed in jeans and a teal blouse, stood behind Kasey, as if offering support. The way she hovered made Mattie think she must be a friend.

"I'm sorry to bother you, Kasey, but Detective LoSasso and I have something we need to discuss with you," Mattie said, looking pointedly at the unfamiliar woman.

"Oh," Kasey said, glancing behind her. "This is my friend, Jasmine Pierce."

Tyler's alibi. Mattie introduced herself before turning to Stella. "And I believe Detective LoSasso has been trying to reach you."

Jasmine looked surprised. "Me?"

"I need to talk to you about last night," Stella said. "I've left messages for you to call me back."

Jasmine also appeared as if she'd been crying, and her red-rimmed eyes widened at Stella's comment. "Kasey couldn't sleep, so she called me, and I've been here since . . . I don't know . . . about four this morning? I think my phone is in my purse. Let me check."

Sounded possible. The two looked like they could have been up all night.

Jasmine disappeared for a few seconds before returning, her hand buried in a large, open handbag, "My phone isn't here. I must've left it at home after hearing the news about Nate. I was in shock when I left."

"May we come in, Kasey?" Stella asked.

"Sure." Kasey opened the screen door wide. "But the place is a mess. I've been so busy helping with Dad the past few months, I've let everything go."

Emerald-tinted draperies covered the two front room windows, and Mattie's eyes adjusted slowly to the dim light. The small living room was crowded with only a few pieces of large, overstuffed furniture: a floral upholstered sofa with wooden trim and two matching armchairs that looked like they could be antiques. A dark walnut coffee table sat against the wall and held a narrow television, and a closer look revealed framed photos on each side—one of the four members of the Redman family in better times when the kids might have been teenagers, the other a wedding picture of Kasey and Nate, smiling and happy as they posed in the traditional white gown and dark tux. Magazines and newspapers lay scattered about, the newspapers still rolled and unread.

After stepping inside, Stella turned to Jasmine. "The reason I called was to find out where you were last night. It's a routine question, and we're asking all the family and close friends."

Jasmine placed her hand on her throat, looking worried despite the detective's reassurance. "I was at the dance with Tyler until we left to go to my house."

"And what time was that?" Stella asked.

"It was about a quarter to eleven. I checked my phone for text messages when we got out to the car, so I remember the time."

"And how long did Tyler stay at your house?"

Jasmine looked as if she was thinking. "Until a little before two? I'm not exactly sure of that time, but we watched a movie and he left right after."

Though Jasmine had provided more detail, her time frames matched what Tyler had told them, and if she was being truthful, he now had an alibi. Although Jasmine appeared stressed, Mattie couldn't read any obvious signs of deception.

"Thank you, Jasmine," Stella said. "Now, if you'll excuse us, we need to talk to Kasey privately for a few minutes. We won't take very long."

Kasey clutched her shawl about herself tighter, as if for protection. "We're best friends. There's nothing about me that Jasmine doesn't know. We can speak in front of her."

Jasmine put her arm around Kasey's shoulders. "It's okay, Kasey. I can wait outside."

Stella was quick to respond. "That would be best."

Mattie held the door while Jasmine went outside and headed toward the red Kia.

Kasey sat on one of the chairs, while Stella sat on the other. Mattie took a seat on the couch.

Stella opened the conversation. "Kasey, we've turned up some information that we need to tell you, and we hope you can clarify some things for us."

Kasey met Stella's eyes with an unwavering gaze. "I'll do anything I can to help."

"This is about what we found in Nate's van." Stella paused for a few beats. "Our K-9 hit on narcotics in Nate's van, and it turned out to be a trace of cocaine."

Kasey looked startled. "Nate didn't use drugs. And anyway, I thought the van had burned."

"It did, but the driver's side door had been opened, so the panel didn't burn completely." Stella leaned forward, her gaze intense. "Kasey, could Nate have been involved in the drug business in any way?"

"Never. Nate liked to party, but beer was his choice," Kasey said, her voice adamant, as if she had no reason to doubt her husband.

Mattie studied Kasey while she spoke. It seemed like she was telling the truth, and her answers corroborated the information given by Rainbow, Cole, and even Flint.

Stella continued to press. "Was he involved with the transportation or sale of drugs?"

Kasey shook her head, her face filling with dismay. "I don't understand. Nate is the victim here. Why are you searching for something to pin on him?"

"That's not what we're trying to do," Stella said. "We're following up on evidence. We need to find Nate's killer. If he was involved with the drug trade, that would give us a whole new direction to take our investigation and a different group of people we need to look at. Does that make sense?"

Kasey stared at the black television screen, obviously trying to put the pieces together, her face tight with distress. A pang of sympathy for the grieving woman made Mattie's thoughts go a different direction. "Kasey, how long have you owned that van?"

"It's fairly new to us. I think we bought it about four months ago."

Mattie exchanged glances with Stella, while the detective's brow lowered in a frown.

"Where did you buy it?" Stella asked.

"At a used car dealership in Denver."

"Could I look at that paperwork?"

"Now?"

"Now would be good," Stella said. "Especially if you're sure that Nate had nothing to do with the drug trade."

"Of course he didn't." Kasey sounded offended as she stood, the bit of anger apparently giving her renewed energy. "Let me see if I can find it in our box of receipts to be filed. I'm behind on things in the office, too."

Mattie decided now was as good a time as any to ask. "Kasey, one more thing. Would you give me permission to bring my dog in here to make sure there's nothing—"

Indignant, Kasey interrupted. "You've got to be kidding me!"

"I was going to say to make sure there was nothing that Nate might have hidden from you. You wouldn't be the first wife who learned about her husband's shady business after his death." Mattie raised both hands in a wait-a-minute gesture as Kasey opened her mouth to protest. "I'm not saying that's what's going on here, Kasey. I'm saying we need to eliminate that possibility if we're going to do a thorough investigation and find Nate's killer. If we find nothing, then we won't need to search your property any further. Right?"

"Oh, good grief." Kasey dropped her shawl on the sofa and turned to march toward the doorway that led to the back part of the house. "Go ahead. You won't find anything."

"I need to have you sign a consent form," Mattie called after her.

Kasey stopped and turned, looking as if a thought had just occurred to her. "That's no problem, but my sister came over last night to stay with me and didn't go to sleep until after sunrise. She's asleep in my bedroom. Do you need to go in there?"

"I'm sorry," Mattie said, "but I'll need to do a thorough job, the bedroom included."

"Poor kid, she was exhausted. I hate to wake her up." Kasey turned left at the hallway before going out of sight.

"I'll help Kasey dig into her files," Stella murmured, "if she'll let me. See if I notice anything useful."

Jasmine was in the red Kia playing music when Mattie stepped outside. The music ended abruptly, and Jasmine opened the car door to get out until Mattie raised a hand. "We're almost done, Jasmine," Mattie called. "Just a few more minutes."

Jasmine frowned but settled back in her seat, closed the door, and turned her music back on.

As always, Robo appeared ecstatic when Mattie put on his narcotics search collar and let him out. She made sure he did his business outside the yard, sacrificing her own car tire, before putting him on a leash. After grabbing a consent form, she led him up the porch steps and let herself back into the house, Robo at heel.

Her short hair smashed against her head, Eve came through a doorway that was straight ahead on the other side of the hall, and Mattie glimpsed a bathroom beyond the open door. Eve's sleepy eyes widened when she saw Robo. "What a gorgeous shepherd."

Mattie smiled and gave a nod of acknowledgment. "I'm sorry to wake you up."

"That's okay. I should get ready to go home and help Mom anyway." She headed toward the kitchen. "But first . . . caffeine."

"Is Kasey back there?" Mattie asked Eve, gesturing toward the hallway.

"Yeah, the room on the right."

Mattie followed the sound of Kasey's voice into a room taken up for the most part by an old oak desk, and caught the tail end of the conversation.

"I have to go through with this fishing trip Nate scheduled," Kasey was saying to Stella. "The clients paid for the trip in advance. We've put a lot of money into equipment for the business and I couldn't afford to refund their payments, so Tyler said he'd run the trip for me."

Kasey was sorting through a stack of papers, but when she glanced up, her eyes were drawn to Robo. She slumped in her chair and audibly exhaled as if all her steam leaked out with her breath. Tears filled her eyes. "He's beautiful. We just lost our dog last winter, an Old English sheepdog." Kasey took the permission form, signed it without reading it, and handed it back to Mattie. "I'm afraid you won't find anything to help with your investigation here in my home, but you're welcome to look."

Mattie folded the form and tucked it into her shirt pocket. "We'll start in the bedroom. Robo, come with me."

As she left, she heard Stella ask a question that should be asked of any spouse in a murder investigation. "Did your husband have life insurance that will help with your expenses?"

Stella had couched the question in nonchallenging terms, and Mattie slowed to listen for Kasey's reply.

"He did, but I'm not sure how much. His parents have the policy. You'll have to ask them about it."

Mattie went into the bedroom. A king-size bed dominated the floor, and its tangled taupe satin sheets looked nothing like the strips of white cotton used in the Molotov cocktail. She clipped Robo's leash to the dead ring on his collar and led him in a counterclockwise sweep of the room's perimeter, taking only a couple minutes for him to slink around, sniffing wherever she indicated, before heading out to the other rooms.

In the living room, a small bench sat beside the front door, boots and shoes scattered on the floor nearby. A pair of work gloves made of leather lay on the bench seat, and they appeared to be a size-small women's glove. Mattie picked them up to keep them from sliding off and tilted open the seat to peer into the compartment. Gloves and hats of all kinds filled the storage space, but none of the gloves matched the one found at the roadside.

When she took Robo through a different internal doorway into the kitchen, she found a quaint and cozy room filled with older appliances, a retro gray-topped Formica table, and four red plastic chairs with aluminum ladder backs and legs. There was no room for a dishwasher in the small space, and dirty dishes filled the sink and cluttered the countertops. Like the rest of the house, the kitchen spoke of the couple's attention being turned toward something other than housework.

Eve sat at the table drinking a cup of coffee. "Should I leave?" she asked.

"Not necessary. Just stay put, and he'll sniff around you."

Mattie and Robo worked the small room in a matter of seconds, swept the office and bathroom, and in the end Robo proved Kasey's prediction to be true—the entire house was free of narcotics.

By this time, Stella and Kasey had come out from the office, Stella carrying paperwork that Mattie assumed belonged to the van.

Mattie made eye contact with Kasey. "You were right. Robo didn't hit on anything here in your home."

Her face filled with sorrow, Kasey nodded, apparently receiving the news graciously. "Do you need anything more from me?"

"Not now," Stella said as she walked toward the door to leave. "I'll be back in touch after I visit with the medical examiner."

Eve came from the kitchen just as Mattie was about to follow Stella through the door. "Can I pet your shepherd?" she asked.

While Stella went ahead and stepped outside, Mattie stayed for a minute, letting both Eve and Kasey pet Robo before going out the door. Just as she stepped onto the porch, a silver Lexus pulled up next to her SUV and parked. A guy with white-blond hair and a ruddy complexion jumped from the driver's side and jogged up the sidewalk. Kasey grabbed her shawl while Mattie stepped aside on the porch to give him room as he charged up the steps. Stella stayed below in the yard, one brow quirked in her bemused expression.

"Kasey!" He embraced her, both arms wrapped around hers while she clutched the shawl around her body. "Aw, Kasey, I'm so sorry. This is terrible."

Kasey turned her face away from his chest, trying to pull away. He let go reluctantly and stepped back to gaze at her with a wounded expression, one hand outstretched for a second before he let it fall. "I came as soon as I heard."

Kasey held the shawl closed at her chest, its edges bunched in her fists. "Thanks, Wilson. But there's really no need."

That felt like a strange response. The whole picture seemed like sort of a shutdown, and Mattie wondered who this Wilson guy was and what was his relationship to Kasey.

He looked hurt but tried to hide it. "I wanted to see if there's something I could do to help."

Kasey shook her head, looking downward as if avoiding eye contact. "There's nothing anyone can do."

She sounded lost, hopeless, and Mattie decided to intervene. She introduced herself and Stella. "We're from the Timber Creek Sheriff's Department. And your name, sir?"

"Excuse me, my head's not on straight. This is all such a tragedy." He offered a handshake, pumping Mattie's arm twice with a firm grip before moving on to Stella. "I'm Wilson Nichol. I've known Tyler and Kasey since we were kids."

Pulling on a jacket over her pajamas as she stepped out onto the porch, Eve stood beside her sister, looking at Wilson with a frown. Jasmine came from her car to join the group.

"Hey, Jasmine," Wilson said to her.

"Wilson," she replied, going up onto the porch to flank Kasey, she and Eve looking like bodyguards.

Since no one seemed happy to see this old friend, Mattie thought she'd better find out more about him. Could he have had something to do with Nate's murder? "Do you live nearby, Mr. Nichol?"

"I live over in Willow Springs," he said, taking out his wallet to hand her a business card. "I own Western Colorado Realty there. We specialize in farm and ranch properties."

While Mattie reached for his card, Wilson's eyes were drawn back to Kasey. Mattie recognized a quality in his gaze that she'd seen lately when Cole looked at her—a spark that went beyond friendship. Meanwhile, Kasey's eyes remained downcast.

Eve was several inches taller than her older sister, and she placed an arm protectively around Kasey's shoulders. "Wilson, Kasey and I haven't had a chance to clean up yet, and we need to go over to Mom and Dad's house. Thanks for stopping by, but we don't have time to visit."

Wilson stared at Eve for a few beats before he looked at Kasey. "I'll come by later then. I just wanted to tell you how sorry I am about Nate. Let me know if there's anything I can do to help."

"I will." Kasey turned to go inside with Eve while Jasmine stayed on the porch.

As Wilson passed by on the way to his car, Robo sniffed at him, and his movement toward the man caught Mattie's eye. Did her dog smell something that interested him, like gunpowder or dope? Or was he merely taking a whiff of a stranger?

She led Robo to her SUV, walking him past Wilson's car to see if he would alert on something. Robo had done hundreds of vehicular drug sweeps since he'd come to work with her in Timber Creek, and it was routine for him to take a free sniff whenever he walked past a car. If Wilson's SUV had transported drugs recently, Robo would tell her.

Her dog walked past the Lexus without interest, so she loaded him up in her unit. Stella had already settled into the passenger seat. But the scowl on Jasmine's face as she watched Wilson turn around and drive away made it impossible for Mattie to leave without finding out what Kasey's friend was thinking.

As Mattie walked back toward her, Jasmine lost the scowl. "Yes?"

Mattie thought she might as well just come right out with it. "I noticed you weren't happy to have Wilson stop by."

Jasmine shook her head. "Was it that obvious?"

Mattie nodded.

Jasmine sighed. "Wilson had a thing for Kasey in high school. They dated for a while, but Kasey ended it when she went to college. He's still Tyler's friend, though."

When Jasmine paused, Mattie prompted her. "And?"

"I suppose Wilson thinks he can move back in on Kasey now that Nate's gone, but she's not interested. The sooner he figures that out, the better off we'll be."

Mattie was glad she'd stayed to ask. Jealousy was a strong motive, and it gave them a good lead to follow. She thanked Jasmine for her candor and left.

As she climbed into her SUV, Stella glanced up from the documents she'd been reading. "What's up?"

Mattie told her about what she'd seen between Wilson and Kasey and what Jasmine had to say. "It strikes me as significant. Here's a man looking at the new widow with love in his eyes. Seems like a motive to me."

Stella pursed her lips and stared out the windshield as she thought about it. "Well, well. I'll call Brody and see what he can find out about Wilson Nichol online. Then let's figure out a time we can go talk to him."

TEN

When Mattie and Stella cruised by the motel on their way through town, the Cadillac SUV was still absent, so they picked up sandwiches at the grocery store and then drove on to the station. Mattie took Robo to the staff office to call Cole. She'd been hesitant to contact him in front of Stella in case the conversation drifted to personal subjects.

He answered on the first ring. "The doctor just left, and I was about to call you."

"How is Garrett doing?"

"Better. Looks like there's been no more bleeding in his brain. He's sleeping off and on. Still has vision problems, but the doctor is hopeful that will resolve."

That news came as a relief. "Sounds good."

"It's the best we can hope for right now."

She wondered when they might be able to interview Garrett and Leslie. "Does the doctor consider him stable?"

"Yeah, I'd say so."

"How is Leslie holding up?"

"She's exhausted, but relieved. She was dozing in the chair when I left the room." Cole paused. "I need to figure out a way to get her vehicle over here so she'll have transportation."

"I might be able to help with that." Mattie thought about it for a moment. "Stella and I need to talk with both Garrett and Leslie. Maybe one of us could drive her truck over to you."

"I'll be leaving here sometime today. We could time it so that I could give you a ride back home."

"We'll work it out. I'll call you back."

Cole sighed. "It'll be good to see you."

Mattie felt a tug in her midsection. "Same here. I'll call you soon and let you know our plans."

Mattie ended the call. Her body seemed to be pulling her toward Cole, even though it had been less than a day since she'd seen him. She missed him, but he was needed at the hospital. Cole was like family to the Hartmans. Thank goodness Leslie had him to help her at a time like this.

Thinking of family made her remember her search for her own. She opened her email on her computer to see if she'd received one about her DNA results, but she was disappointed to find there was still no word.

She joined Brody and Stella in the war room, where she chose a ham and Swiss on rye for lunch and Robo ducked under the table to lie down.

Brody pulled up Kasey's Facebook page on his laptop and turned the computer so Mattie and Stella could see the screen. "Lucky for us, hardly anyone uses the privacy settings. Here's the most interesting thing I've found."

Kasey's latest post had been made the previous week, and it was a shot of her from the past. Dressed in a pink tailored western suit and matching colored Stetson, she sat astride a handsome black-and-white paint horse, a banner proclaiming MISS TIMBER CREEK COUNTY stretched diagonally across her chest. Kasey's caption stated, THOSE WERE THE DAYS! HERE I AM ON GOOD OLE BOSS, RODEO QUEEN MY SENIOR YEAR OF HIGH SCHOOL.

"Take a look at the comments," Brody said.

There it was, right at the top, a comment made by Wilson Nichol: HEY, GORGEOUS. LOVED YOU THEN, STILL LOVE YOU NOW.

"Wears his heart on his sleeve, doesn't he?" Stella muttered. "Wonder what Kasey and Nate thought of that."

"Kasey liked the comment," Brody said. "From what I can tell, though, Nate didn't use Facebook much. He's got a business page, but there's very little on it. He didn't comment on any of Kasey's posts, so he might not have even seen it. Go ahead and read some of the others. There seems to be a lot of love going around in that group."

Sure enough—many of the posts made by men and women alike expressed their love for Kasey. Mattie shrugged one shoulder. "Seems like most people love her. Friendship? Romance? Hard to say. But in Wilson's case, considering what I saw and what Jasmine said, I'd bet on romance."

Stella scrolled down Kasey's Facebook page. "Yeah, but did she love him back? Knowing that would make a difference."

"Jasmine says she doesn't," Mattie said.

Nodding acknowledgment, Stella rose from her chair to go to the whiteboard that held notes about Nate's case. She picked up the marker and started to write. "I contacted Cabela's in Sidney, where everyone thought Nate had gone, and they were willing to cooperate when I explained I was investigating his homicide. According to their records, there's been no activity on Nate's business account for months. If he was at their store yesterday, he didn't purchase anything. So why wasn't he where he was supposed to be?"

Mattie didn't have the answer to that yet, but the question did stir up others. Had Nate been having an affair with someone? And what about Wilson? Had he killed Nate out of jealousy? Or did he know something about Nate that had enraged him enough to motivate him to homicide? "We've got to get to Wilson as soon as we can. Maybe he'll give us some answers."

Mattie shared Cole's news about Garrett's condition, suggesting they drive over to Willow Springs to interview Wilson Nichol and the Hartmans as well as help Leslie by delivering their truck. "Then I can catch a ride back to Timber Creek with Cole."

"All right," Stella said. "I'll take my car so I can drive on to the autopsy afterward. We'll talk to Wilson first and then Garrett."

Mattie felt anxious to be on the way. "I'll call and make an appointment with Wilson Nichol. I don't want to give him a chance to avoid us."

Stella gave her a nod. "Don't worry. We'll pin him down."

★ ★ ★

Mattie swung by her house to drop off her vehicle and settle Robo in for the afternoon. She hated to part with him, but it was too hot to leave him in the car for long periods, even if he did have his own air conditioning in the back. After Stella picked her up, they went to get the Hartman truck so that Mattie could drive it to Willow Springs.

It took just under an hour to reach their destination, and they dropped off the truck in the hospital parking lot before taking Stella's car to the office of Western Colorado Realty, an attractive log building with a red metal roof. The sign out front confirmed that the business specialized in the sale of rural properties as well as rental of vacation homes and cabins.

Before Stella could pull into a parking space, Mattie leaned forward and waved for her to keep on driving. "I'd like to swing into the alley and check out the back of the building."

"Why's that?"

Maybe it was her years of patrol or maybe her narcotics detection training, but Mattie usually liked to know the layout of the building before she went inside. Partly to know if there were backdoor exits, and partly just to know what kind of outbuildings were on the property. She explained her reasoning to Stella.

"Okay," Stella said, "we'll go satisfy your curiosity. Never hurts to have too much information."

Stella swung around the block and entered the alley that ran behind the building. There was no fence to block the view, and she slowed to a stop as they came to a dumpster that sat outside a small garden shed. Mattie got out to poke around, and the glint of glass at the base of the shed caught her eye. A flat of old jars, their labels faded and missing from sitting out in the weather. She felt a buzz of excitement. These were the same type of jar as the one used in the Molotov cocktail.

She motioned Stella to join her, and being careful to stay in the alley and not venture onto Wilson's property, she walked where she could see the edge of the building. Anything found open to the eye from public roadways was fair game and could possibly be used to get a search warrant. Mattie spotted a red plastic fuel can leaning against the side of the shed next to the padlocked door and pointed it out to Stella. The detective swiped her phone camera to zoom in and take photos of both the fuel can and jars.

"This will give us some talking points," Stella said, shooting Mattie a pleased glance. "Way to go."

After parking in front, they went inside, where a pretty receptionist with red lacquered nails and silver bangles on her wrists offered them something to drink. They both declined, and she used the interoffice phone to tell Wilson they'd arrived. "He'll see you in just a few minutes."

Mattie let her gaze travel around the lobby. Western paintings adorned the walls as well as aerial photos of various ranch houses surrounded by green meadows and mountainous settings. One wall appeared dedicated to photos of rental properties: cabins surrounded by forests or sitting beside lakes and rivers, vacationers in chest-high waders fly-fishing in the water.

As promised, Wilson arrived within a few minutes, his right hand outstretched. When he came close, Mattie could smell the alcohol on his breath with an undertone of peppermint he'd most likely used to try to mask it. She was particularly sensitive to the scent of liquor, an aftereffect of being raised by an alcoholic. It wasn't a big deal—he might have had a drink over a business lunch—but the odor hadn't been present when she spoke to him this morning. Maybe Kasey's rebuff had set him to drinking.

"Did Tara offer you something to drink?" he asked. "Can I get you anything?"

"Tara did offer, but no, thank you." Stella glanced at her watch. "I have another appointment soon, so perhaps we could speak with you privately?"

"Of course. Come this way." Wilson escorted them back to an inner office and then ushered them toward a dark leather sofa and chairs that circled a glass coffee table near the window. "Please, have a seat."

Mattie and Stella sat on a sofa against the wall while Wilson settled into a plush chair. A handsome oak desk dominated the other side of the room, dark leather armchairs poised in front of it. Framed photographs of Wilson playing golf, riding a horse, and posing midhandshake with formally dressed individuals hung on the wall.

"How can I help you?"

Stella sat forward on the edge of the sofa. "I understand that you've been friends with Tyler and Kasey Redman for years."

"We go way back. In fact, the three of us grew up together."

"So you know them well."

"Almost as well as my own family. The Redmans have had it tough this past year." Wilson was shaking his head in dismay. "What a terrible tragedy—Nate's death. I hope you can find out who killed him."

"Do you have any information that might help us with that?"

Wilson looked startled. "Me? No, ma'am. I know the Redmans, but I'm not that familiar with Nate. Or the people in his life."

"Don't you socialize with Tyler and the Redman family?"

Wilson's complexion turned rosy. "Well . . . I did. I mean, I do. Some. But not so much since Kasey and Nate married. I mean, I see Kasey now and then around town or at her parents' house, but not Nate."

That was a lot of stammering around just to say "not much anymore."

"Why would that be?" Stella asked.

Wilson fiddled with the cuff on his tailored blue shirt. "No reason, really. Kasey runs in a different social crowd, I guess. I live and work here in Willow Springs. Don't go over to Timber Creek as much as I used to."

It seemed like this line of questioning was making him nervous. To Mattie, his body language confirmed that he had feelings for Kasey, and she thought it was a safe bet that he'd been jealous of Nate.

Stella's brow lowered as she pursued it. "I understand that you and Kasey were high school sweethearts."

"Yeah. A long time ago."

"Some speculate that you might still have feelings for her."

Above his navy-blue silk tie, Wilson's neck and face flushed a deep red. "Who said that?"

Stella shrugged. "Someone who knows Kasey quite well."

"Probably Jasmine," Wilson said, sighing. "She always sticks her nose where it doesn't belong. Sure, I still care about Kasey. Like I would care about a sister, you know."

Men don't gaze at their sisters the way you looked at Kasey this morning, Mattie thought. "How well did you know Nate?" she asked.

He turned toward Mattie. "I met him a few years ago when he and Kasey married. Went to their wedding and wished them well. But other than that, like I said, I don't see him."

Mattie pursued the topic. "You're friends with Tyler, though. Did he ever talk about his brother-in-law? Did you get to know Nate through him?"

"Nope. I mean, maybe Tyler mentioned him a time or two. He didn't think much of Nate, but no, we didn't spend time talking about him."

Stella picked up the questioning, zeroing in on Wilson's words. "Tyler didn't like Nate?"

Wilson tugged at his collar. "I didn't mean to say he didn't like him. He liked him well enough, I guess. I should have said that Nate just wasn't the subject of our conversations. You know what I mean."

"You said Tyler didn't think much of Nate. In my book that means he didn't like him." Stella pinned the full force of her gaze on him. "Why didn't Tyler think much of him?"

"Look, I'm not pointing a finger at Tyler in any way. Maybe Tyler didn't get along with Nate as well as he hoped. But that doesn't make either of them a bad guy, especially not Tyler."

Mattie threw out exactly what she was thinking. "Maybe Tyler hoped that you would be his brother-in-law someday, not Nate."

Wilson stared at her for a few beats. "Maybe, but that wasn't in the cards. Kasey fell in love with another guy. I moved on. End of story. There's no more to it than that."

Stella asked the question that had to be answered. "Where were you last night around eleven o'clock?"

Wilson's eyebrows shot up. "Here in Willow Springs."

"With whom?" Stella asked.

Wilson's skin was starting to look dewy with sweat. "I was at home all evening watching movies. I went to bed early."

Stella looked skeptical. "On a Saturday night?"

Knowing that was exactly how the detective had spent her own Saturday night, Mattie had to suppress her amusement.

Worry lines etched Wilson's forehead. "Absolutely. I'd been out late on Friday, and Saturday is a big workday for me. I have more appointments on Saturday than any other day of the week. I was beat. I took the night off."

"And can anyone verify that?"

"Not really." It looked like a flash of insight erased his worried expression. "Wait a minute. I made some phone calls during the evening. You can take a look at my cell phone records, can't you? Isn't that how it's done these days? I wasn't anywhere near Timber Creek, so you won't get any pings off that tower."

Mattie studied him as he settled back in his chair, once again sure of himself. *Must watch his share of detective shows on television.* She sorted through the ways a person could give himself an alibi with a cell phone: leave it at home, leave it with a friend to make some calls, make some calls from home and then turn it off when you travel. But still, she thought, it would be worth checking out. "Will you sign a release form so that we can obtain your records?"

"Absolutely. I have nothing to hide here."

Stella handed him a form from her notebook and settled back on the sofa, crossing one trouser-covered leg over the other while he gave the form a cursory glance and signed it. "One more thing, Mr. Wilson. There's a container of gasoline or some kind of fuel behind your shed out back. What can you tell me about it?"

He looked puzzled. "What?"

Mattie studied him, trying to determine what he was thinking while both she and Stella awaited his next response.

He shook his head, narrowing his eyes. "I don't know what you're talking about."

Stella showed him the picture of the container and jars on her cell phone.

"I have no idea how those things got there. They're not mine." He looked at the photo again. "Anyone could have put that can there. It's outside the shed."

"Can we take a look inside the shed?" Stella asked.

Wilson eyed her, shaking his head. "I don't know what's going on here, but I don't like it. I heard somebody set fire to Nate's van. You're thinking it was me because you found a gas can sitting out beside my shed?"

His defensiveness was unmistakable, but still, he had a point. Most criminals didn't leave the tools of their trade sitting out in the open like that. And yes, anyone could have come down the alley and placed them there. Mattie knew the Timber Creek County prosecutor wouldn't be able to take this discovery to court as evidence. But why would someone plant these things? Was someone trying to frame Wilson?

"The gas can alone doesn't point to guilt," Stella said. "We're taking a broad look at everything right now. So is it all right if we take a look inside the shed?"

"I don't think so," Wilson said, standing and adjusting his cuffs. "I've told you everything I know about Nate Fletcher, so if you'll excuse me, I've got another appointment that I need to get to."

Stella closed her notebook and stood. "All right. But if those aren't your things, can we take them with us?"

Wilson looked cornered, his eyes shifting while he paused, as if trying to analyze the consequences of his choices. "I suppose if I say no, you'll sit out there until you get a warrant to take them."

Stella nodded. "It wouldn't take long to get one. This *is* a homicide investigation."

Wilson waved a hand in dismissal. "Go ahead. Take the trash someone dumped. My fingerprints won't be on anything."

Stella handed him one of her cards. "Thank you for your cooperation, Mr. Nichol. Let me know if you think of anything that might help us in our investigation or if anything comes up."

Wilson stood to escort them out of the office, closing the door firmly behind them.

Missing Robo's familiar greeting from the back, Mattie took the passenger seat. Stella started the engine and drove to the back alley. After bagging the items and loading them into the car trunk, they headed for the hospital.

"Sounds like Wilson and Tyler are close but there was no love lost between Tyler and Nate," Stella said. "That doesn't give us a motive for murder, but it's a lead. We've got to take another look at Tyler. Can we trust an alibi given to us by his girlfriend?"

"I know what you mean. But what would be Tyler's motive? Any thoughts on that?"

Stella frowned, obviously thinking about it. "I don't know. Could he have learned that Nate was cheating on Kasey, making him angry enough to snap?"

That didn't fit. The crime scene indicated someone who'd planned the murder in advance, not someone who'd snapped.

But before Mattie could speak, Stella nixed the theory herself. "No, too organized."

"Could Wilson be the one who discovered Nate was cheating and killed him to supposedly protect Kasey?"

Stella pursed her lips, nodding slowly. "But I think those items could've been planted outside Wilson's shed by someone who wanted to throw us off."

"But who?" If that was a theory worth looking at, it might point back to Tyler. Or maybe Jasmine? Or could they have planned it together? She shared her thoughts with Stella.

They were back at the hospital, and Stella made the turn into the parking lot. "Everything's muddy right now, but the one thing that's clear is that Wilson still has a thing for Kasey. I'll follow up on those phone records to see who Wilson was talking to last night. We'll see if that sheds light on anything. But first we'll go ahead as planned and see if Garrett and Leslie have remembered anything new, and then I'll head on to Nate's autopsy."

Though she was frustrated by the lack of clarity in the case, something inside Mattie's stomach fluttered at the thought of seeing Cole again. And after the interview, she could look forward to an entire uninterrupted hour with him in his truck as they drove home. Maybe she would have an opportunity to bring up that hard conversation she'd wanted to initiate last night.

ELEVEN

It had done Cole's heart good to see Mattie with Garrett and Leslie. She and Stella had both questioned the Hartmans gently, and Mattie's warmth toward his friends had been obvious.

Since Garrett's condition had stabilized, Cole felt comfortable with heading home. Early this morning, he'd called Tess, his office assistant, to ask her to feed and water his animals, but he needed to get home to take care of afternoon chores himself. Then he would head out to the Hartman ranch to check on Garrett's livestock and make arrangements for a neighbor to help over the next few days. When it came to animal care, there was always something to do.

But in the meantime, he had Mattie all to himself while they drove back to Timber Creek. Though he was bone tired, handing her up into the passenger seat of his truck gave his outlook on life a fresh, new face-lift.

After settling into his seat, he turned to study her to see how she was holding up. Fatigue registered itself in the lines around her eyes along with a saddened expression. He reached for her, and she slipped her hand into his. When she turned to face him, he noticed her dark-brown eyes were liquid.

"How are you?" he asked.

She shook her head. "It's hard to see Garrett like that. Will he be able to see normally again?"

"The doctor thinks it's possible. It's early yet."

"And poor Leslie, she loves him so much. Cole, it breaks my heart. They've been through more than anyone should this year, and to think he got hurt trying to save a neighbor. He's such a good person."

"The salt of the earth." He squeezed her hand. "Knowing Garrett, he'd do it all over again if he had to."

She was searching his face, and he knew she was trying to read him just as he'd done with her. "How are you doing? Did you get any sleep?"

"I dozed in the chair a little after the doctor told us the bleeding had stopped."

"Do you want me to drive so that you can sleep?"

"Are you kidding? And miss out on getting to be with you? I don't want to waste time sleeping."

She shook her head at him, but the tiniest of smiles told him she was pleased. "Let me know if you change your mind. Talking to me might not be as awesome as you think."

"Being with you always gives me a lift, Mattie." Cole released her hand long enough to start the engine and back out of the parking space, but then he reached for it again. Hand-holding might be all they had time for today, but it was the best he could do under the circumstances. "I take it you left Robo home."

"Yeah. You can drop me off there."

Cole glanced at her, wondering if he could possibly have more of her attention after they took care of their various responsibilities. "When do you plan to wrap things up tonight?"

"I've got to check in with Brody, and we still have a couple people we need to find and interview—some guys from out of town."

He remembered their earlier conversation. "Why were you asking me about Nate and drugs?"

"Robo hit on the driver's side door panel of Nate's van. The lab found traces of cocaine there."

"That's a surprise. I wouldn't have guessed that Nate had anything to do with the drug trade."

"We're still not sure of it ourselves. The van is fairly new to them, and we need to track down the previous owners. Brody's working on that. Kasey swears that Nate wasn't involved with drugs in any way, and Robo found nothing in their house."

Cole was about to reply when his phone vibrated in his pocket. He grimaced as he released Mattie's hand to fish it out to see who was calling. He didn't have time today for a client emergency, and he hoped one wasn't in the works. Caller ID told him that his oldest, Angela, was calling. "Mattie, this is Angie. I need to take this."

"Of course."

He connected the call with his hands-free system. "Hey, Angel. How are you doing today?"

"Oh Dad." Her plaintive voice came through the truck speakers, loud and clear. "Thank goodness I reached you."

Cole leaned forward in alarm. "What's going on, sweetheart?"

"Mom's flaking out on us, and Sophie's so upset she's crying. We need to come home, Dad."

Olivia, his ex-wife, had been suffering with depression for over a year. In recent months she'd been feeling better, and she'd thought she was ready to reconnect with her daughters by having them stay with her, but this didn't sound good. "What's going on with your mom?"

"Hard to say, since she locks herself away in her room most of the day." Angie sounded stressed. "I can't handle this, Dad. I don't know what to tell Sophie, and she's getting so sad, and . . . and well, we need to come home."

Out of the corner of his eye, he could see Mattie's concern. She loved his kids, too. "Of course you can come home. We just need to figure out how to get you here. Are you safe there at your mom's house for the time being?"

"Sure. We're totally safe, Dad. It's just . . . well, when Sophie started to cry, I got upset, too."

"I'm glad you called." He and the kids had been through some dangerous situations this past year, and how to stay safe was the issue they dwelled on almost daily. Olivia might neglect her kids, but he was relieved to know that at least she hadn't compromised their safety. "I've got some things to take care of for the Hartmans, but then I'll hit the road and come get you."

Mattie was frowning now. "Can you drive to Denver tonight without sleep?" she murmured.

"Dad, I wonder about calling Aunt Jessie. We're supposed to go stay with her later this week. Maybe she could come get us and let us spend the night with her. What do you think?"

His sister Jessie was an attorney who lived in Denver. At sixteen, his daughter was getting a level head on her shoulders, and at the moment she seemed better at problem solving than he. "That's a great idea, Angel. But let me call her, okay? First let me talk to Sophie."

"Here she is."

A great deal of sniffling preceded Sophie's small voice. "Dad?"

Cole's heart ached for his nine-year-old. She, out of all of them, had the hardest time understanding her mother's condition. "Hey, Sophie-bug. I hear that Mom might not be feeling well."

Sophie's breath hitched as she struggled to speak through her tears. "She doesn't want us here, Dad."

Movement from Mattie's side of the truck caught his eye, and a quick glance told him she'd placed her hand on her heart. "Of course she wants you, Sophie. Trust me when I say that. But you know how she struggles with being sad, and something must have set that off. It has nothing to do with you."

"But . . . but Dad . . . it does. She doesn't love me anymore. She doesn't want me here."

Cole focused his tired mind on his daughter, reaching out to her over the miles. "Did she tell you that?"

"Well . . . no. . ."

"Sophie, don't read more into this than what's there. Your mom has an illness. She loves you and wanted you to come stay with her, but her illness is getting in the way of doing what she wants. Your mom loves you, Sophie. Don't forget that."

More sniffling before Sophie could manage a squeaky sound of agreement.

"I'm going to call Aunt Jessie to see if she can come get you, okay? Everything's going to be all right. You'll see."

"But I don't want to leave Mom."

With a glance, Cole shared his frustration with Mattie, and she gave him a look of encouragement. "I understand that, Sophie. But if staying there makes you sad, I think you should come home, and we'll work out another visit with your mom later in the summer. I'll drive you up to Denver over the week-end and we'll do some daytime visits. Something a little shorter than what we planned for this time. How does that sound?"

"Okay, I guess."

Cole could tell Sophie was trying hard to get herself under control. He wasn't above dangling a carrot that he thought she couldn't resist. "Besides, Belle misses you. She'll probably want to come along with me to Denver so she can ride home with you."

Belle was their Bernese mountain dog and the first indoor pet the kids had ever been allowed. Olivia had established a strict no-pets-in-the-house policy, but after she left, Cole had decided that was one of her rules that should be reconsidered. Belle loved all of her new family, but she had a special connection with the youngest member.

"I miss her, too."

Done. He hoped he'd soothed her enough to carry her over until Jessie could arrive. "Are you feeling better now? Can you stop crying and help Angie pack your things?"

"Okay." Her voice was shaky, but she sounded like she was beginning to hold it together. "What do we tell Mom?"

"I'll talk to Mom. Just tell her you love her and you'll be back to see her later, okay?"

"Okay."

"Call me if you want to talk again, Sophie. Will you do that?" He waited for her to agree. "Let me talk to your sister now."

A quick check in with Mattie told him she was brushing tears from her eyes, looking out the passenger's side window and trying to hide it. When Angie came back on the phone, he summed up the plan and told her he would call her back as soon as he talked to her aunt. "Are you okay now, Angie?"

She released a sigh in an audible huff. "I guess so, Dad. It just makes me mad. Sophie has been looking forward to this for a month!"

"I know it's frustrating, and I know your mom has been looking forward to your visit, too. I'll talk to her. I can't help but think she's doing the best she can. Try not to be mad at her, okay?"

"Her best isn't good enough."

Cole could see the distress on Mattie's face. She suffered when his kids did—there was no doubt about it. It was one of the things he loved about her. "Take it easy, Angel. Be careful what you say. Remember that you don't want to say anything hurtful right now in anger. We'll talk it through when you get home. Better yet, we'll talk it over this evening. And I'll call you back after I make plans with Aunt Jessie."

They said their goodbyes, and Cole disconnected the call while his eyes connected with Mattie's. She looked like she'd been through the wringer. His own temper flared. "Damn it. I thought Olivia could handle a visit with her daughters."

"From what you've said, she thought she could, too."

He'd been able to keep his anger under control while talking to the kids, but now he couldn't help letting it out. "I'm all for the kids having a relationship with their mom, but not if it hurts them. I won't let that happen again."

Mattie nodded as she averted her eyes and looked out the windshield. "I know. I know you can't let the kids get hurt. But, well . . ."

Cole looked at her and could see she was trying to organize her thoughts. It was so easy for her to withdraw from family stress and conflict, and it was important for him to know what she was thinking. "What, Mattie? I want to know what you think. In your line of work, I'm sure you've had experience with families that struggle with these kinds of issues."

"Not to mention my own family." Mattie tipped him a sideways glance. "I've told you I've been getting therapy to work on issues from my childhood. One of the things we talk about is my feelings about being abandoned by my mother. It dredges up all kinds of bad emotions, like feeling unloved or unwanted."

"I know that can happen when parents leave their children. I'm doing the best I can to assure the kids that their mother loves them, but Olivia isn't helping much. She isn't pulling her weight in that arena."

"Yes, it seems that way. But what if she bit off more than she could chew, Cole? I mean . . . a week with the kids is a big first step. My therapist and I talk about taking small steps toward building relationships. I think you're on the right track when you said you could take the kids up for a short weekend visit or even for only a day at first. Surely Olivia could handle that."

Cole reacted to her logic by trying to cool down. He took a breath. "You're right. When Sophie cries like that, I can't help but get mad."

Mattie's expression was full of empathy. "I know. Me too."

"I'd better call Jessie and see what she's got planned for the rest of the day." He gave Mattie a grimace as he told his system to dial his sister. He felt relieved when she answered right away.

"Hey, Cole. What's up?"

After greeting her, he explained the situation. "Is there any way you can go get the kids and let them spend the night with you? I'll come up this evening to get them or maybe tomorrow morning."

"Sure, I could do that. Is Olivia okay with this plan?"

"It doesn't matter. As far as I'm concerned, the visit's over."

"I think maybe Olivia should have a say in this, too."

His temper prodded, Cole frowned. His sister, the attorney—she loved the role of devil's advocate. "I'll call her and let her know what's going on, but with the kids so upset, I'm not willing for them to stay there any longer than they have to."

"All right, Cole. You don't have to get all bent out of shape. I'll go get them."

Sheesh—finally. "Thanks, Jessie. I owe you one."

"I like the sound of that. Hey, I've got an even better idea. I'll take a few days off and bring the kids down myself. Then you'll owe me big time."

Cole felt a weight lift from his shoulders. The thought of planning a trip while helping the Hartmans with their animal care as well as taking care of his own had become overwhelming, especially under the added burden of fatigue. "I *will* owe you big time. I appreciate it, Jessie."

"I'll pick the girls up and we'll head down to Timber Creek tonight. Then you can help me deal with the aftermath of their shortened visit."

"Sounds great. Send me a text when you leave Denver, and remind the girls that they can call me if they want to talk. And thanks, Jessie."

"You can thank me later when I call in that big favor you owe me."

They said their goodbyes, and then Cole signed off. When he looked at Mattie, she gave him a soft smile.

"It's nice to have a sister to help out when you need her," she said.

"Yes, but I hate to think what she'll be asking me to do for her in the future." He knew how much family meant to Mattie, and he knew how the losses she'd suffered hurt her. "You're right. I'm lucky to have Jessie. Okay, now for the hard call. I need to talk to Olivia. I'm going to take it off speaker so I can really focus. Is that okay with you?"

"Of course it is." She sent him a teasing smile. "As a cop, I need to tell you that hands-free is safer, but using your phone isn't illegal, so go for it."

He had to admit it would be easier if Mattie couldn't hear his half of this next conversation, but he didn't have time to put it off. He turned off the Bluetooth connection and dialed Olivia. When she didn't answer, he disconnected and redialed.

She answered on his third try, and she sounded sleepy. "What is it, Cole?"

Her terse greeting triggered his temper again. He forced himself to give a civil reply. "Thanks for picking up the phone, Liv. Were you asleep?"

"I was taking a nap. What do you need?"

Cole drew a breath, fighting to stay in control. How to proceed? Well, he might as well just get down to it. He reminded himself to stay as neutral as possible, something his own family counselor had taught him. "I got a phone call from the kids. They say you've been spending a lot of time in your room. They were upset, Liv."

"Oh." It sounded like a guilty-as-charged kind of *oh*.

"Sophie was crying and, well . . . I made the decision to end the visit and bring them home. Jessie will be over soon to get them."

Silence.

"Olivia?"

"I can't believe you'd do that without consulting me first, Cole."

Believe it, Liv, he wanted to say. "As you know only too well, we sometimes have to do what we think is best without consulting each other. I think this first visit was scheduled for too long, and as far as I can tell, it's been too much for you. Am I wrong?"

No reply.

"Talk to me, Liv. I'm just trying to do what's right for the kids. Has it been harder on you than you thought it would be?"

"I guess so." She sounded wan and listless. "I wanted them here so badly, but I felt myself slipping into old patterns on the second day. I guess I've ruined it."

"You haven't ruined it. We'll set up a shorter visit in a few weeks if you feel up to it."

"Angela has become so difficult. I think she hates me. And, well . . . Sophie can be so demanding."

Welcome back to parenting. "First of all, Angie doesn't hate you. She's a teenager, Liv. She just acts that way sometimes. And Sophie probably needs reassurance. It's been a while since she's seen you. She worries that you don't love her."

Olivia's breath caught in a sob. "I've really messed things up."

Cole felt sorry for her, but the kids were his priority. "It's not forever, Liv. Do you want to see them again in a few weeks, maybe a month?"

"Yes." He could tell she was trying to hold back her tears. "Maybe we could try a Saturday."

"All right." He thought he shouldn't have to tell her what to do, but then again, maybe he did. "Can you talk to the kids and tell them you love them before they go? Reassure them that you want to try again in a few weeks."

"Things aren't that easy, Cole."

That had at least roused a bit of energy in her. "I know, Liv. I'm just trying to do right by the kids here."

She released an audible breath, but he couldn't tell if it was in exasperation or determination. "I'll talk to you later."

And with that, she disconnected the call.

He shot a glance at Mattie, but she was gazing out the passenger's side window. He thought she might be trying to give him all the privacy she could. He didn't want her to feel like she wasn't a part of this thing with his family, because someday . . . well, she might be. "I hope I didn't screw that up, but it is what it is. I'm afraid we overestimated her ability to take care of the kids for a week."

Mattie reached out her hand, and he grasped it. "The kids aren't in their usual routine either, and that probably makes it even harder."

"I should have thought of these things."

"You can't anticipate everything. But now you and Olivia both know. Things will go better next time."

He squeezed her hand and sighed. "I need to call Angie back now. According to Olivia, she's been giving her mom a hard time. I guess I better tell her to take it easy."

"You're a good dad, Cole."

"Just doing the best I can."

He released her hand so that he could reconnect the Bluetooth for his call to Angie. Mattie had a way of accepting things and making the best of them, and he appreciated that quality in her more than he could say.

Her previous comment about her childhood nagged at him. Last night, he'd hoped to confess that he knew about the abuse she'd suffered during her childhood and to assure her that it wouldn't affect their relationship, but right now he just couldn't bring himself to do it. Even though Mattie was opening up to him more than ever before, their bond still felt fragile, and he didn't want to say anything that might break it.

His dream of romancing her over the weekend had fallen by the wayside. He wished it could be different, but he'd have to follow her example of accepting things that couldn't be changed.

Sometimes life just gets in the way of love.

TWELVE

As Mattie entered her house, she placed her hand on the ache in her stomach that Cole's goodbye kiss had given her. The way he'd managed to respond to his kids, his sister, and even his ex-wife made her love him even more.

Robo trotted out of the bedroom, yawning and wagging his tail. It was obvious how he'd spent the afternoon, and she knew he'd be even more energetic than usual once he awakened fully. "Did you have a good sleep? Hmm? Do you need to go outside?"

She let him into the backyard, going out onto the porch to watch him circle the perimeter as he sniffed along the fence line below the seven-foot-tall chain-link fence topped with barbed wire. Despite the county's precautions, two different individuals had tried to take Robo's life in her very own yard, and she felt like she could never let down her guard. She rounded the corner of her house to make sure the lock on the gate was secure.

After throwing the ball for Robo to retrieve for about fifteen minutes, she loaded him into the Explorer and headed for the station. Sam Corns was on dispatch duty, and she waved at him as she made her way through the lobby toward Brody's office. She tapped on the door, resulting in Brody's gruff invitation to come in.

"I'm back from Willow Springs," she told him as she settled into one of the cheap plastic chairs in front of his desk. Robo sat on the floor beside her. "We found a fuel container and a box of jars that need to be sent to the lab for processing. Stella has them in her car."

Brody had been working on his computer, and he turned away from the screen to look at her. "LoSasso called and briefed me. I've got a courier ready to take them as soon as she gets back."

"She thinks it'll be another hour or so."

"She'll call me when she knows her ETA." Brody leaned forward, placing his elbows on his desk. "I also tracked the previous owners of Nate's van, Leonard and Dixie Easley. They ran a flower store in Denver, owned the van for years and used it for deliveries. They both turned seventy last year and decided to retire, so they traded in the van at the dealership." Brody looked skeptical. "Call me crazy, but I have trouble believing that Grandpa and Grandma were using that van for drug running."

"Well, I guess you never know, but the odds are against it."

"I saved the best for last." Brody wore his self-satisfied smile. "You know that revolver we found at the scene? I was able to trace the registration number on it myself."

This *was* good news. "And I can tell you found something useful."

"Just did. Haven't even had time to notify LoSasso yet." Brody paused as if waiting for a drumroll. "The gun is registered to Wilson Nichol."

Mattie almost leaped from her chair. This could break the case wide open. "Can we get a warrant for his arrest?"

"There's only one problem. Nichol filed a stolen gun report on it three weeks ago. That's why I was able to trace it so fast."

That did complicate things. "Do you think the report is legit? Or did he plan this murder in advance and file it to muddy the water?"

"That's a good question. I'll notify LoSasso and see which way she wants to go with this. At the very least, this combined with the items you found on Nichol's property could get us a warrant to search his office and home."

A niggling doubt undermined Mattie's excitement. "And we can't forget that leaving the gun at the scene and those items in plain sight behind Nichol's shed makes this whole thing look like he's being framed. Would Nichol be dumb enough to leave such a trail of evidence?"

The buzzer on Brody's phone interrupted them, and Mattie leaned back in her chair while he took the call.

Brody straightened, his eyes drilling Mattie's. "Did you get an exact location?"

Something's happened, Mattie thought as she shifted to the edge of her chair.

"We'll be right out." Brody hung up the receiver as he stood. "Nine-one-one. Caller said he'd been shot."

Adrenaline loaded Mattie's system, launching her from her chair. Robo leaped up to join her. "Who is it?"

"Don't know. Male caller said he was beside Timber Creek up in the mountains west of town, and then he quit talking. The phone wasn't disconnected, but Sam can't get him to speak again." Brody was rounding his desk to head out the door.

Mattie beat him to it and hurried into the lobby with Robo rushing out front.

Sam was still trying to get the caller to respond. "Sir? Sir, can you tell me where you are?"

Mattie hovered near the dispatcher's desk. "What have you got?" she murmured as Sam held the receiver to his ear, staring in front of him as he strained to listen.

Sam shook his head and glanced up at her. "Nothing more. All he said was he's in the mountains west of town on Timber Creek. I've got a cell phone number here but no name."

Mattie looked at Brody. "Can we get any help from the cell phone tower for location?"

Brody shook his head. "One tower in the area. All it will tell us is the call came from the west. If he's got the phone's navigation turned on, we might locate it, but that'll take some time."

Robo was pumped full of energy, and he danced beside her, shifting his weight from one front paw to the other. As usual, her emotion had gone straight to her dog.

"Keep this line open as long as you've got a connection to the caller," Brody told Sam. "Let's activate Search and Rescue, and we'll send them out to the banks of the creek in pairs."

Mattie was as eager to start as Robo. "I'll head out now."

Brody hesitated. "We're short-staffed. I'm going to have to stay and organize the volunteers as they come in."

"I know. I'll go on my own. Maybe we can find this guy in time."

Brody eyed her. "Where will you start?"

Mattie thought for a brief moment. "Timber Creek runs down through the BLM land before it hits the meadows of the Redman Ranch. I'll drive as far as I can into the foothills as long as the road runs beside the creek, but once the creek splits off, I'll leave my vehicle and go along the bank on foot."

"All right. You go. I'll send Johnson as soon as I can get him out there."

★ ★ ★

Always grateful that the county had bought an SUV for the K-9 unit, Mattie was even more so now. Robo stood behind her with his eyes pinned outside the windshield as the Explorer lurched up the rocky two-track that led into the high country above the Redman Ranch. Mattie had accessed the BLM property by leaving the highway and bumping over a cattle guard, and she was now on the four-wheel-drive road that headed upward beside the creek. Light from the setting sun slanted in, touching on bubbles made by eddies and swirls as water rushed downhill around rocks and boulders within the creek bed.

Willows crowded the creek banks, blocking her view as she looked for the man who'd been shot, and she realized she needed to leave her unit and search on foot. She pulled off the two-track and parked, ratcheting on the emergency brake. After hopping out, she wedged rocks behind the tires to reinforce the brakes and keep her vehicle from sliding downhill.

Robo leaped from his compartment. She made him wait long enough for her to put on his blue nylon search harness and to take a few laps of water. He was pumped up and ready to go, so she patted him on the side while she told him, "Let's go find someone."

She had no scent article for direction, but the mere presence of his harness told him he was looking for a person, and she knew it was all he needed to direct his considerable energy toward a search. She sprinted alongside him toward the creek bank.

Once she reached the water's edge, she paused long enough to get Robo started. "Let's find someone. Search!"

Nose down, Robo began to quarter the area, and as he trotted away from the creek, Mattie realized she hadn't thought this through. How could she let Robo know that he was supposed to search along the creek bank?

She called him back to her, clipped a short leash on his harness, and started leading him upstream, staying as near the creek as vegetation would allow. She had a feeling the caller had been at a location higher up in the mountains than this, and she knew that keeping Robo on a leash was going to be too slow and cumbersome as they climbed in elevation. She needed a better plan.

She began to talk to him. "We need to find someone here. By the creek." She said it over and over as she lifted branches of willows and pulled back shrubbery to direct him to search. Within a few minutes, he began searching without direction.

She unclipped the leash as she kept up her chatter, directing Robo with gestures and keeping up with him. He stayed beside the creek and started sniffing through the vegetation on his own. She felt a surge of pride. This dog was so smart, and she felt honored to have him for a partner.

They made better time heading uphill. The creek was about fifteen feet wide here, narrower and deeper in places where it tumbled downhill around granite stones and over falls. Mattie jogged along beside it, dodging rocks, fallen branches, and boulders.

Within the first fifteen minutes, they entered the forest, where pine, spruce, and piñon trees grew sparse but created new obstacles. The fresh scent of pine filled the air. Robo continued to beat around the willows and shrubs by the creek while Mattie ranged beside him to the best of her ability.

There had been no time to think about the danger associated with the search. Nate Fletcher had been shot less than twenty-four hours ago. Why had this caller been shot? Was it an accident? A long-range rifle shot? But it wasn't hunting season right now, and an accident didn't make sense.

It had been almost an hour since the call first came in to the station, and if this man was bleeding out, time was of the essence. She pushed a feeling of hopelessness aside and focused on the mission, whether it be recovery or rescue.

She jogged uphill, glad she trained each morning by running the hills that surrounded town. Robo continued to quarter the area beside the creek, searching under and around willows. When the creek traveled along steeper areas, the vegetation grew sparse, opening up the banks to view. Mattie took advantage of it to scan the banks and run ahead, calling Robo to join her.

Her phone jingled in her pocket, and she paused, letting Robo continue to search. The terrain was too rough to try to read the screen and run at the same time, and she was puffing hard, so she stopped to look at caller ID.

It was Brody, and she connected the call. "Hey."

"Where are you? Johnson is on his way."

"I parked close to the cattle guard. He'll see my vehicle beside the road. By now, I'm about a mile farther uphill on the creek."

"All right. He should arrive at your vehicle within ten minutes."

Mattie began to jog uphill again. "Anything else from the caller?"

"Nah. We lost the connection."

She puffed out a breath. Had the shooter found the victim and disconnected the call? Was there an armed shooter somewhere up ahead? "Okay. I'm going on up. Still have a cell phone signal, so have Johnson call me when he gets here."

"Will do."

In the dim light of dusk, she'd lost sight of Robo, and she stepped up her pace. She focused on dodging tree roots, deadfall, rocks, and other barriers that seemed bent on catching her toe. She kept her eye on the ground with an occasional glance uphill to try to spot her dog. She hated to call him back and interrupt his drive to search, but she had begun to wonder if she should.

As she broke free from some trees, she finally saw Robo up ahead, still near the creek. The sun had set, and his black fur and tawny markings blended into the forest in the waning light. He was skirting the area, winding around a cluster of bushes, when he stopped, sniffing the air.

As Mattie neared, she could see his hackles rise. "What do you smell?" she murmured as she reached him. He was standing still, sniffing as if trying to sift through the air. She wished she possessed his special power and could help.

A low growl rumbled in his chest.

"What is it?" Mattie squinted, peering through the forest, struggling to detect something in the shadows that her dog could smell but she couldn't see. "What's out there?"

Robo edged closer, hovering at her left heel, growling as he searched the area with his eyes as well as his nose. A chill ran down her spine, and Mattie drew her Glock from its holster. She had no idea what they were facing, but she understood her partner's warning.

The forest was still, all the normal evening sounds hushed. A low-pitched roar rumbled from somewhere uphill, a primordial sound that shook Mattie to her core. For a few seconds, she and Robo froze, and then he broke into a furious bark. Several rattling chuffs from uphill answered, followed by the long, drawn-out growl of an apex predator.

The hair at the back of her neck stood at attention. What on earth was that? A bear? A cougar?

Her first concern was for her dog. She sure as hell didn't want him trying to protect her by charging to attack. "Robo, heel! Stay!"

She backed up to a pine tree, taking shelter against its rough bark. Robo stayed with her but continued to carry on, barking and snarling.

The predator responded with a rattling growl that ended in a roar. Mattie strained to see through the feeble light of dusk. Nothing but trees. She grabbed her flashlight from her belt and directed its powerful beam uphill. Again, nothing.

Robo hovered at her side, his front paws lifting from the ground with every ferocious bark. A downward glance told her where he was looking, and she shone her light in that direction. She glimpsed the shape of a large cat before it whirled and darted away.

Her dog's hair bristled, and it reminded her of a strategy to use during a wildlife encounter—look big. She raised the flashlight above her head with her left arm while keeping her handgun trained in the direction of Robo's line of sight. The light beam wavered in her trembling hand.

Another roar echoed through the forest, but this time it sounded like it was farther uphill. Was the cougar going away?

Mattie huddled against the tree, her heart pounding at a fearful pace. Robo continued to bark and growl, and she decided to let him. She held the flashlight aloft until her arm felt numb. After a series of fading growls from up above, the forest fell silent and Robo settled at her heel.

When she decided it was safe to move, she lowered the light and reached for her cell phone. There were enough bars on the screen to try a call. A quick swipe brought up Brody's number.

"Where are you, Cobb?"

She spoke quietly into the phone, hoping her voice wouldn't quiver. "Not far from when I talked to you last, maybe a mile and a half from my vehicle. Where's Johnson?"

"He just passed your unit, but he's sticking to the road. He should be near."

"Tell him to stay in his cruiser. There's a big cat out here, and it's on the hunt."

"Just a minute." She heard Brody pass on her message to Sam, who would notify Johnson. "Are you safe?"

"I don't know, but I think so. As far as I can tell, Robo barked enough to make it go away. I don't want Johnson coming up on it unaware."

"He's still in his cruiser. He's driven a mile uphill, but that's as far as he can go. The road's too bad for him to get closer. Retreat downhill so you can get to the safety of his unit."

Despite the terror she'd felt a few minutes ago, she hadn't forgotten the urgency of her mission, and evidently Robo hadn't forgotten either. He paced a few feet out in front, sniffing the air, and then turned to stand at attention and pin her with his eyes.

"I think Robo's hit on something, Brody. I've got to go uphill to check it out."

"Don't be stupid, Cobb."

"I'm not. Robo scented the cougar, and now his body language tells me it's gone. He's got a hit on human scent this time."

There was a long pause before Brody responded. "Keep this line open as you move forward."

"Will do." Mattie put her cell on speakerphone and shoved it into her pocket before clipping a leash on Robo's collar. She wasn't going to take the chance of losing him in the dark. "Okay, Robo, let's go find someone."

With Robo's leash in one hand and her flashlight in the other, Mattie followed him uphill. She watched the hair on his back while keeping an eye on the rugged terrain at her feet. Robo didn't hesitate as he led her straight uphill, his nose to the air instead of the ground.

Her flashlight showed her a still form beneath the trees, and as they approached, it gradually assumed the shape of a human lying spread-eagle, faceup.

Robo sat a short distance from the body, as if he'd taken Mattie as close as he dared. She scanned the form, but her eyes were drawn to its most ghastly aspect. The body's shirt had been ripped open and its belly plundered, skin and viscera torn apart, bloody organs and tissue scattered. Mattie tore her eyes from the nightmarish sight and shone her light on the face.

It was Wilson Nichol, his mouth frozen open in a final scream. His passing had not been peaceful. Mattie recalled the low-pitched, rattling growl of the mountain lion that had fed on this man, and it touched a spark of terror in her soul. She reached for her phone.

"Brody, Robo found him. It's Wilson Nichol. He's dead."

"Are you in a safe place, Cobb?"

She scanned the dark forest around her. A branch snapped off to her right, and she whirled to train her light in that direction. Nothing. She looked at Robo. He sat calmly, staring up at her.

"I think so, but tell the others to be careful as they approach. Have the posse come in a group, and tell them to bring lots of lights and make lots of noise."

"Stay with me on the line, Cobb, while I get you some help. I'm coming, too, as soon as I can get there."

THIRTEEN

At the crime scene, Stella, Brody, and Mattie stood in a knot beside a campfire that one of the posse members had built. Memory of the mountain lion's growl made Mattie shiver, and she threw on an extra log, making the fire pop and flare. Robo stayed close at her side. She brushed the butt of her service weapon with her hand, reassured that the posse members had come armed with rifles and stood guard around the perimeter of the crime scene.

"It had to be one big cat." Brody gestured toward the prints by the body, which were marked with orange flagging tape anchored to short metal spikes. "I've never seen cougar prints that big."

Classifying the large cat as a cougar still didn't feel quite right. "I've heard a cougar's scream before, Brody. It's high-pitched like a woman's scream. This was a low-pitched rattle."

He eyed her, thinking. "Probably growled to warn you when you approached. Might not have used the full scream."

Her experience with cougars was limited to only one encounter last October, so she wasn't the expert. "I suppose that's possible. But is it likely that a cougar would feed on a human?"

Stella wore a perplexed scowl. "In the nine-one-one call, Wilson Nichol said he'd been shot and was bleeding to death. I think the cougar attack came after, or at least I hope so."

Brody continued to look thoughtful. "Cougars are usually shy of humans, but if one was hungry, or if a mother was feeding cubs, she might have taken advantage of an easy food source. She could have judged Nichol to be fallen prey, that's all. It doesn't necessarily mean we have a man killer on our hands."

Mattie hoped that was true, but the fact remained that they did have a killer on their hands. Only the killer was human. "Who is that new wildlife manager? I think we should call her in to take a look at these prints."

"Glenna Dalton. I'll give her a call, see if she can meet us up here tomorrow morning." Brody squinted at Stella. "He has an entry wound on his chest with an exit wound on his back. How does that compare with what the ME discovered during Nate Fletcher's autopsy?"

"He recovered the lead from Nate's body. Two .38 caliber bullets to the chest. Both penetrated the heart. Hollow-point projectiles for maximum expansion, so the shooter came armed to kill. Stippling on Nate's shirt indicated gunpowder burn. He was shot at close range, which supports the theory that he knew his killer."

Brody frowned. "Two taps to the heart makes me think of a hired hit."

Mattie couldn't dismiss the fact that Robo had found a trace of narcotics inside the van door panel. "Leads me back to drug running, which could mean we have an unknown suspect."

"That might work for Nate, but there's no evidence that he and Wilson were into drug running together," Stella said. "In fact, what we know about them contradicts any kind of partnership."

Mattie realized they could be jumping to conclusions about these two homicides being related. "How can we be so sure we've got only one shooter here?"

"That's right," Stella said. "At this point, we have nothing. If we could recover the bullet at Wilson's scene, we could see if it was from a handgun or a rifle and at least determine if he was shot at close range like Nate. A similar MO might make me lean more toward the one-shooter theory."

"Robo and I will do an evidence search in the morning."

"Those scuff marks indicate the cougar dragged him a ways," Brody said. "It'll be impossible to determine trajectory that shows you where to search."

"We still have to try," Mattie said. "And we need to locate Ben Underwood and Zach Irving. Those two have a connection to Nate Fletcher, and they're from out of town. I'd love to let Robo sweep that Cadillac of theirs for narcotics."

Brody nodded. "You two go ahead and see if you can track them down at the motel. I'll stay here until the techs are done with the crime scene. We'll keep a guard on it overnight and take a fresh look early tomorrow morning. Sheriff McCoy is coming back to town tonight, so he'll be available soon."

"We'll stay in touch," Stella said before turning to leave.

Grateful that Robo, Stella, and a powerful flashlight accompanied her, Mattie turned away from the fire to head into the darkness, still wondering if a cougar could produce the low-pitched growl she'd heard.

★ ★ ★

When they arrived at the Big Sky Motel, four cars were parked inside the well-lit courtyard, and Mattie was pleased to see Zach Irving's silver Cadillac Escalade among them.

"There it is," she said. "I'm going to get permission from the manager for Robo to take a sniff of the cars here in their lot."

"Good idea."

The owner of the motel was on duty, and as one of the merchants on the committee that had funded Robo's purchase, he was more than willing to cooperate, though he said he would contact the owners of the Cadillac in question and let them know she wanted to talk to them.

As Mattie stepped out of the office, the door to room eight opened, and the cowboy that Rainbow had been dancing with the night before stepped outside and stood under the porch light. He appeared to be looking at her SUV while another man exited the room and stood behind him.

Stella went to meet them while Mattie passed by her unit to leave the driver's side door open before following. Robo's cage was equipped with a latch that could be opened remotely with a button attached to her utility belt, and it had paid off before to leave an open exit so that her partner could provide backup if she needed him.

Stella introduced herself and then Mattie while Ben Underwood performed the introductions on their side. They offered handshakes all around.

Mattie remembered Ben's dark good looks from the dance. In the courtyard's spotlights, his brown eyes twinkled with friendliness; he was about six two and lean. Last night he'd worn a Stetson, but tonight he was bareheaded, revealing dark-brown hair clipped close on the sides with the top about three inches long.

Zach Irving was a couple inches shorter than Ben. He had sandy hair and the same dark eyes, though not quite as friendly. Both were dressed in jeans, boots, and short-sleeved shirts. Judging from the bronze tone of their skin, it looked like they might spend a large amount of time outdoors.

"We want to talk to you about Nate Fletcher," Stella said, cutting right to the chase.

Ben's eyes took on a serious cast. "Tyler Redman called early this morning. Horrible news."

"What do you know about it?"

"Just what I was told. That someone shot and killed Nate last night."

Mattie studied the two. While Ben showed the appropriate amount of dismay, Zach appeared to be searching their faces, his eyes darting between hers and Stella's. Nervous.

"When did you meet Nate?" Stella asked.

"We never had the chance to. We found his website and signed up for a fishing trip. I spoke to him on the phone once to be sure all the arrangements had been made, but we never met in person."

So far Ben seemed to be doing all the talking, which Mattie thought rather odd.

Stella continued to question both of them. "Where were you last night?"

"I was at the dance here in town. Zach's engaged to be married soon, so he stayed here at the motel like a good boy." Ben tossed a smile in his friend's direction. "Evidently, that puts an end to all his fun."

Stella gave him a tight smile. "Could I see some identification, please?"

Zach cleared his throat, his voice crackling with tension as he spoke for the first time. "Are we in some kind of trouble here?"

"No trouble. You're in the unfortunate position of having an appointment with a man who was shot and killed last night. We need to clear you in order to move on with our investigation."

Both men produced California driver's licenses, the identification on which matched the names they'd given earlier. Mattie recorded the license numbers and their addresses, then handed them back to their owners.

Stella continued with the drill. "I need to ask a few more questions."

Zach gave her a hard stare. "Do we need an attorney?"

Since he'd mentioned it, Mattie had to wonder the very same thing.

Stella answered. "Not that I'm aware of, sir. This is strictly routine."

True. Typically, interviews were strictly routine . . . until they weren't. Zach's nervous behavior and his lack of an alibi made Mattie's radar light up.

"And where were the two of you this evening around six o'clock?" Stella asked, moving on to Wilson's death.

His body language still open and relaxed, Ben Underwood answered for both of them. "We took a drive into the high country." He paused, apparently thinking. "I think we were somewhere on the pass west of Willow Springs around six."

"Can anyone vouch for seeing you around that time?" Stella asked. "Did you stop for dinner or gasoline so that you have receipts?"

Ben and Zach exchanged looks before Ben answered. "We ate dinner here in Timber Creek at that little diner."

Clucken House, Mattie thought. It would be easy enough to check to see if they were telling the truth.

"What time?" Stella asked.

"We got back to town about eight. Went to dinner soon after," Ben said.

That would've been well after the time Wilson Nichol was shot. The two could've easily killed him and made it back to town to eat around eight.

"Do either of you know a real estate broker from Willow Springs named Wilson Nichol?" Stella asked, addressing both of them, evidently trying to draw a response from Zach.

Zach gave Ben a sidelong glance before he spoke. "I know who he is. I've spoken with him on the phone recently."

The glance and his reply sharpened Mattie's attention. This admission linked Zach Irving to both Nate and Wilson.

Stella pursued more information. "What did you discuss with Mr. Nichol?"

"Business," Zach said. "I'm interested in rural property development. He and I spoke about various properties he could show me."

"And you, Mr. Underwood," Stella said. "Do you know Wilson Nichol?"

"I don't, ma'am. I'm a building contractor. Zach and I work together after he acquires the property he wants to develop, so I haven't met or spoken with Mr. Nichol."

Stella trained her gaze on Zach. "I'm sorry to tell you that Mr. Nichol was killed this evening."

His brow shot up and he took a step back. "What?"

Stella remained silent, and Mattie studied both men's reactions. While Zach appeared surprised and then shaken, Ben's reaction was less specific. He seemed surprised at first, but the affable expression he wore returned within seconds, which made Mattie wonder if he used it as a mask.

Zach stared at Stella. "Wilson was killed. How?"

"He was shot."

Zach's posture was tight with tension. "Like Nate?"

"Both homicides are under investigation," Stella said.

Zach's gaze jumped from Stella to Mattie. "What's going on in this town? Two men have been shot and killed?"

"That's right," Stella said, focusing on Zach. "Do you know anything about either of these men that might help us in our investigation?"

Mattie continued to study the pair while they held eye contact with each other. They didn't use words, but she wondered if they were sharing some type of nonverbal communication just the same.

Ben gave a small nod to his friend, and Zach was the first to answer. "I truly don't know much about either of these men except for the business we've talked about over the phone. I'm sorry, but I can't help you."

"And I know even less than he does," Ben said, tipping an open palm toward his friend.

Zach looked at Stella. "Is it safe for us to even go on this fishing trip?"

"I don't know," Stella said. "You might consider canceling it."

The two looked at each other again before Ben spoke. "The trip's bought and paid for, and Nate's wife says she can't afford to give us a refund. We're here, so we might as well go ahead with it."

"I'll talk to Tyler," Zach said, straightening his shoulders as if to release tightness.

Ben looked at Stella. "Is there anything more you need from us tonight, Detective?"

"Just one more thing. We have a strict no-narcotics policy in our town. It's routine that we use our K-9 to sweep vehicles passing through on the highway. We'd like your permission to do a quick narcotics sweep of your vehicle here, and then we'll be on our way."

Zach crossed his arms over his chest. "Absolutely not! This feels like harassment. Small-town cops trying to pin something on the out-of-town guys."

So far Mattie had been observing in silence, but it was her turn to step up. "Our local businesses cooperate with our policy, and I have permission for my dog to take a sniff here in this parking lot."

Zach looked at her, shaking his head. "If that dog scratches the paint, I'll sue your department for damages."

"He's trained in a passive method of indication, so he doesn't damage property. You can observe."

She turned to go to her Explorer, and as she approached, Robo started his happy dance, his head bobbing behind the front seats. He'd probably been watching the entire time, wondering when it would be his turn to play. It took mere seconds to prep him, and when she slipped on his narcotics detection collar, it focused all that eagerness into work. She clipped on his leash and used the phrase that would communicate his mission. "You want to find some dope? Let's go!"

As she led Robo to the Cadillac, he trotted beside her at heel, his eyes pinned to her face. She noticed that Zach had removed himself from the others and was standing back on the sidewalk, arms crossed, his face darkened by a scowl. "This is ridiculous," he muttered as Mattie drew near.

She ignored him. After one last thump on Robo's rib cage, she told him again to search. It was what he'd been wanting and all he needed to transform into a slinky, sniffing machine. Ears pinned, Robo took in scent while Mattie guided him in a counterclockwise search of the car. She asked him to pay extra attention by using her hand to direct his nose to the cracks at the doors, into wheel wells, and under bumpers. When he finished, he turned his head toward Mattie, his eyes glued to her face as he awaited his next instruction.

No hit. She trusted Robo's talent and training—the Cadillac was clean of narcotics. Disappointed that her drug-running theory involving these out-of-towners—which could have suggested a motive for both homicides—no longer existed, Mattie looked at Stella and then Zach. "It's clean."

With Robo latched onto her heel, she led him toward her unit while Stella wrapped up the interview. Even though she'd found no trace of narcotics, there was something about these two that bothered her. It was as if they were keeping some type of secret. And if it wasn't drugs, maybe it was murder.

FOURTEEN

Eager to see his kids, Cole stood on the front porch, waiting for them to arrive while watching the dogs patrol the yard. Angie had called him after they crossed the last mountain pass to let him know they were about a half hour away, and that had been twenty-five minutes ago.

Their Bernese mountain dog, Belle, finished her business first and came to stand with him on the porch, while his Doberman pinscher, Bruno, continued to circle the yard, sniffing every flower bed and bush he came to. Cole placed a hand on Belle's head and stroked the satiny fur between her ears while she looked up at him with her soft, dark eyes. He knew she would be especially excited to see Sophie, while Bruno was always happy to see anyone who would play with him, though he seemed to be most attached to Cole.

Lights pierced the darkness at the end of the lane, turning from the highway toward the house. Belle and Bruno both alerted, ears pricked and barking.

"Okay, you two, that's enough. I see it." Cole moved down the steps to the sidewalk with the dogs trotting out ahead, woofing under their breath.

Jessie steered her red Toyota Prius up to the edge of the yard and parked. Sophie sprang from the car as soon as it stopped.

"Belle!" Sophie ran to her dog with open arms while Belle frolicked to greet her, tail beating a breakneck rhythm, the limp from last summer's gunshot wound the only thing slowing her down.

By this time, Sophie was down in the grass, cooing to Belle as she hugged her and making Cole feel like chopped liver. "Hey, Sophie-bug, you got a hug for your poor old dad?"

Sophie giggled as she stood and turned toward Cole, her brown eyes lit and her freckled cheeks bunched in a grin. Nine years old and she could make his heart melt with one smile. He hated to think about her growing into a more reserved teenager, but he supposed that would happen someday. He gathered her into his arms for a hug, sweeping her off her feet and then setting her back on the ground near Bruno, who was prancing around with an open-mouthed, tongue-lolling grin of his own. He was just as smitten with Sophie as Belle.

Sophie gave him his due, spreading her hugs around freely. "Bruno, you big old boy! How ya been?"

Speaking of reserved teens, sixteen-year-old Angela had stepped out of the car and was observing Sophie's homecoming with a pleased expression. Cole registered the look and thought how much his eldest had matured this past year. Before, she'd picked on her younger sister at every turn, and now she'd adopted an almost maternal relationship with her. He didn't know if that was good or bad. Was it a normal part of her getting older, or a residual from Sophie's kidnapping? He hoped for the former.

"Glad you're home, Angel," he said as he approached her for a hug. She gave him a peck on his cheek, which told him he must be in her good graces—at least for the moment. Angela was tall and willowy and had the white-blond hair and blue eyes of her mother. Dark circles under her eyes spoke to the stress she'd been under. He drew her up against his side and held her close while he leaned forward to wave at his sister through the open door. "Hey, Jessie. How was the trip down?"

"Uneventful." Jessie was gathering up her cell phone and her glasses case and putting them into her handbag, a large turquoise-leather affair that looked like it held everything but the kitchen sink. His kid sister, who'd once been a rugged tomboy, had the appearance of the attorney she was, her light-brown hair highlighted and cut into a wispy style. "Did you already eat dinner?"

It was well after ten o'clock, so her question surprised him. "I did. Did you guys skip dinner?"

"Oh, no. We stopped along the way, but Sophie says she's hungry."

"Well, come inside, little bit. I've got some leftover lasagna in the fridge that Mrs. Gibbs made. We can make you a hot plate special." While Sophie scooted for the front porch, the dogs galloping behind her, Cole stayed and helped carry in luggage. As they breached the entryway, he spoke to Jessie. "I don't think Mrs. Gibbs would mind if you stayed in her room."

Jessie shook her head. "I wouldn't intrude on her private space. I'll take the extra twin bed in Sophie's room."

They left the bags at the base of the stairs and followed Sophie into the kitchen. Cole was surprised that Angela came, too, having thought she might prefer to head on up to her own room. Pleased that she wanted to join them, he gave her another quick hug. "It's nice to have you kids home again."

"We need to talk, Dad."

Uh-oh, he should have guessed. "In private or with Sophie?"

Angie gave him an impatient look, the kind that said he'd asked a stupid question. "All of us. Sophie has questions that are way beyond my ability to answer."

"Let's get some food on the table, and we'll sit down and talk things over." Sophie was already shoulders-deep into the refrigerator, so he went over to help her sort through things to find the pan of lasagna.

He and Jessie kept up the chitchat while they heated leftovers. Angela set forks on the table, and soon they were all at their seats. Belle took her place beside Sophie, hoping for a tidbit, while Bruno settled beneath the table at Cole's feet. He had the feeling they both sighed with pleasure that their family was all in one place again.

In years past, this situation with Olivia would have made Cole talk "at" his kids, but months of family counseling had taught him to become a better listener. Once they'd polished off enough of the meal to banish the hungries, Cole turned to his oldest. "What do you want to talk about, Angel?"

"About Mom."

"Sure. Anything specific?"

She turned to her sister. "Sophie . . ."

Sophie put her fork down and leaned forward, a shadow crossing her face. "She acted like she didn't want us there, Dad. Even on the first day."

"How so, sweetheart?"

"I wanted to sit by her to watch TV, and she got up and moved away. Then I asked her to read me a story before bed, and she said she was too tired. And she didn't have a happy face on. You know."

Cole did know, and he recognized that Sophie's happy face had also disappeared. He knew better than to make light of the rejection she must have felt. He looked at Angela to see if she wanted to add anything, but she remained silent and stony-faced. "Mom told me she wanted you there for the whole week," he said. "I know she was excited to have you come visit."

Sophie's eyes brimmed. "Can a mom fall out of love with her kids?"

Cole looked at Jessie, and she raised her brows at him, an invitation to field the question. The slow burn that had started when he first received the call from his distressed kids threatened to flare. He didn't want to say the wrong thing and make matters worse between Liv and her children, but by golly, she wasn't making this any easier. "I'm not sure I know how to answer that question, Sophie. I don't know about other moms; I just have some ideas about *your* mom."

He could tell she was fighting tears and trying to put on a brave face. "What about my mom?"

"I don't think she's fallen out of love with you and Angie. You know this has been complicated. Mom has an illness that we can't see, but it's still an illness. Her depression comes and goes, and evidently she's still struggling with it more than we were aware of."

A tear slipped down Sophie's cheek. "But why does she act like she doesn't like us? I don't get it."

Cole felt like he'd reached a dead end. "To tell the truth, I don't get it either. But when I talked to your mom on the phone, I did understand one thing. She does love you, and she wants to spend time with you."

"But why does she act like she doesn't?"

Judging by Sophie's sad face, Cole would guess he hadn't helped her very much, even though he wished more than anything that he could. "Sophie, try to understand that your mom has an illness. She takes medicine for it and she works in counseling just like we do . . . you know, to try to get in touch with our feelings so that we can handle them. But your mom's sadness is bigger than what we feel. It's not so easily managed, but she's doing the best she can."

Cole hoped he'd hit on a comparison that Sophie could relate to. "Imagine how sad you are right now, only make it much, much bigger. That's what your mom deals with, and it can make her feel tired. She might want to go to her room and lie down. Sometimes she needs a nap. That's what was going on with your mom the past few days. She hasn't fallen out of love with you. She loves you more than ever."

He remembered what Mattie had said about small steps. "We just took too big a step, Sophie. We tried to do too much at once. Instead of visiting Mom for a week, we're going to go for a day next time. I think that will work much better, don't you?"

Sophie's attention had been riveted on him the whole time, and she looked like her tearfulness had resolved for the moment. That didn't mean they wouldn't have to revisit this conversation in the future, but it was now almost eleven o'clock, and she looked as tired as he felt.

"It's getting late. How about we stack the dishes in the sink, and I'll take care of them tomorrow. If you hurry and brush your teeth, Sophie, I'll read you a short story."

"Okay." She jumped up from her chair with dishes in hand, dropped them off at the sink, and scurried up the stairs, pausing long enough to grab her suitcase. Belle and Bruno trailed after her. Stories always worked wonders for getting Sophie to bed.

But with Angela, things weren't so easy. "Are you okay for now, Angie?"

Her frown told him she wasn't. "It's not that simple, Dad. You can't brush off the way Mom treated us with a story."

"I know. We've got more to talk about, but we can't solve everything tonight. We'll spend some time deciding what we want to do about all this over the next few days."

"I know one thing for sure. I don't want to go back to Denver to see Mom ever again."

He wanted his kids to have a relationship with their mom. He couldn't imagine letting Angela's frustration and hurt keep her away from her mother forever. But for now, understanding might be more effective than argument. "It was rough, huh?"

"Sophie started crying the first night." Angie's anger seemed to melt and her eyes brimmed. "I didn't know what to do. When she cried again last night, I couldn't take it anymore."

"Of course not. You did the right thing, sweetheart." Cole reached out with an open palm, and she placed her hand in it. "You can always call me when you're in a bind, whether it's related to Mom or not."

Jessie leaned forward. "And you can call me whenever you're in Denver. I'm just a phone call away."

Angie dashed a tear from her cheek. "I don't want to be a baby about it."

Jessie was quick to respond. "You're not. It hurts to feel rejected."

Cole could tell that Jessie's words came from the heart, and he appreciated her support. "We'll see how you feel about visiting Mom again after we've had more time to mull it over and talk about it. I know we won't try an overnight visit again anytime soon. We're all tired. Let's get some sleep and see if things don't look brighter in the morning."

If he wasn't mistaken, Jessie brushed a tear from her eye as she stood to clear her dishes before carrying her bag up the staircase. It made him wonder when she'd felt the rejection she'd mentioned. *We all have our crosses to bear,* he thought, *we just don't always know what the other guy's are.*

Troubled enough by the discussion to know that sleep wouldn't come to him anytime soon, he decided to clean up the kitchen. As he loaded the dishes into the dishwasher, he thought of Mattie and the burdens she must bear. He hoped he could at least talk to her before this night ended.

FIFTEEN

It was approaching midnight when Mattie let Robo out of the station and headed to her vehicle. Brody had told her to go home to get some shut-eye while he waited for Sheriff McCoy to arrive. He would brief the sheriff tonight, and she should be ready at first light to go up to the crime scene.

She was loading Robo into their unit when her phone pinged with a text message from Cole that said, KIDS ARE HOME AND IN BED. ARE YOU STILL UP?

Her heart lifted at the thought of talking to him before bed, something she'd become accustomed to lately. She texted a YES, and her phone rang in her hand.

She answered it. "How are the kids doing?"

He sighed. "They're still upset, but I hope they feel better after they've rested. They seem pretty tired."

His words shot straight to her heart. She'd grown to love Cole's kids as if they were her own. "I hope they feel better in the morning."

He made a sound of agreement. "Where are you now?"

"Just leaving the station."

"Do you need to eat? We've got lasagna."

It was his way of tempting her to stop by, because he knew the typically empty state of her refrigerator. The thought of being with him tonight made her ache with longing, but he didn't need to know that. "I haven't eaten since noon, and the restaurants are closed. I'd love to come over."

"See you soon."

Mattie drove the mile to Cole's house with Robo standing in his compartment, wagging his tail and looking out the windshield. He seemed to know the route as well as she did. As she parked beside the Prius near Cole's front yard, Bruno rushed out to greet them. Cole was standing on the front porch, but he came down the steps and moved toward her car.

She opened the front door of Robo's cage, and he bailed out, eager to play with Bruno. The two chased each other in joyous delight, roughhousing in the grass.

Cole took her in his arms, and she rested in his embrace for a few heartbeats before tilting her head back for his kiss. His warm lips on hers made her wonder what it would be like to come home to this every night after a hard day. After the kiss, Cole tucked her under his arm to walk with her up to the porch.

"Where's Belle?"

"She's in bed with Sophie." The porch light revealed Cole's smile. "I'm glad you could come over. I've missed you."

"What have you heard from Garrett?"

"He's resting comfortably." Cole frowned. "His vision's about the same. The rehab team will evaluate him tomorrow."

She wished the news had been better. "I guess that's the best we can hope for tonight."

"It's early yet. Things can still resolve." He tightened the arm around her shoulders. "How is the burn on your arm?"

"It looked better this morning. I put on more ointment and a clean bandage. It's going to be fine."

Cole nodded, taking her hand as they climbed the porch steps. They turned and watched the dogs for a moment while the twosome ended their rambunctious greeting. "Does Robo need some food?"

"He's all right. I fed him at the station."

"I think we can take them into the house now without waking everyone."

Mattie told Robo to heel, breaking him out of his play mode, and they led the dogs into the kitchen, where they checked on empty food bowls and lapped water before settling down. Cole heated a serving of lasagna while she helped herself to salad, and they sat at the table. After eating, she broke the news about Wilson Nichol's death.

Cole looked astonished. "Good grief! What's going on up there?"

"I wish I knew. But that's not all." She told him about hearing the mountain lion's growl and the results of its predation.

"Geez, Mattie. You were alone when this happened?"

"I had Robo with me."

"He wouldn't fare well in a cougar attack."

"His barking seemed to scare it off."

"Thank goodness for that. It's not right for you to go up into the high country without backup."

She sent him a warning look. She knew he worried about her, but it wasn't like Cole to tell her how to do her job. "We're shorthanded this weekend, and Brody was needed at the station. Since it's atypical cougar behavior, I wondered what you thought about the attack."

Behind Cole, Angie appeared in the kitchen doorway, wearing shorts and a tank that she used for pajamas. "What attack?"

"Angie!" Delighted to see the girl, Mattie rose from her chair to give her a hug. "It's good to see you. Sorry your trip didn't work out."

Angie returned the hug and stepped back to give her dad a look. "We should've known it wouldn't."

Cole frowned. "How could we have known, Angie?"

"Mom hasn't wanted to have anything to do with us for over a year. This visit was just her pretending to be a mom."

"That's not true, Angie." Cole looked upset. "We've talked about this."

This father–daughter conflict made Mattie uncomfortable, but instead of withdrawing as usual, she hoped to say something that would ease Angie's pain. After all, that's where her anger was coming from, and Mattie knew the torment only too well. She touched Angie on the arm to get her attention. "Let's go to the den and sit for a minute. I have something to tell you."

After sitting on the couch, Angie gave Mattie an expectant look. "What?"

Mattie drew in a deep breath—this kind of sharing was something she was still getting used to. "I think you know that my mom left me and my brother when I was six years old, right?"

Angie nodded.

"Well, I grew up feeling abandoned. I thought she left because of something I did. All I knew when I was a kid was that my mom had left me and it hurt."

Angie's gaze didn't waver, her eyes fixed on Mattie's.

Mattie's gut tightened. She'd spared Cole's kids the details of her ordeal on Redstone Ridge the night of last month's forest fire, and she planned to share only a small bit of it now. "Just last month, I learned that my mom left because she was running away from someone she feared. It had nothing to do with me or my brother. In fact, I think she believed she was protecting us."

"Wow." Angie appeared to be thinking it through.

"So, what I'm saying is, you might think your mom's decision to leave had something to do with you, or Sophie, or even your dad. But it really had to do with her and what she's going through. None of you can fix it for her, even though I'm sure she still loves you."

Angie sat in silence, but Mattie sensed her anger had lost some of its edge.

She needed to share one last thing. "I used to think my mom should be perfect, and she should come try to find me. But now I know that dwelling on that and dwelling on my hurt feelings doesn't do anyone any good. Especially me."

Angie nodded as if that made sense to her.

"Maybe it's best to continue to give your mom some space. We can't tell what the future will bring with her, but you can focus on the summer and having fun with the other people in your life."

Angie shrugged. "What really made me mad was how she hurt Sophie's feelings."

With a slight smile, Mattie leaned back on the cushion. "I guess that doesn't surprise me . . . you get that from your dad."

Angie looked at Cole, who squirmed in his chair before giving his daughter a sheepish smile. "Guilty as charged," he said.

"Of course you want to protect your sister. It's important for you to help her as much as you can," Mattie said. "But it's not all on your shoulders. You've got your dad and your aunt who are willing to help. And besides, you can't shelter Sophie from everything. Part of your anger might be because you felt helpless at first, when in reality you did the very best thing."

Angie cast her eyes down toward the expanse of sofa between them.

Cole spoke up. "Angela, it's been a long day, and we're all tired. Do you think you could go to sleep now?"

Angie stood. "I guess so."

Mattie drew a breath, trying to relieve the tightness in her chest caused by sharing her private thoughts and feelings. Was this what being part of a family required? She wondered how people could interact like this, day after day—she'd rather break up a bar fight. She stood to give Angie a hug before the girl hugged her dad and left to go upstairs.

Mattie felt depleted. Though she wanted to slump back onto the couch, there were only a few hours left before sunrise and she needed to go home. She awakened Robo and told him it was time to go. He arose, stretching and blinking before trotting toward the door. Cole went with them out to the porch.

He put his arm around her as they went down the steps. "Thanks for talking to Angie tonight. I think you might have made her feel better."

If that was true, this emotional exhaustion would be worth it. "I hope so."

"I hate for you to have to leave, but I bet you're going to have a big day tomorrow and an early start."

It seemed like a night for sharing secrets. As they walked toward her unit, darkness enclosed them and Cole's arm on her shoulders gave her reassurance, shoring up her reserves. Tension mounted inside her as she realized what she was about to do. This was the moment she'd been waiting for. She couldn't put it off any longer. "Cole, I need to tell you something."

"You know you can tell me anything." He held out his arms and she stepped into his embrace, squeezing him so tightly that every inch of their bodies touched.

"You don't know everything about me," she said, her voice sounding timid even to her own ears.

"And you don't know everything about me. That's not a problem, is it?"

This man often tried to bring levity to serious situations, but she couldn't go there with him right now. "It's not like that for me, Cole. There's a part of my past that feels so degrading and horrible that I just can't bring it into your world. You have no idea."

Cole sighed, tightening his embrace even more. "Mattie, sweetheart . . . I can tell there's something eating away at you. All I can do is assure you that there is absolutely nothing you can tell me that will change the way I feel about you."

She burrowed her face into his chest, and he stroked her hair, soothing her much like she'd seen him soothe a frightened animal. "I need to tell you, Cole."

"I can't let you struggle with this," he said, his lips against her hair. "I have to tell you that I know Harold Cobb took advantage of you when you were a child."

Mattie froze. She couldn't believe what she'd just heard. She tried to take a step back, to create some distance between them, but he continued to hold her. "You know?"

"It pains me that you have to deal with the aftermath of that, but it doesn't change anything between us." Cole's voice had become husky.

Coldness snowballed inside her, and she feared it would make her heart stop. Stella was the only person she'd shared her dark secret with, the only one she'd trusted with it. Had her friend betrayed her? "How did you find out? Did Stella tell you?"

"No one told me, Mattie. Sheriff McCoy was talking about Harold Cobb, and I figured it out." Cole sounded anguished, as if he could sense the turmoil his words had stirred up. "No one violated your privacy."

But someone must have. How else would he know? And he must have known for a whole month without telling her. Were they all talking about her in her absence? She pressed her hands against his chest.

Cole loosened his embrace enough for her to see the distress on his face. "Mattie, listen. I put two and two together. Please tell me if I got it wrong."

She pushed against him hard enough that he was forced to let her go. "You waited a month before you said anything about this? A whole month? That feels like a . . . a stab in the back. You should have said something."

Cole flinched. "No, Mattie, I couldn't. Don't you see? I couldn't bring it up unless I knew you wanted to talk about it.

If that was the wrong choice, I apologize. But think about it, Mattie, and tell me if you wouldn't have reacted the same way."

But she didn't want to see it from his viewpoint; she wanted to get away. "My baggage is nothing you should expose your family to. You can see why I don't want to burden you or your kids with it."

His distress was apparent in his expression and his voice. "I'm not afraid of it, and I'm not afraid of it harming my kids. I need you to understand something. The only way this knowledge affects me is the pain of seeing how it affects you. It hurts to see you suffer like this."

That's what she'd feared most. She didn't want the things she still dealt with—the nightmares, flashbacks, and anxiety—to bring hardship to Cole or his kids. This day had proven that they had enough of their own family problems without taking on hers. "You'll get tired of having to deal with me and my issues."

"Never." He reached for her, and she longed to let him hold her again, but she shrugged off his hands and retreated until she felt the security of her Explorer against her back. All she wanted now was to get away, to go to the safety of her own home where she didn't have to deal with Cole or this conversation.

Cole moved forward as if unwilling to let her go. "Mattie, there's only one thing I'm afraid of. I couldn't bear it if you let Harold Cobb drive us apart."

But she could already feel herself pulling away. "Maybe not, but his actions are still a part of me."

"You were just an innocent child." Cole sounded like his heart was breaking, too.

"I know that." She knew all that stuff about perpetrators and victims, but at times like this, it didn't help. The way the two of them had been raised was light years apart. Cole wouldn't understand. "It's late. I need to go home so we can both get some sleep."

"The last thing I want to do is sleep," he said, sounding desperate. "Mattie, stay. Stay so we can talk about this."

"I'm exhausted, Cole. I need time to think this through." She called Robo and went to load him into the back of her unit.

Cole waited for her at her car door, blocking the handle. She couldn't see his eyes in the darkness, but she could feel their intensity. "I'm sorry I've upset you, Mattie, but I had to tell you. I didn't want there to be secrets between us any more than you did. You can trust me to be honest and to never hurt you on purpose. If there's one thing you take away from here tonight, let that be it."

Honesty? She knew he wouldn't *try* to hurt her, but he'd kept this secret for weeks. She felt so tired she couldn't think, and she didn't know what else to say. All she wanted was escape. She reached for the door handle.

He opened the door so she could climb in. Even before she could settle into her seat, he leaned forward so their faces were inches apart. "I'm falling in love with you. And I hope like crazy that you won't hold this against me."

Mattie started the engine. "I've got to go."

Her overhead light revealed his anguish. He touched her cheek tenderly, backed away, and closed the door. He stood in the glow of her headlights as they swept over him, shoulders slumped and thumbs tucked inside his jeans pockets. Looking dejected, he raised one hand in farewell as she pulled away.

She supposed the whole team at the station had been in on that conversation. Had it changed their opinion of her? How could she show her face at work again? An icy coldness filled her chest, making her shiver, and she thought her heart might break. How could she ever survive this betrayal?

SIXTEEN

Monday morning

Exhausted from a night with very little sleep, Mattie sipped coffee while she drove through dawn's first light toward Wilson Nichol's crime scene. She'd spent her early hours in bed tossing, turning, and thinking about Cole's words until she'd finally dozed. Nightmares filled with twisted images of fire and the sensation of running through the forest awakened her at four, her legs thrashing the covers, tossing them off to the floor.

She had dressed in running gear and taken Robo outside to jog along the lanes of Timber Creek. With her dog beside her, she'd passed from one island of light under streetlamps to another, staying on the move while she tried to work through her feelings. Running had served her well in the past when she needed to ease her anxiety, and it was something she turned to still whenever that growing tightness threatened to take over her chest.

One thing came clear to her while she ran: she would not allow herself to become Harold Cobb's victim. Though love might feel complicated at times, she knew Cole was the man she wanted, and she wouldn't let a scumbag like Harold Cobb cheat her out of leading a happy life.

By the time she returned home, she'd decided it wasn't Cole's fault that Sheriff McCoy had brought up details from her childhood during an investigative team meeting. What bothered her most was that he'd never said anything about it to her.

Not until after she'd wrestled with herself for weeks, working up the courage to broach the subject.

And yet . . . he'd had a point when he'd said he couldn't discuss her past unless he knew she wanted to. If she were to be completely honest, she'd have to admit that's probably the way she would have handled the situation, too.

Cole had said she could trust him—and that was the crux of her problem. He had no way of knowing the extent of her trust issues and how hard she struggled with them. She dealt with the subject with a trauma therapist in Denver, but she'd only touched on it lightly with Cole. She'd been coping well lately and working toward improving her mental health—keeping a journal, learning yoga and breath training. These things all helped, but she'd been surprised by her body's response when Cole shared what he knew, bombarding her with such a painful feeling of betrayal.

It was like a column of ice had surrounded her. She couldn't move. She couldn't think. She'd needed to run away, and she'd barely been able to manage that.

Fight or flight. Both Mattie's work and personal life made her more than familiar with the bursts of adrenaline associated with this phenomenon. But rarely had they left her immobile, like last night. Now that she'd had time to separate and think about it analytically, she realized how large this trust issue loomed for her, especially as it related to someone she loved.

And she did love Cole. But could she trust him enough to give him her heart? Could she open herself to the possibility of being hurt by him?

By the time she reached Wilson Nichol's crime scene, sunrise lit the eastern horizon with shades of vermillion and orange. Members of the sheriff's posse stood guard around the crime scene tape while thirty feet away others huddled near the campfire, its smoke billowing up and drifting off on the breeze.

Mattie shelved her thoughts for later and exited her SUV. The high-altitude morning air combined with exhaustion made her shiver, so she grabbed her jacket and slipped it on.

Sheriff McCoy and Brody pulled up behind her in McCoy's Jeep. The sheriff unfolded his tall frame from the driver's seat and got out, shutting the door as he shrugged on a jacket. Brody stepped out on the passenger side.

Abraham McCoy, one of the few Black men in the Timber Creek community, was built like a tree trunk and had a deep voice that Mattie had seen soothe even the most rattled of victims. She'd experienced it herself as a six-year-old child when, as a young deputy, he'd answered her 911 call the night Harold Cobb tried to kill her mother. When he'd picked her up in his strong arms, she'd never felt so safe.

But now, she felt confused about how much he'd known about her childhood suffering, and yet . . . he'd done nothing to address it. She'd gone straight into foster care, bounced from home to home for years until she'd found a place with Mama T, and he'd never referred her for the services she needed as a child to work through her pain. Maybe that was putting too much responsibility on his broad shoulders, but she believed that's what she would have done if she'd been in his shoes.

She decided to act as though nothing had changed. Work always served her well when she needed to escape the reality of her personal life. She straightened her spine as she approached the Jeep and didn't waver when she looked him in the eye. "Welcome back, Sheriff. This is a heck of a thing to come home to."

Her breath hung in the cold air before dissipating.

"It certainly is. I hear you and Robo have been hard at work."

Business as usual felt like the way to go. "We'll see if we can find some evidence as soon as the sun rises enough to help us out."

McCoy nodded and glanced toward the fire as the cook called out a greeting. "Looks like they've got a pot of coffee going. Let's warm up and see how the night went while we wait for daylight."

Mattie could smell the coffee's aroma as she approached. She warmed her hands around a tin cup filled with dark, bitter brew and listened to Frank Sullivan, one of the posse members, brief them on the happenings during the night. After the coroner, local physician Dr. McGinnis, had made it to the site to pronounce the death, the ambulance had arrived, parking down below as close to the scene as it could. Members of the posse had teamed up with the EMTs to carry the body down to the ambulance on a stretcher.

Though they'd stayed on the lookout all night, no one else had heard the cougar. Everything in the forest had gone quiet. "Too quiet," Frank said, looking at Mattie. "It might still be out there. Hard to say."

Mattie nodded and sipped her coffee. Robo stayed close, as if they needed to huddle after their experience in this spot last night.

"I think things are clear again this morning," Frank said. "The birds are chirping."

He was right. As the sunlight slanted through the evergreens, the birds were warming up to greet the day.

"How do you suggest we go about this?" McCoy asked Mattie.

Before she could answer, Frank interjected. "After the body was removed, we kept everyone out of the area, just like you told us."

"That's good." Mattie gave him a nod of appreciation. "I'll see if Robo picks up anything first. Then we can decide where to go from there."

Brody looked up at the sky. "I think it's light enough to get started."

Mattie tossed the remainder of her coffee aside, glad for an excuse to get rid of it. Campfire brew had never been one of her favorites. She took Robo back to her SUV to prep him for an evidence search. She put on his blue nylon collar, snapped a leash on the dead ring, and gave him a few slurps of water.

Yellow tape marked off a circle about thirty feet in diameter around the crime scene. Mattie ducked under it, scanning the ground for where she'd found the victim. Bloodstains marked the exact spot.

Robo hovered at her heel, not as eager to get to work as usual. He'd once been injured in a cougar attack, and she wondered if that was the reason for his hesitation. She patted his sides, ruffled his fur, and began the chatter meant to rev up his prey drive. He raised up on his hind feet at her side, bouncing on his back paws a couple of times, his eyes pinned to hers as if to say her encouragement was working.

"Okay, buddy. Let's go. Seek!"

Holding the leash in her left hand, she used her right to direct him to search a grid by sweeping it with his nose. It didn't take long to clear the area around where Wilson's body had lain, and at the uphill side, Robo scooted under the crime scene tape, making Mattie duck under to stay close behind him.

It took only a moment to figure out that Robo had decided to backtrack the victim's trail, which she agreed was a good idea. Typically she would have unclipped his leash and let him range out in front, but there was no way she was going to allow him to stumble into a cougar's ambush. She kept him on his short leash, the six-foot spread between them close enough to set her mind at ease.

Brody fell in behind as Robo led them upstream, staying outside the heavy vegetation along the creek bank. She could see occasional spots of blood in the grass as they went. A sharp-eyed tracker could have followed this trail, but she was glad her dog's nose could lead her quickly up the hillside.

"Blood," Brody murmured, evidently seeing the same thing she had.

The terrain underfoot grew steeper, and scuff marks on the rocky ground showed them where Nichol had fallen and then picked himself up to continue his struggle downhill to try to save himself. A knot formed in her stomach as she imagined his helplessness as blood from the exit wound in his back saturated his clothing and dripped on the rocks.

The trail moved closer to the creek, where the ground was soft and moist. Robo's fur bristled on the back of his neck, making the fine hair on the back of hers rise and sending prickles down her back. He sniffed the ground and looked up at her as if to say, *Are you getting a whiff of this?*

She spotted several huge paw prints in the moist dirt, right beside footprints that Mattie assumed had been left by Wilson Nichol. If she hadn't been spooked already, this would do it. "Robo, wait."

Robo paused and Brody drew up beside her. "What did he find?"

"Paw prints." Mattie pointed to the ground. "The cougar followed Nichol's blood trail downhill."

Brody stared at the ground, frowning. "Damn. That's what it looks like."

Mattie pulled a short spike with orange flagging tape tied to it from her belt and tagged the prints so they could examine them later. "Is that game warden coming up to help us this morning?"

Brody nodded. "She said she would. She might be down at the crime scene already."

"We'll need her to take a look at this area, too." Mattie hugged Robo close to her leg and told him to search, the command she used for tracking a person.

He put his nose to the ground and continued to climb, winding through thorny bushes, willows, and evergreens that grew beside the creek. After about a hundred yards of rough sledding, he came to a halt and again looked over his shoulder at Mattie. Their eyes met.

"What did you find?" Mattie scanned the area, spotting a large splash of blood on a patch of flattened grass. As Brody drew up beside her, she pointed it out to him. "I think this might be where Nichol was shot."

Brody knelt and surveyed the area. He gestured toward some very faint footprints. "Let's flag these. I don't know if they're Nichol's or if they belong to the person that shot him."

Mattie placed a spike near the prints. Moving carefully to avoid disturbing any evidence, she studied the area, looking for the bullet that had penetrated Nichol's chest. The thick vegetation along the creek bank would hide anything that small. "I'm going to ask Robo to do an evidence search here, even though it looks impossible."

"Go ahead. I'll contact the sheriff and see if the game warden is down there with him." Brody moved away, leaving Mattie space to search.

She decided that if she kept Robo close, it was safe to unclip his leash. She told him to seek and watched as he sniffed the grass, his head parting the tall green stuff in waves. He clearly knew what he was doing as he entered a thicket of willows too dense for Mattie to follow. She cruised along the edge, keeping him in sight so that she could call him back if he started to leave the area.

About ten feet into the willows, Robo disappeared, and Mattie squatted to find him. His black shape materialized within the shadows, and his tawny markings gave him enough definition for her to realize that he'd sat and was looking back at her over his shoulder.

Her pulse quickened. He'd found something.

She edged through the willow branches to reach him. "What is it? What did you find?"

After her eyes adjusted to the dim light, Mattie could see a pair of high-powered binoculars, lenses down in the muddy soil.

"Good boy," she murmured as she stroked Robo's head. "What a good job you did."

By this time, Brody had moved to the edge of the bushes. "What is it?"

"Binoculars," she called to him. "I'll photograph them before I pick them up."

Broken ends of willow branches poked her as she took out her cell phone and snapped shots of Robo's find. Black field glasses lying in shadow against a background of dark mud required the use of a flash. No one would ever have seen them here within the willows.

Had some fisherman who was angling the stream lost the binoculars? Or did they belong to Wilson, or his killer? She hoped the lab would be able to find prints.

After taking photos, she pulled a latex glove from her pocket and put it on. From behind, Brody thrust a paper evidence bag toward her through the branches.

When she picked up the set of binoculars, she avoided the barrels of the lenses so she wouldn't smudge fingerprints that might have been left. She carefully placed them inside the bag and folded it closed before edging out from under the dense thicket.

She handed the bag to Brody. "Take a look."

He peered into the bag. "Mud on the lenses, but otherwise in pristine condition. Haven't been out here long."

She turned to praise Robo and realized he hadn't followed her from the willows. She bent to search for him within the branches and was about to call him to come, but stopped herself when she saw him. He'd moved farther through the thicket toward the creek and now sat, looking at her as if wondering what was taking her so long. "Brody, he's found something else."

After grabbing another evidence bag, she went upstream to press through the willows toward the creek side and slowly made her way down to where Robo waited. "What you got, buddy?" she murmured as she crept through roots and branches to get to him.

Robo's find lay beside him—a lead bullet, flattened at the tip. The binoculars had drawn Robo into the thicket, which had allowed him to find the smaller object.

"He found the lead," she called to Brody. "It's short, from a handgun and not a rifle."

"Well, I'll be damned!"

Mattie photographed and bagged the projectile, and this time Robo followed her out to join back up with Brody. They both patted and praised him while he danced in place, staring at the pouch on Mattie's utility belt where she kept the tennis ball they played with for his reward. "Hold on a second," she told him, stroking his head. "Let's get away from this scene before we play."

Mattie clipped on Robo's leash while she studied the ground darkened by blood. "Wilson was shot at close range here, and the bullet went through his chest, losing velocity in the willows."

"Ballistics can probably determine the caliber," Brody said, "but I think you're right; this eliminates the possibility of a long-range rifle shot."

"I don't know if the binoculars belonged to Wilson or his killer." Turning slowly, Mattie scanned the area's entire circumference, trying to determine what the person using the binoculars could have been looking at. The forest blocked her line of vision in every direction but downhill. That one afforded her a view of the valley where the Redman Ranch and its headquarters were located.

Brody was looking downhill, too. "The Redman Ranch?"

Who would find this view so interesting? And why? "Let me play with Robo for a few minutes, and then we'll get back to work."

"Sounds like a plan."

SEVENTEEN

Mattie and Robo searched the area around Wilson Nichol's crime scene but didn't find anything new. When two members of the sheriff's posse arrived to guard the site, she thought she might call it quits, but then she noticed Robo's head go up, and he stared into the forest. Within seconds, he put his nose to the ground to sniff, shifting his head side to side in the way that meant he was zeroing in on human scent.

She called to Brody. "Robo's got another hit. I think he's still following Wilson Nichol's track."

"Go for it. I'll follow."

Mattie spoke softly to Robo, encouraging him as he guided her upstream. They trekked about one hundred yards through steep and rugged terrain before Robo veered away from the creek. Mattie figured this was the path Wilson had taken prior to being shot.

Not long after they left the creek bank, Robo led her to a silver Lexus SUV parked within a pine grove as if it had been hidden in a spot far from the main road, which looped back and forth up the mountain in a series of switchbacks. Robo led her straight to the driver's side door and sat while Mattie rewarded him with hugs and pats.

She looked over her shoulder at Brody. "This is Wilson Nichol's Lexus."

He raised one eyebrow as he scanned the small clearing within the trees. "Now we've got to wonder who hid it here."

"True. But Robo led me straight to the driver's side door, so I think Nichol parked it here himself."

"What's inside?"

Mattie peered into the window. Since he was standing right next to her, Mattie figured it was a rhetorical question and didn't answer, but she spotted several scrolls that looked like architectural drawings, rolled and secured with rubber bands, lying on the passenger seat beside an empty case for binoculars. Otherwise, the car's interior appeared uncluttered and immaculate.

Careful not to touch anything, Brody leaned forward. "Keys are in it, and it's probably unlocked. We'll seal it and have it towed to the crime scene lab for a thorough search. Maybe it'll give us some kind of evidence."

"It looks like he might have left it here while he got out to take a look around with the binoculars."

Brody scanned the area, his eyes following the two-track that led away from the trees where the car had been parked. "I can't see the main road from here, but it probably connects with this one. Apparently Nichol headed downhill after he was shot instead of trying to get back here."

Mattie thought about it. "That chest wound looked like it took out one of his lungs. Maybe he couldn't get enough breath to try to go uphill."

Robo had been sniffing the vehicle from all angles, reminding Mattie that she wanted to do a drug sweep on it. She called him to her and asked him to sweep the exterior in a methodical way, sniffing wheel wells and the undercarriage at her direction.

Nothing. This vehicle was free of the scent of narcotics. Although the lack of evidence didn't wipe away her previous theory that Nate Fletcher and Wilson Nichol might have partnered in drug trafficking, it certainly didn't support it.

Brody had called Sheriff McCoy to give him an update, and he disconnected the call just as Mattie was finishing up.

"No sign of drugs," she told him.

"The sheriff will send Johnson to guard the car until it can be processed. I'll stay here until he arrives, but you need to go down to where Nichol was shot. The game warden and McCoy are headed there now."

Mattie acknowledged his words with a short salute and turned to jog downhill, Robo keeping pace beside her. She'd not traveled far, careful to watch her step and avoid stones and dead-fall, when her phone rang. She stopped, and as she called Robo back to her, she withdrew her phone and checked caller ID.

Cole. She wanted to talk to him—they had a lot to discuss—but she felt like she should talk to him in person, face-to-face. She needed to join up with Sheriff McCoy as well, so she pushed the call to voice mail.

But as soon as she silenced the phone, she regretted it. What if Cole was calling with news about Garrett? Or the kids? Her life had expanded this past year so that not everything focused solely on her.

She hit Cole's number on speed dial, resuming her quick pace down the mountain.

The phone rang once before Cole answered. "Mattie. I'm glad you called back."

She could hear the stress in his voice. "I'm on my way to meet the sheriff, so I have only a minute."

"I'll just say it, then. I feel terrible about how we left things last night. I never wanted to hurt you, and I've gone over it a hundred times in my mind. I don't know how I could have changed things, but I'm sorry if I made a mistake."

Cole sounded so contrite that her heart went out to him. She had to let him know that she didn't blame him. "Not your fault, Cole. It is what it is. We need to talk, but it might be late before I get off work."

"Call me no matter when. I need to talk to you."

She could tell he wanted to resolve things as much as she did, but now wasn't the time. "Do you have news from Garrett?"

"He had a good night. They took him downstairs to the rehab department for evaluation, and he's been there all morning."

It was a relief to hear that at least Garrett had rested well. She caught a glimpse of McCoy's large frame through the trees. "I've got to go."

"Don't forget to call me tonight."

"Okay." She ended the call, feeling tired and overwhelmed. Did she have it in her to navigate an intimate relationship? She didn't have time to think it through, because she'd reached her destination.

When she entered the small clearing, McCoy and a woman were squatting beside the paw prints Mattie had flagged earlier. They both stood to greet her.

"Deputy Cobb," McCoy said, "this is Glenna Dalton, the new wildlife manager."

Mattie extended her hand. "Pleased to meet you."

Glenna returned Mattie's handshake while her eyes went to Robo. "Likewise. I've only been in town a few weeks, but I've already heard about you and your partner."

Mattie knew that Robo's successes over the past year had built his reputation, so she wasn't surprised. "What do you think of this cougar attack?"

Glenna stood at least six inches taller than Mattie's five foot four, and she was built strong and solid. She wore khaki shorts and a shirt with the Colorado Parks and Wildlife logo on the upper sleeve. Her curly brunette hair was caught loosely in a long ponytail at her nape, and her hazel eyes studied Mattie from under a floppy, wide-brimmed hat.

"It was a little hard to believe at first," Glenna said. "Not typical mountain lion behavior. I've been driving this territory since I was hired, and it looks like rabbits and rodents are plentiful up here. You know, a cougar's usual fare. I have trouble believing a big cat would be hungry enough to feed off a human, unless something's wrong with it. Maybe it's been injured and unable to hunt."

Glenna squatted back down near the paw prints. She reached into her pocket and took out a ballpoint pen, laying it down alongside the clearest print before taking out her phone and snapping pictures. "These prints are quite large. Bigger than any I've seen before."

"Do you have experience studying cougar prints?" McCoy asked.

Glenna rocked back on her heel, bracing her arm against her knee while she looked up at the sheriff. "I was involved with a cougar project up in Montana prior to moving here. For six months we tracked and tagged mountain lions. I've seen some large cats, but this one is bigger than the norm."

Glenna was studying the photos she'd taken, zooming in as she stared at the screen. She stood, offering her phone to McCoy first and then Mattie.

"Notice the toe shape here." Glenna's finger hovered over the screen as she pointed. "It's shaped like an oval."

Mattie didn't know the significance of toe shape and assumed the sheriff didn't either, but Glenna had taken back her phone and was swiping through photos again.

"Here," Glenna said. "This is a photo I have from our project. Notice the toes. They're teardrop shaped. That's the hallmark of a cougar print. This print is smaller, too."

Mattie took the phone and looked at a smaller print in the photo, lined up beside the same type of ballpoint pen. *She's right. These toes are shaped like a tear.* "Are we looking at a different animal, then?"

Glenna shook her head. "I don't know for sure. But the prints don't match, do they?"

"They don't." Mattie decided she should mention the different sound the cat made. "When I heard this cat growl, it was deep-pitched, so deep that it rattled. I've only heard a cougar scream once, but it was nothing like what I heard last night."

"What else could it be? A bobcat?" McCoy asked, but even as he spoke, he was shaking his head. "I know. Not big enough."

Glenna stood and looked upward at the mountainside that loomed to the north. Mattie followed suit and scanned above the forest, noting cliffs and rocky outcroppings, canyons filled with the bright-green leaves of aspen, spires and crags, all places where a cougar could hide. Or lie in wait for his prey to pass by.

"I guess I need to go on a lion hunt," Glenna said.

"How do you plan to do that?" McCoy said.

She turned away from the mountainside and looked back at the sheriff. "I don't have a horse yet. Can you help me find one I can use?"

Cole could help, Mattie thought. He and his dad often supplied horses for search parties up in the wilderness area.

"Maybe," McCoy said. "But you'll never find a cougar up in that country. They've got a million places to hide and are rarely seen."

"I've got a dog that's trained for tracking game." Glenna pointed at the paw prints and then traced her finger along an invisible pathway that traveled upward to an indefinite spot on the mountain. "If I start out first thing in the morning, I can pick up the track here and follow it to its territory. I should be able to find it."

As soon as she uttered the words, Mattie thought of Cole's Doberman pinscher. Bruno's previous owner had used him to track deer and elk that she hunted up on her mountain property. With the right dog, it could be done. "That's a dangerous mission for a dog," Mattie said. "Tracking a big cat."

The sincere expression on Glenna's face projected the confidence she had in her dog. "Mine's a Rhodesian ridgeback. They're used for tracking lions in Africa. I use an e-collar with an audio signal that tells him to come back to me, and he knows I'm serious when I call him."

Mattie considered all the things that could go wrong: the dog could get out of signal range, the cat could ambush Glenna from above, and since this new wildlife manager was unfamiliar with the rugged country she was headed into, she could even get lost. "You're going to need some help."

"I hoped someone would offer." Glenna looked directly at Mattie.

McCoy shifted his weight from one foot to the other, a rare sign that he'd grown restless. A quick glance told Mattie he was frowning. "I don't know if this is a good idea. I need to loop in Cole Walker and discuss it with him—he'd be the one to line up the horses. We need to think this through before we go off half-cocked."

"He's the local vet, right?" Glenna asked.

McCoy nodded. "I'm calling a team meeting at four this afternoon, Ms. Dalton—"

"Glenna," she interjected.

"Glenna," McCoy said. "Can you meet with us at the station? By then I'll have discussed this with Dr. Walker. Perhaps he can come, too."

Mattie didn't like the idea of Cole going on a man-eating lion hunt in the mountains when his daughters needed him. Sophie and Angela should come first. But Glenna's hazel eyes lit with anticipation.

"Having a vet on the hunt would be perfect," she said. "I'd like to sedate the cat instead of killing it, and a vet could help. I'll come to your meeting."

The thought of Cole riding into harm's way made Mattie's stomach drop. She would lobby against it, but she supposed the final decision would be up to Cole. The best she could hope for would be for him to decline the mission, but she doubted that would be the case. If it meant saving the life of an animal, whether it was wise or not, choosing to stand aside wouldn't be the Cole Walker way.

EIGHTEEN

Mattie drove by the Big Sky Motel on her way to the station, noticed the Cadillac's absence, and wondered where Zach Irving and Ben Underwood had gone. Had they headed back to California, or were they going forward with their fishing trip? Stella would know, and she made a mental note to find out.

Sheriff McCoy's Jeep was already parked in the lot at the station, as was Stella's Honda. Mattie unloaded Robo and went inside, but as soon as she entered, Stella came from her office and headed toward McCoy's, beckoning for Mattie to join her.

Stella spoke softly. "The sheriff has Nate Fletcher's parents here in his office. I want you to hear what they have to say."

"All right." Mattie followed Stella through McCoy's office door.

Bent with grief, Tom and Helen Fletcher looked like they hadn't slept for days. Sheriff McCoy had settled them into visitors' chairs, cups of coffee placed on the desk in front of them. Helen hunched forward in her chair, her arms wrapped around her middle, while Tom sat with knees splayed, elbows propped on his thighs as if holding him up. Their eyes were reddened, lids swollen.

Stella and McCoy took their seats, while Mattie and Robo lingered in the doorway. Tom Fletcher stood and offered his chair, but Mattie told him she'd rather stand. He sighed heavily as he sank back into his seat, the weight of the world on his bent shoulders.

McCoy cleared his throat. "Mr. Fletcher, would you repeat what you've told me for Detective LoSasso?"

Tom nodded and set his gaze on Stella. "We knew we needed to come talk to you in person, because we know how it is in small communities."

"How's that, Mr. Fletcher?"

"Nate was the outsider here. Hometown folks get the benefit of the doubt."

Stella frowned. "I can assure you that's not how we're running our investigation."

"The sheriff has already assured me of that. But still, it's important for us to be here."

"I'm sure that's true. And it's important for us to hear what you have to say."

Tom leaned forward. "There'd been something eating away at Nate for the past few months. He's never been the kind who would talk openly about his troubles, but when we spoke on the phone, I could tell he was unhappy."

Stella nodded, apparently waiting while he collected his thoughts.

"He quit calling me and his mother. If we wanted to touch base, it was up to one of us to reach out." Tom looked at his wife. "A few months ago, he told Helen that things weren't going well at home and he was considering leaving Kasey. When she asked him why . . . Well, you tell them, honey."

This came as a surprise. Everything she and Stella had gleaned from Kasey and her family suggested that the two had been happily married.

Helen picked up the story. "Nate said Kasey had expectations that he couldn't fulfill. That seemed to be all he wanted to say about it, and I gathered it was a private matter so I shouldn't probe." A slight tinge of pink colored her pale cheeks, and she brushed a strand of dark hair shot with gray back from her face.

Helen choked up, so Tom continued. "A couple months ago, Nate asked to borrow money. Quite a large sum, in fact. I asked why he needed so much, and he said the original loan for starting his business had come due and he hadn't generated enough income to cover it. That didn't seem right to me, so I asked if I could view his financials before making a commitment."

There'd been a hint that Nate and Kasey had been dealing with financial trouble, but this bit of news provided confirmation. Mattie wondered if the couple was deeper in debt than she'd thought.

Tom braced his elbows on his knees, hanging his head in utter desolation. "In hindsight, I wish I hadn't done that. Nate got his feathers ruffled, and it took some explaining to make him understand that his mother and I wanted to help, but we needed to be assured that his business could pay back the loan eventually."

Helen interjected, placing her hand on her husband's shoulder. "Tom has a lot more business experience than Nate. He's managed his own insurance company for over thirty years."

"It's made a living for us, but we don't have large sums of money on hand to loan out." Tom placed his hand on hers. "When Nate was a child, we covered him with a generous life insurance policy, in part to be used to borrow against if he needed college money or start-up money for a business. I suggested we look into borrowing against the policy if he was interested."

"What's the death benefit on that policy?" Stella asked.

Tom raised a brow. "I was getting to that. Half a million dollars."

Mattie was blown away.

"That's a large amount for someone so young," Stella said.

Tom shrugged. "It's our business. It's what we believe in."

"Did Nate go ahead and use the policy to borrow the money?"

"No, we didn't get around to that. I explained the details to him, and he said he'd talk it over with Kasey and get back to me. That's as far as it went."

Helen looked at Stella. "Shortly after we spoke to you yesterday, Kasey called to ask about filing a claim on the policy for the death benefit. We packed up our car and headed down here to talk to the authorities."

Mattie figured she knew why they had, and she guessed Stella did too, but the detective was waiting for them to say more. When they didn't, Stella offered a prompt. "What did Kasey say when she called you?"

Lines of concern on Tom's face added to those already etched by grief. "I told Kasey we'd need to have a copy of Nate's death certificate before I could file a claim for her."

Tom took a moment to struggle with tears that brimmed in his eyes. "And then I explained that in cases of homicide, the company would probably launch an investigation before paying. That upset her, and I was worried that she needed the money right away to pay back the bank. I thought we should help her with it if we could. But when I asked, I found out that Kasey's dad, Doyle Redman, is the one who loaned Nate start-up money years ago. There was no bank involved. Then she said that Nate owed money for gambling debt and he'd been unable to pay back her father. I had no idea—" Tom's voice broke and trailed off.

Helen reached for her husband's hand. "We had no idea about any of this. The loan, the gambling. None of it."

Nate's parents were obviously devastated, and Mattie's heart went out to them. But she also felt a sense of irritation. Why was this the first time anyone had mentioned the bit about gambling debt to law enforcement? Kasey had had plenty of opportunities to tell either her or Stella about it. Who did Nate owe gambling money to? And why hadn't Kasey shared this piece of the puzzle with the police?

"What did Kasey tell you about the gambling debt?" Stella asked.

"She said he'd been to Vegas and racked up debt on all their credit cards," Tom said. "I remembered Nate telling me that he'd been driving from California to Nebraska a lot and was tired of it, but I was shocked to learn he had a gambling problem. And once I promised Kasey I'd get back to her about the life insurance, she couldn't get off the phone fast enough. Then Helen and I started talking, and we got worried."

Repetitive trips from California to Nebraska—to Mattie, that meant drug running.

"Did Nate say why he was making these trips back and forth across the country?" Stella asked.

"He said it was for his business. Supplies and working to get clients. In hindsight, I have to wonder about that." Tom paused while his gaze shifted between Stella and the sheriff. Mattie wondered exactly what he was thinking. He'd brought up some hard information with serious consequences that implicated Kasey.

Stella leaned forward, placing her elbows against her legs in a posture that matched Tom's, although unlike his downtrodden body language, her energy fairly snapped between them. "Is Kasey the *only* beneficiary on the insurance policy?"

Tom nodded. "I suggested that Nate make the change shortly after he married. In those days, it seemed like he'd found the love of his life."

"Kasey is our daughter-in-law, and we've always thought she was a sweet girl." The pain caused by thinking anything different was evident on Helen's face. "If it turns out that she has nothing to do with Nate's murder, it would be devastating to let her know we've even brought it up. I hope you can understand our position."

"We handle these things carefully, Mrs. Fletcher," McCoy said. "It's a theory that should be examined, and you can be assured that we'll proceed with discretion."

Tom cleared his throat. "The Redmans are important people in Timber Creek."

"Like Detective LoSasso said, that won't influence our investigation," McCoy told him.

But Mattie knew that statement wasn't necessarily true. Status had an impact on judgments no matter where people lived or in what profession they were involved. Even the local judge sometimes seemed to sign search warrants based on family connections.

"We're dedicated to finding your son's killer," Stella said. "Do you have any other concerns you'd like to discuss?"

As Tom shook his head, he looked at his wife. "I think that's all."

"Will you be staying in Timber Creek?"

"At least for a few days. We need to see Kasey and help her with arrangements for our son's funeral." Helen's cheeks were flushed with stress. "It's hard to explain, but Kasey was our son's choice, and we've loved her as if she were one of our own. It's a terrible thing to harbor such an evil suspicion about someone you love. What if we're wrong? We don't want to color her life with such a horrible accusation."

Mattie thought these two were perhaps among the wisest people she'd ever encountered. Even in the face of their own grief, they were weighing their words and striving to protect another from unwarranted suspicion.

Stella retrieved her card from her pants pocket. "You can call me to talk anytime, day or night. And let us have your contact information in case we need to get in touch."

After the Fletchers gave Stella their cell phone numbers, the meeting broke up. Mattie opened the door she'd been standing beside, asking Robo to heel as she stepped back out of the way.

On his way out, Tom made eye contact before glancing down at her dog. "I admire the work you do. And he's a beauty."

"Robo's responsible for finding the bulk of the evidence we have in your son's case," McCoy said.

Tom's gaze conveyed intense sincerity. "Thank you for that."

"We'll stay on it." And as Tom reached to pet her dog's head, Mattie was quick to prompt Robo. "It's okay, Robo. Say hello."

Robo stood and wagged his tail. Most people didn't seem to realize how dangerous it was to reach out toward a strange dog, especially a protective one like hers. But good genetics and years of training paid off. Take a dog with a friendly personality, add socialization and behavioral training as a puppy, and then top it off with months and months of continuous training in police work and obedience, and here was the result. This type of police dog earned back every one of the thousands of dollars spent to acquire him. Mattie never took having such a valuable asset for granted.

Tom stroked Robo's head and then escorted his wife through the lobby to leave. McCoy held the door for them as he said goodbye.

"That's the best motive we've got, at least in Nate's case," Stella muttered under her breath to Mattie.

"Wives have killed for less," she replied. "So evidently Nate's been stopping in Vegas, and he told his wife he was in Nebraska when he wasn't. Things between them aren't as rosy as she's led us to believe."

"It's time I pulled her in and talked to her here at the station," Stella said.

Mattie nodded. "The insurance money works as a motive for Nate, but what about Wilson?"

"Maybe there was some kind of a love triangle gone bad. Right now, I'm skeptical about any of the information we've learned from Kasey Redman."

"Cross-country trips could mean drug running, but you know who else is from California?" Mattie eyed Stella.

"Zach Irving and Ben Underwood. And right now they're supposedly on a fishing trip up in the mountains north of town with our first victim's brother-in-law."

"Do we know that for sure?"

Stella nodded. "Their car's parked out at the Redman Ranch. Spotted it there early this morning."

McCoy came back through the lobby to join them. "Let's take a thirty-minute break and then meet in the briefing room before Glenna Dalton and Dr. Walker arrive. We need to plan how we're going to keep our promise to proceed with the utmost care when what we really need to do is bring in the victim's wife and sweat her."

NINETEEN

During her break, Mattie caught up on paperwork while Robo sacked out on his cushion. Soon, a light snore coming from his direction made her look to see him settled on his chest, his front legs splayed to each side in a position that looked far from comfortable.

Her partner made her smile, even in the most serious of times.

She'd grown to love him more and more as the months passed. He was her friend, her protector, and her comfort when she was feeling down. She was one lucky cop.

She turned back to her computer to check her email, scrolling through the list, replying to those that needed her attention. There was one from Jim Madsen, Robo's trainer, setting up an interdepartmental training session in Denver in a few weeks, which caught her eye. It was always fun to mingle with other K-9 handlers, and any day spent with Sergeant Jim Madsen was a good day. But there were still no results on the DNA she'd submitted to the database previously, and she wondered how much longer it would take. She was growing impatient with the wait.

At three, she rose from her chair, and that movement alone sent Robo scrambling to his feet. He yawned and stretched, blinking the sleep from his eyes before standing on his bed, ears pricked and fully alert.

"Let's go to the briefing room," she told him, and he headed off in that direction.

The others were already there, including Brody, and Mattie took a seat at the front table while Robo settled beside her chair. She had a disturbing thought: all of her colleagues seated at this table knew her childhood secrets, whereas before she'd thought only Stella knew. She pushed the thought away, unwilling to let it interfere with her work. Nothing had changed except her own awareness—these people were professionals, and their interactions had remained the same as always during the past month.

The sheriff's presence always lent a certain level of stability to their group. Mattie had learned something about "being grounded" during her weekly yoga lessons with Rainbow, and Sheriff McCoy was probably the most grounded individual she knew. And as far as she could tell, his unflappable nature came to him easily; she doubted he spent much time learning to steady himself with asana poses and meditation like she did.

But as she studied him, she had to wonder if he knew other secrets about her, leaving her with an unsettled feeling. She still suffered from repressed memories from her childhood, and it haunted her to think he might know more than she did about her past.

Stella was writing lists on the whiteboard she'd developed for Wilson Nichol. "All right, everyone, this is getting complicated. Two homicides, both with gunshot wounds. You've notified Wilson's family, Sheriff?"

"His parents," McCoy said. "They moved from here to Arizona last year and don't seem to know much about his current life. They plan to come to Timber Creek as soon as they can make arrangements to be gone from their business."

Stella turned to the whiteboard to review the points she'd written from the autopsy, ticking off each one with her marking pen. "There was one through-and-through gunshot wound to

Nichol's chest, going front to back. From the appearance of the exit wound, the bullet was designed to expand upon impact, similar to the hollow points found in Nate Fletcher."

Stella moved on to the next point. "Examination of his organs and the cavity left by the predator indicates Nichol bled out and his heart had stopped beating before the cat got to him. The ME is listing the cause of death as exsanguination from a gunshot wound."

Mattie had hoped that was the case, and she was relieved to hear it confirmed.

"Let's move on to what we've learned about the evidence left at the scene." Stella pointed to a photo of the boot prints found in the soil beside Wilson's body. "These prints and the victim's footwear don't match, so let's assume they were left by his killer. Of course we don't know if the killer came up that close to Wilson during or after the shooting, but the trajectory of the bullet that Robo found in the willows matches with the position of the footprints. It looks like the shooter was standing right there when he shot Wilson."

A little jolt of adrenaline did a lot to boost Mattie's flagging energy level. This was good news. If the killer had been close in proximity when he'd shot Wilson and had used a handgun, the same MO had been used for both victims.

Stella went on. "Analysis suggests the prints are approximately a man's size eight and a half to nine and a half, which converts to a woman's size ten to eleven."

Stella eyed her, and Mattie decided to voice what she figured the detective was thinking. "And I would guess Kasey Redman wears a shoe about my size, a size seven."

"You read my mind," Stella said. "When you take into consideration the dampness of the soil, it looks like this print was left by a man of slender build. Though I advise we take this with a grain of salt. It's hard to read much into print depth in different soil types."

"Agreed, but the glove found at Nate Fletcher's scene was large enough to suggest a male killer, too." Mattie scanned the list of persons of interest. "Tyler Redman is a husky guy, but Flint Thornton, Ben Underwood, and Zach Irving are all lean."

"Right," Stella said, shifting her gaze to Brody. "Brody, what's your opinion of Flint Thornton as our killer?"

He scratched the stubble on his chin. "Flint has no history of violent crime. He was into petty theft, property damage, and smoking pot as a teenager, but we never busted him for any of the hard drugs. As far as I know, he's kept his nose clean for years."

Mattie would like to believe that a record of juvenile crime didn't necessarily lead to a record as an adult, but in many cases it did. "We can't eliminate him yet."

Brody shrugged and looked at her with tired eyes. "No, we can't."

Mattie focused on the next point in Stella's list. "Let's talk about the revolver Robo found at Nate Fletcher's crime scene."

"Smith and Wesson .38 Special," Stella said. "Four hollow-point rounds in the cylinder and two spent cartridges, which as you well know matches the number of shots used to kill Nate. The gun had been wiped clean: no prints."

Mattie spun back to the evidence they'd found at Wilson's place—the jars and the can of fuel. "We know now that the gun was registered to Wilson Nichol, and he reported it stolen a few weeks ago. That and the items we found behind his office point to someone trying to set Wilson up as Nate Fletcher's killer."

"I think it's possible," Stella agreed.

McCoy tapped a finger on the table. "Which begs the question: if the killer went to all the trouble to plant this evidence against Wilson, why did he turn right around and kill him?"

"True," Stella said. "I wonder if something happened after Nate that made the shooter decide he needed to kill Wilson as well."

During the silence that followed, Mattie wondered how they might find the answer to that question. "We need to trace Wilson's activities between the filing of the report and the time of his death, especially focusing on these last few days," she said at last. "We've got to see who he's crossed paths with."

"I've started that, but first let's finish talking through our evidence," Stella said. "Wilson's fingerprints were the only ones found on the binoculars, so it's safe to assume they belonged to him. And the scrolls found inside his car were blueprints of the Redman Ranch. One was of the buildings on the property, and one was the general layout of the entire acreage."

"Why would he have those in his possession? And why was he carrying them around in his car?" Mattie paused to think for a moment. "Maybe the Redmans are planning to sell their place and use him as the agent. He could have been up there checking out the lay of the land."

McCoy shifted in his chair. "We need to follow up with the Redmans to see if they plan to sell their property."

"Already done," Stella said. "I called Lillian; they have no desire or plan to sell their property."

Mattie sorted through details she knew, trying to match the pieces. "All right, when we look at the real estate angle, here sits a valuable piece of property owned by Lillian and Doyle Redman. Wilson Nichol is in real estate sales, Zach Irving is a real estate developer and Ben Underwood a builder. That's one way these three men tie in together."

"Agreed," Stella said. "But Lillian also told me she'd never met the two men from California until this morning when they left with Tyler to go fishing. As far as she knows, they're merely Nate's customers."

Sheriff McCoy interjected by raising his hand. "I've got a warrant to search Wilson's business and home to see if we can find anything associated with his death. Perhaps we can find something there that sheds light on Wilson's relationship with these two men or anyone else on our list."

Tyler Redman. He was Wilson's friend. "What about Tyler?" Mattie said. "Could he be the one interested in selling the land?"

"And now he's the one hobnobbing with the developers," Brody added.

"Hard to say," Stella said, "but that doesn't provide motive for killing Nate *or* Wilson. In fact, killing Wilson would throw a wrench into that plan. We've still got to dig for motive, and I'll execute that search warrant first thing tomorrow."

Stella turned back to the whiteboard, putting her marker on the next point. "Let's talk about this information from Wilson's phone records."

Stella had listed a phone number, and now Mattie took her notebook from her pocket to record it.

"This is the number for the last incoming call on Wilson's cell phone. It's the last person he talked to before he dialed nine-one-one." Stella tapped the end of her marker against the number on the whiteboard. "We need to find out who called him."

Mattie checked the records in her notebook. "And that number doesn't match either Ben Underwood's or Zach Irving's."

"Right. But I got some help from CBI tech support. The number isn't registered to anyone and belongs to a prepaid phone. They're trying to trace where the phone was sold, so we can find out if we can get a receipt or even the store's CCTV recording of the person who bought it," Stella said, referring to closed-circuit television used by security.

"That's good work," McCoy said in a low tone.

"Maybe it was Kasey," Mattie said. "She's another link between Nate and Wilson."

"True," Stella said, adding Kasey back on the Persons of Interest list. "We have to take another look at her, especially in light of the fact that she's got a strong motive for Nate."

It took a few minutes for Stella to update Brody on the information Nate's parents had shared, giving Mattie time to think about the money.

She tried to draw the triangle she'd come up with for the others. "Kasey said earlier that she and Nate had all their assets tied up in his business. Now we find out she's also buried in credit card debt due to his gambling. The insurance money gives her motive to kill Nate. And maybe Wilson found out, and she had to get rid of him."

Stella nodded, her lips pursed. "And the fishermen are just who they say they are—Nate's clients on a Colorado vacation?"

"Maybe." Mattie brought up the point that still bothered her. "But Robo *did* find trace cocaine in Nate's van. He's been driving from California to Nebraska, which suggests drug running, and these two are from California. Perhaps Nate decided to take on drug trafficking to solve his money problems, and they're part of it."

Stella eyed the sheriff. "I know we hate to lean on the widow too hard, but we need to bring Kasey in and talk to her again."

"I have no problem with that," McCoy said, frowning. "But I want to protect Nate's parents. Find a way to keep their suspicions confidential."

"I can do that."

A knock sounded outside, followed by Rainbow poking her head though the door's opening. "Cole Walker and Glenna Dalton are here to see you, Sheriff."

"Send them in," he said, rising to help Stella wheel the two whiteboards around to face the wall. "And could you help me round up coffee for them?"

"Already done," Rainbow said, giving him her cheerful smile before leaving.

As they shuffled around to make room at the table for more chairs, the heat on Mattie's cheeks began to rise. *Business as usual*, she reminded herself, lowering her face as she pushed an empty chair up next to hers.

She'd hoped to use the cover of darkness tonight for her first face-to-face meeting with Cole, but no such luck. She'd tried to prepare for seeing him again, but she could feel her body starting to betray her before he even stepped into the room.

She needed to get past these feelings of being exposed soon—with her colleagues and with Cole—because they all had serious work to do together. And two murder cases to solve.

TWENTY

Mattie let Robo trot over to greet Cole when he entered the room. Cole bent to pet him, but his eyes went straight to hers, checking in silently to see how she was doing. Concern and fatigue lined his face, and she nodded, hoping to send the message that she was okay. Maybe a little bruised around the heart, but basically all right.

Though McCoy was quick to introduce Glenna, Cole mentioned that they'd met in the lobby. Stella stepped forward to shake hands, introducing herself before gesturing toward the table in an invitation to sit.

Cole took the seat beside Mattie and they settled in—Mattie painfully aware of where his arm brushed hers—while Robo went back to his place on the floor at her other side. He circled, lay down, and heaved a sigh as he relaxed his head down on his paws, everything apparently right in his world. She leaned down to stroke his back, once again taking a lesson from her dog: relax and rest when you can.

Glenna had taken a seat across the table, and she began to set up an iPad she'd carried in with her. "Could I have your Wi-Fi password?" she asked McCoy.

He gave it to her before addressing the group. "We all know why we're here. We have a problem with this cougar, and I hope we can determine what we're going to do about it."

"Well," Stella said, "we now know that Wilson Nichol died from a gunshot wound. So this isn't a man-killing lion we're dealing with. It's just a man-eating one."

Glenna looked up from her computer screen to look at Cole. "I've been doing some research this afternoon. This morning, I talked to Sheriff McCoy and Deputy . . ." Her eyes went to Mattie's name tag.

"Mattie," she told Glenna.

Glenna nodded at her before looking back at Cole. "We talked about how the paw prints of this cat didn't match up with what I know about cougar prints, and how the growl Mattie heard didn't match the scream of the cougar she'd heard in the past. So I did some research. Let me play some animal sounds I found on You Tube. Mattie, I want to see if one matches what you heard in the forest."

Glenna tapped her screen, waited a few seconds for it to load, and tapped it again. A bloodcurdling screech filled the room, followed by throaty growls, none with the deep timbre Mattie remembered from last night. Robo scrambled to his feet to stand by Mattie. He cocked his head, his eyes homing in on the tablet.

"That's a cougar," Mattie said, putting her hand on Robo to soothe him.

"Right," Glenna said. "How about this?"

A couple taps initiated a loud roar, followed by some chuffing growls.

"Not the same," Mattie said, "and not what I heard yesterday. African lion?"

Glenna nodded. "Right. Now try this one."

A deep, throaty growl emanated from the tablet's speaker, making the skin on the back of Mattie's neck crawl. Robo's hackles stood on end and he barked, his shoulders shuddering beneath her hand. The growl from the iPad escalated into a roar and then lingered in a deep prolonged rattle that shook Mattie to her core.

"That's it," she said softly, meeting Glenna's gaze. She sensed Cole turn in his seat to look at her. "That's what I heard."

"Siberian tiger," Glenna responded.

Mattie's heart thudded in her ears. She had no idea how a tiger could be loose in the Colorado mountains, but she had no doubt that Glenna had played a recording of the same growl she'd heard last night. Though hard to believe, she and Robo had been within yards of a Siberian tiger, a fearsome predator no matter where it was found.

Cole shifted in his chair, clearly uneasy. "How can that be?"

"That's what I'd like to know," Glenna said. "I checked on all the tiger permits in the state for zoos and wildlife parks. All tigers are present and accounted for, no reports of an escape."

"It's illegal to transport a tiger into the state," Brody said, "much less release one into the mountains."

"But I think that's what someone has done," Glenna said. "We have a tiger on the loose, in unfamiliar habitat. Maybe it's never lived in the wild before; maybe it doesn't know how to hunt. It's hungry. It follows a blood trail, finds dead prey, and it feeds on it."

Stella looked incredulous. "So you're saying this tiger isn't to be blamed for eating a man?"

"I'm saying that any large cat is dangerous and will attack if it's hungry or has its back to the wall." Glenna focused on Cole, her face passionate. "But what I'm also saying is that this tiger is a victim, too. Someone has brought it here, released it, and left it to survive on its own. It deserves a chance to live. I hope we can give it that chance. Sedate it and capture it."

"I can provide horses, and I've got a BAM kit in my office," Cole said, referring to a sedative used on wildlife. "But I don't have a dart projector."

"I have one that we can use," Glenna said.

"I don't know how we're going to find this tiger," Cole said. "I doubt it stays in one place."

"I have a dog trained to hunt cougar," Glenna said. "I'm sure he can track it. All he'll smell is cat."

Mattie's heart made a slow downward slide within her chest. Hearing the tiger's growl had reminded her of what Wilson Nichol looked like after the tiger had been at him, and she didn't want Cole anywhere near it. "This is too dangerous. I'm not a fan of tracking down this tiger and killing it, but that's what has to be done."

"Hold on a minute," McCoy said, his mellow voice dampening the emotion in the room. "We need to look at the big picture here. Why would someone bring a tiger into our county?"

"I've been thinking about that," Glenna said. "I'm not sure I have the exact answer, but tigers have become the target of wildlife trafficking over the last few years. At first, poachers were killing them to sell their parts on the black market. But lately we've had reports of live tigers being involved. Just a few months ago, traffickers with three tiger cubs in duffel bags were busted in Arizona while transporting them from Mexico to Texas."

Mattie thought of the large dog crate in the back of Nate's van. Even in its burnt and torqued condition, she'd noted its strong, steel mesh, much heavier than that needed to hold an Old English sheepdog, the pet Kasey mentioned they'd lost recently. And Nate's route seemed to be California to Nebraska. "Is wildlife trafficking often done through Mexico?" she asked Glenna.

"A large part of it. Easier to get into the U.S. from there."

Narcotics still hadn't been mentioned, and Mattie needed to know about that piece. "Is drug running associated with wildlife trafficking?"

"As a matter of fact, it is," Glenna said. "These guys often make the most of their trips. Drugs, wildlife, guns. Makes a trip across country all the more profitable."

The picture was becoming clearer now. Nate could have been running illegal goods from California to Nebraska on the interstate highway and then passing them on to someone who ran them farther east. It was a trafficking route well known to law enforcement. Nate might not have been an end user or a supplier, but he certainly could have been a link in the trafficking chain.

"Were drugs found in the van?" Glenna asked Mattie.

"My dog found a trace in the door panel."

"Good boy," Glenna said with a quick smile for Robo before sobering. "I'm still not certain why a tiger would be released into the wilderness area of Colorado. Unless someone intends to hunt it."

Tyler Redman and the fishermen up in the mountains north of Timber Creek. Mattie would bet anything the party hadn't taken fishing poles on their trip this morning but were instead armed with hunting rifles. Her energy surged as she made eye contact with Stella and determined that the detective had come to the same conclusion.

They both looked to Sheriff McCoy. The decision to share case details would be up to him. He'd leaned back in his chair and was staring at the backside of the whiteboards. Brody cleared his throat and shifted in his chair.

McCoy tapped one finger lightly on the table. "Let's talk theoretically for a moment. Let's say we have circumstantial evidence that such a hunting party exists."

"I'd say that falls under my jurisdiction," Glenna replied, looking the sheriff in the eye. "Any animal being hunted illegally in the state of Colorado is within my purview."

"Right," McCoy said.

Mattie thought of the men who were bound to have traveled well up into the high country by now: Tyler Redman, Flint Thornton, Ben Underwood, and Zach Irving. One or more of these men could be responsible for planning and carrying out a double homicide. Any one of them could be a murderer.

McCoy propped his elbows on the table as he leaned toward the game warden. "But let's say members of that hunting party might include suspects in a murder investigation."

Glenna's eyebrows rose. "Then I'd say we'd better pool our resources and get together a hunting party of our own."

TWENTY-ONE

Sheriff McCoy called Kasey Redman to tell her to come speak with them at the station, and she arrived around six in the evening with her friend Jasmine. Stella had suggested that both McCoy and Mattie participate with her in the interrogation as a subliminal way to ramp up the pressure on Kasey. But oddly enough, it put a strain on Mattie, too. She felt like she'd not had time to work through her feelings about the sheriff, and joining him in such close quarters seemed to crank up her sensitivity.

She worried her claustrophobia would interfere with her ability to concentrate. Bringing Robo in with her would help, but since the space was so small, she'd left him on his cushion in her office.

Kasey evidently wanted some support, too, and asked if Jasmine could come in to the interview with her, but McCoy stood firm and wouldn't allow it. McCoy and Stella went to one side of the table while Mattie took the seat next to Kasey, angling her chair so that she could observe Kasey's reactions and body language. They had decided beforehand that their main objectives would be to use this interrogation as an information-gathering session as well as to see if they could catch Kasey in a blatant lie or cover-up.

"Thank you for coming in, Kasey," McCoy said, settling into a chair beside Stella. "As I said, we've found some additional information that we need to discuss with you."

Kasey was nodding, her eyes red-rimmed and sorrowful as she watched the sheriff's face. Mattie's front-row seat afforded her a full view of Kasey's facial expressions. She forced herself to focus on Kasey's every word and movement and forget her own feelings. After all, she'd grown used to compartmentalizing, and now was the time to practice that strategy.

McCoy continued. "We'll be recording this interview today, because we're trying to clarify details in Nate's investigation."

Kasey looked startled. "Am I a suspect?"

Not an unusual response. Most people said that when told they were being recorded.

Stella replied with the usual assurances that this was merely routine. "First we want to discuss the information I received from your father-in-law when I spoke with him. Remember you told me to call him about the insurance?"

Mattie had to hand it to her, Stella had come up with a good opener—no lies, no misleading, but not specifically the truth either.

Kasey nodded. "I talked with Tom and Helen this afternoon, too. They're in town now."

"Mr. Fletcher said the benefit on Nate's insurance policy is for half a million dollars," Stella said.

Kasey sat slumped as if tired, cupped by one of the room's hard plastic chairs, but she maintained eye contact with Stella. "I was surprised it was that much. Nate and I had talked about taking a loan out on the policy to pay some bills, but we hadn't done it yet."

"So when did you learn the exact amount of the death benefit?"

"Just today, when Tom came to the house. He said he'd handle the details for me as soon as the investigation is over." Kasey looked at Sheriff McCoy. "Do you have any idea when that might be?"

"These things take time," he said. "It's hard to say."

"It's just that . . ." Kasey glanced down at the table. "Well, I need the money."

Wow. Mattie hadn't expected that admission right up front.

Stella's face remained passive, but Mattie could feel heat from the gaze she'd locked onto Kasey. "Yes, you mentioned you had money tied up in Nate's business. Any other debt that's troubling you?"

Kasey pressed her hands to her face and leaned forward, elbows to the table. Mattie read embarrassment, distress, both? "I hate to say this, but we have a lot of credit card debt. It's been killing us."

Strange word choice.

"Credit card debt?" Mattie prompted, jumping in where she could to keep the questions coming from all sides, another technique to ramp up the pressure.

"Yeah, I'm sorry to say this and I hope you'll keep it confidential." Kasey sighed, dropping her hands from her face but keeping her head bowed. "Nate had a problem, a gambling addiction."

"It's helpful for us to know these things for our investigation, Kasey," McCoy said gently. "What else was going on with Nate?"

Mattie recognized that the sheriff was using a sympathy approach to keep Kasey talking. He was good at winning people over; she'd seen him use the technique many a time.

Kasey raised her eyes to meet McCoy's. "He drove out to Vegas a lot. Told me he was going for supplies. I should've known better, but I believed him at first. Nate did the bookkeeping for his business, but a few months ago I found one of his credit card bills. There were more bills I discovered later."

"That must have been difficult for you," McCoy murmured.

"We went through a rough patch a few months ago, but we'd worked it out. We were in this together and we hoped to work through it."

Kasey was saying all the right things, and they matched the time frame Nate's parents had mentioned for when he'd told them he was having marital problems, but Mattie had to wonder why she was so forthcoming now when she'd avoided mentioning all this before. "Did Nate travel anywhere else in addition to Vegas?" she asked, wanting to see if Kasey would lie.

Kasey leaned back in her chair. "Yes, he would stop in Vegas to spend the night, but he usually went on to California. San Diego mostly, but sometimes Los Angeles."

"I thought Nate got the bulk of his supplies in Nebraska. Why did he drive out to California?" Stella said.

Kasey glanced down at the table. "Oh, conferences, meetings with clients. He was working on some videos for advertising."

Mattie noted Kasey's break in eye contact and doubted these kinds of meetings were necessary for an outfitting business in Colorado. Clients would want to come here to see horses, the equipment, and the mountains for themselves, and people who were strapped for cash rarely attended conferences. If Kasey was innocent and really believed this about Nate's whereabouts, Mattie had a wheat farm at the top of Pikes Peak she wanted to sell her. "Can you provide receipts from conferences and the video work for us?" she asked. "We need to pin down Nate's travels and contacts prior to his death."

For the first time, Kasey squirmed before answering. Was that a tell that she had been lying? Or was she about to?

"I'll look," Kasey said. "As you know, our office is a mess. I'll see what I can find."

"Thank you," McCoy said. "Was there any other debt owed that we should know about?"

Kasey looked at him. "Not really."

Stella leaned forward, subtly shifting Kasey's attention from McCoy to her. "Maybe a loan from your parents?"

Kasey looked startled, and Mattie could tell Stella had dropped a bomb. She could read Kasey's mind: *How do they know about that?*

"Well . . . we owe Mom and Dad some money, but they won't press me for it."

But Nate's parents had indicated otherwise, making Mattie want to push for more. "They don't need to be paid back?"

Kasey shifted in her seat as she turned toward Mattie. "Well, eventually maybe, but they know I can't pay them now."

Mattie pushed a bit more. Unlike Sheriff McCoy, she didn't mind being the prickly one. "So you'll pay when the insurance money comes in?"

Kasey's eyes narrowed ever so slightly, the only indication of her annoyance. "Yes, probably then."

"Speaking of your parents," Stella said, taking the conversation in a different direction, "do they have plans to sell the ranch?"

"Oh, gosh no," Kasey said, looking relieved to turn away from Mattie and back to Stella.

"It's just that we found blueprints to the ranch in Wilson Nichol's car."

"They plan to pass the ranch down to us kids. Why would Wilson have blueprints to our place in his car?"

"We'd like to know the answer to that, too," Stella said. "So there's three of you kids, and one ranch. Do any of you kids want to sell the place?"

"We love that place. It's where we grew up. It's our heritage. Selling it isn't in the picture." Kasey's expression appeared sincere.

Mattie decided to slip in again with a follow-up question. "How about Tyler? Does he feel that way, too?"

When Kasey turned toward her, Mattie caught a glimpse of irritation on her face. "As far as I know."

"And can a ranch like that support four families in the future, when in the past it only needed to support one?"

That appeared to strike a chord. Kasey straightened and didn't try to hide her exasperation. "We'll figure it out. That's why Nate and I started our own business."

"Yes," McCoy said, "and it underscores the importance of the fishing trip. Where is Tyler now with that party? Where do you camp?"

Prior to the interview, they'd decided not to mention wildlife trafficking and their suspicions of a tiger hunt. If Kasey was involved, she could tip off Tyler, ruining any chance for surprising the hunting party.

"I don't know where they've camped this time," Kasey said. "It's summer, so they're going to a higher elevation than usual. Tyler even talked about riding the peaks above the BLM, just to give our customers a taste of the wilderness area. They could be anywhere."

"One last thing, Kasey," Stella said. "Have you thought of anything at all that might help us with our investigation of Nate's death or the death of Wilson Nichol?"

Kasey sat with her head lowered for a moment before swiping a tear from her cheek and looking up. From Mattie's viewpoint, it appeared she was looking back and forth to take in both Stella and the sheriff. "I've racked my brain, but I can't think of anything that might help. I promise to call you if I do."

"Good," Stella said. "Could you open your cell phone to settings and show me its number, Kasey?"

Her eyebrows arched, surprised. "I can tell you my number."

"I'd like to see it, please."

Kasey's mouth puckered slightly as if in distaste, but she fished her cell phone from her handbag, made the swipes, and handed it to Stella. Stella read the number aloud as she jotted it down—probably for Mattie's sake as well as the recording—and handed it back.

The number did *not* match the last one called to Wilson's cell phone prior to his death.

"Sheriff?" Stella said, turning to him. "Anything else?"

"That will do for now, Kasey," he said, pushing back his chair to stand. "Please give my regards to your parents."

McCoy escorted Kasey to the lobby, while Mattie and Stella sat looking at each other.

"She looked like she was lying when we asked her about Nate's trips to California," Mattie said.

"Oh, yeah. She knows more about this trafficking thing than she's saying."

Mattie paused a moment to think. "But what about the murders? So far the evidence just doesn't support her as the shooter."

Sheriff McCoy entered the room as Mattie spoke. "All our evidence points to a male shooter, but I wouldn't cross Kasey off the list for conspiracy yet."

"I'll look for connections tomorrow when I search Wilson's office and home," Stella said. "Maybe his receptionist can give me information about who's been to his office and who might have stolen his revolver. We have to keep digging for some hard evidence before we can make any arrests."

"We'll keep at it." McCoy looked at Mattie. "Now go home and get some sleep. You and Deputy Brody have an early start in the morning to go track down a tiger. You might even lead us to solving this thing."

Mattie was going on thirty-six hours with very little sleep, and she figured Sheriff McCoy could see it. But before she went to bed tonight, she needed to talk things over with Cole. Much as she hated conflict and intimate conversation, her peace of mind—and a good night's sleep—depended on going through with it.

Her duty as a law enforcement officer required it.

TWENTY-TWO

Out on the back patio, Cole opened the grill to flip burgers and glanced at Sophie, sitting at the picnic table with her sketch pad and crayons. She seemed much happier than she'd been yesterday, settled back into home life and no longer tearful. *The resilience of childhood.*

After closing the grill, he went to peer over her shoulder. "What are you drawing, Sophie-bug?"

"Flowers." She showed him a picture of a florist's bouquet she'd pulled up on her tablet, which she was trying to duplicate on her sketch pad—sort of a technological still life. "I'm making a picture for Mom. I hope she'll like it."

Okay then, so she hadn't moved on quite yet. "I'm sure she will. You're doing a great job."

He went back into the kitchen to finish the salad he'd started, enjoying the solitude after such a hectic day. Angela was up in her room and Jessie had decided to eat supper with their parents so he could have time alone with his kids. Tomorrow Jessie planned to take the girls out to the ranch to visit their grandparents in the afternoon and then spend the night. It would work out great, since he planned to leave home before sunrise to try to track down that tiger.

A tiger . . . it was still hard to wrap his head around. And to think, Mattie had been in the forest within yards of it while it was protecting its meal. The thought made him shudder.

Someone needed to capture this animal, and despite misgivings about leaving his kids alone for the whole day, he knew he was the person to help do it. His kids would be with family and well taken care of. Jessie and his parents would be a great distraction for them, and his dad planned to take them all horseback riding. Angela and Sophie always loved that.

His cell phone was on its charger on the kitchen counter, and he glanced at it to see if he'd missed a call or a text from Mattie. Before he'd left the station earlier, she'd promised to call when she got off work, and he couldn't spend another sleepless night without talking things over with her. But no message had come in while he'd been outside.

Cole washed and chopped a stalk of celery, thinking how confusing relationships could be. He felt like he'd contributed to his ex-wife's depression and ultimately driven her away because he'd spent so much time at work and lost touch with her. And yet he feared he'd said too much to Mattie last night. Too much, or he'd chosen the wrong moment.

Sometimes he couldn't win for losing.

He remembered the days—not quite twenty years ago— when things got serious with Olivia. He'd been a young buck then, driven by hormones, but falling in love was different this time around. Sure, he wanted a physical relationship with Mattie, but that type of intimacy was something he would never push on her. In fact, knowing what he did about her childhood, the thought of it made him kind of nervous. And it made him worry—could he give her the happiness in life that she deserved?

Angie drifted into the kitchen, saving him from his thoughts. "Hey, Dad," she said, going to the cutting board to snag a baby carrot. "Do you need some help with dinner?"

"I do. You'd be an *Angel* if you finished this salad." He grinned, extending the knife handle toward her with a flourish.

Angie grimaced as she took it. "Sometimes you're so ridiculous."

"That hurts," he said, tapping his chest over his heart. "I'll go check those burgers and be right back."

He grabbed a plate on his way out the door, checked the burgers to find them fully cooked, and moved them off the grill. "Dinner's ready, Sophie. We'll eat out here on the picnic table, but come inside to fix your plate."

Sophie banged the storm door behind her as she followed him into the kitchen, smeared ketchup on her burger, grabbed salad and chips, and hurried back outside, evidently eager to get back to her drawing. Cole and Angie filled their plates at a more sedate pace.

After turning the assembly of burger, bun, and toppings into a delicate art form, Angie lifted her plate and headed for the door. "You coming, Dad?"

"I'm right behind you." He went to the counter to take his phone with him, but it rang just as he got there. He checked caller ID. "This is Aunt Jessie," he said to Angie. "Just a minute, I'll be right out."

"City zoo," he said, connecting the call.

"Ha-ha, that's so funny I forgot to laugh. Some things never change," she said, a smile in her voice. "I'm just calling to tell you I'm going for drinks with Ginger and won't be home until late."

Ginger was one of Jessie's high school friends who still lived in town. "Did you already have supper?"

"Sure did. Mom had it on the table by six sharp. You?"

"Just about to eat."

"Ah . . . it's getting late," Jessie said. "I should've made you guys something before I left."

"Not at all. The kids and I made burgers. Have a good time."

"I will." Jessie paused. "Cole, I need to ask you something."

Oh boy, now what? "Okay."

"Are you in love with Mattie?"

He wasn't expecting that. He looked over his shoulder to see if either of the girls had come back inside, but he was still alone. "That's kind of a personal question, don't you think?"

"Yes, but it's necessary. The consensus out on the ranch is that you are."

"What? You've been talking about me with Mom and Dad?"

"There's not much else we have to talk about."

"You could talk about your work, the kids, your own love life."

Jessie scoffed. "Yeah, like that even exists. Oh never mind, I already know the answer. Just so you know, Dad's all for it, but Mom doesn't like the idea of you getting married to a cop."

"She didn't like the idea of me being married to a house-wife either," Cole said, before doing a double take. "Wait a minute. You guys have us married now?"

"You're the marrying type, Cole. And I guess the whole town is buzzing about you two. I'll have to see what Ginger has to say."

There was no way to reply to that.

But Jessie wasn't done yet. "What do the girls think?"

"The girls haven't mentioned it. I don't think they know."

"Don't be so sure. Especially with Angela. She's not a kid anymore, and she's probably completely aware of what's going on. You should talk to them about it."

"Jessie! Look, this isn't your business, but maybe Mattie and I aren't totally clear about what's going on yet ourselves. Besides, now isn't the time to bring this up with the kids."

"Of course not now," Jessie said, using a tone reminiscent of their mother's. "I'm just saying you should address it soon. Don't let things go on forever. That's all I'm saying."

"You sound like Mom, Jessie. Look, I've got to go. The kids are outside waiting for me."

Cole stuffed his cell phone into his pocket and headed outside, muttering to himself, "Sheesh." He knew he had to talk to his kids about Mattie, but he had no idea what to say. Or when. Especially now.

For Pete's sake, things were getting complicated.

The girls had a head start on him and were just finishing up when his cell phone rang again. This time caller ID surprised him. It was Olivia, and she'd never initiated a call before; he was the one who always had to chase her down.

Hoping she was all right, he hurried to connect the call. "Hi, Liv."

"Cole." Her voice sounded stronger than when he'd talked to her yesterday. "I've been worried about the girls. How are they?"

He decided it was a good sign—she was reaching out about the kids and not just about herself. "They're doing all right. Getting back into their routine."

Both girls were frozen in place, examining him closely. He put his game face on and gave them a slight smile that said, *All is well.* Holding up a hand, he mouthed, "I'll be right back," and rose to go into the house. As he closed the storm door, he looked over his shoulder to see that neither of them looked very happy— Sophie looked sad and Angie was scowling—but it couldn't be helped. He had no idea how this conversation was going to go, and he didn't want the girls privy to it if it headed south.

"I hate to wait too long to schedule the visit you mentioned," Olivia was saying. "I think it would be best to see the girls again soon."

"That sounds fine, Liv." As long as he could convince Angie to cooperate, but he'd cross that bridge when he came to it. "Do you feel up to it?"

"I will." She sighed. "I got overwhelmed, Cole. I've been thinking of what you said about small steps."

Small steps, that's what Mattie had told him. "And?"

"I'd like to start talking to the kids on the phone, if that's all right. If it doesn't upset them, I mean."

Cole could see Sophie watching him through the glass door. "I think that would be good. We could try it and see."

"And when you bring the kids here, maybe we could go to the Museum of Natural History. It's got something of interest for everyone. And . . . and could you come with us, too?"

She was tiptoeing along, and he felt how hard this was for her. He appreciated her effort. "Sure. Sounds like fun, and I've got nothing else to do in Denver to pass the time. When shall we do this?"

"Is two weeks all right, on Saturday?"

He glanced at the calendar. "Looks like we could do it then."

"Thanks, Cole." She sounded relieved. "I really want to make this work."

"Me too. The kids do, too."

She drew in a deep breath and released it, and he could tell this call had taken a lot out of her. "Do you think the kids would talk to me now?"

He had no doubt their younger daughter would want to, but he'd have to work on the older. "Let me give the phone to Sophie; she's right outside at the picnic table. Then I'll see what Angie's up to."

"She might not want to talk to me, huh? She was pretty angry when she left."

Olivia wasn't born yesterday; she knew the score. "Let me talk to her while you visit with Sophie. I'm sure she'll come around, but she might need more of a cooling-off period."

"Okay." Olivia hesitated. "You're a good dad, Cole."

She must be feeling charitable this evening, and it was in the kids' best interest for him to respond in kind. "I try to be. I've always thought you were a good mom, Liv. You'll get back in the swing of things. Just give it time."

"Thank you," she said in a hushed voice.

"Are you ready for Sophie now?"

Another deep breath. "I am."

Cole went outside, placing his thumb over the speaker on his phone. The kids were watching his every step. "You guys know this is your mom. She wants to talk to you."

Sophie leapt to her feet and reached for the phone. "Mommy!" she said into the speaker, sounding years younger than her nine-year-old self. But Angela was still frowning. Cole gestured for her to follow him inside, leaving Sophie alone on the deck, happily talking to her mother. "Mom wants to talk to you, too."

Angie was shaking her head.

"I'm not gonna force you, Angela, but I want you to reconsider. This is the very first time your mom has reached out to you girls, and it took a lot for her to do it."

Angie looked sulky. "She gets to talk to Sophie."

"You're being stubborn." Cole struggled to maintain an even keel. "We've discussed what your mom's dealing with. You're not a child anymore, and I know you must understand. It will hurt if you walk away. Not just your mom—it'll hurt all of us. Even you. Maybe especially you."

Angie's face clouded, her eyes misty.

"Your mother's sorry for what happened, and she couldn't help it when it did. You need to forgive her and move on. She loves you, and if you're honest with yourself, you know you love her, too."

Tears brimmed in her eyes, and for a moment he feared he'd been too forceful. He reached for a tissue to give her. "Just talk to her for a few minutes. Will it hurt to listen to what she has to say?"

She sniffled into the tissue. "I guess not."

"That's doing the adult thing, Angie." Cole put his arm around her shoulders and guided her toward the door. "Let's go see if Sophie's ready to hand over the phone and let you get a word in edgewise."

"Sometimes that's hard with her."

Cole chuckled softly, giving her a quick squeeze before moving outside. "Yes, it is. Your little sister can keep up with the best of them."

★ ★ ★

Mattie texted Cole but didn't receive a reply. He'd mentioned dinner earlier, but since she hadn't known when she would get off work, she'd declined. Now, after finishing her paperwork, she thought it was too late to show up on his doorstep. With the kids home and his sister there, it didn't feel right. And at this stage, she was too exhausted to even think, much less have a heart-to-heart talk.

She drove to Crane's Market and grabbed a chicken salad sandwich from the cooler, some chips, and a knucklebone for Robo before going to the cashier to check out. She was standing in line behind other late-evening shoppers, who mostly carried twelve-packs of beer, when her phone rang. It was Cole. She juggled her purchases and connected the call.

"Sorry for the delay," he said. "The kids were on my phone talking to their mom, and I didn't get your text until now."

Hearing the news about the kids gave her heart a lift. "Oh, wow. How did that go?"

"It was touch-and-go with Angie, but in the end, I think it went fine. And Sophie is over the moon."

It was amazing how much that little bit could help a child. "Is Angie going to be okay?"

"I think so. She seems to be inching in the right direction. I've got some work to do before we get together with their mom in two weeks, but I think we'll all make it."

"So you scheduled a visit."

While Cole told her the plan, she developed a melancholy ache in her chest, and insecurity knocked at her door. *Maybe he wants his family back together after all.*

"That sounds good," she murmured as she moved up in line so that she would be next at the checkout counter. "I'm about to check out at the store, Cole. Let me call you back."

"Come over. I cooked a burger for you. And I need to see you tonight, Mattie. You can come here, or I'll come to your house after Jessie gets home."

The person in front of her finished his transaction. "I'll call you."

Mattie made her purchase and went out to her SUV, where Robo greeted her exuberantly. As always, his smiling face lifted her flagging spirits. She started to turn on the engine to head home but hesitated midreach. Instead she leaned forward to rest her forehead on the steering wheel. God, she was dead tired.

She sorted through her sluggish thoughts. Maybe this ache in her chest was caused by fatigue, but she suspected it was really lovesickness, which was utterly ridiculous. She was a grown woman, not a teenager. Cole had said he wanted to see her, and she wanted to see him, too. She had some responsibility here, and if she wanted this relationship, she needed to do something about it, not just scuttle about moping.

She texted Cole to tell him she was on her way.

After parking in front of the Walker home, Mattie let Robo out of his compartment, and he romped with Bruno, streaking in circles around the yard. Cole came to meet her, leaving the well-lit porch to hug her in the semidarkness at the end of the sidewalk. She tried to avoid displays of affection in front of the kids, and she glanced toward the house to make sure they hadn't followed him outside.

"Thanks for coming," he said, taking her arm to walk toward the porch with her. "I've got a plate for you, and after the kids get a chance to say hello, I'll see if I can send them off to bed. Even Angie's tired, and they have a big day with their grandparents planned for tomorrow."

Mattie's plate was waiting for her on the table where Sophie was seated, working on a drawing of a horse. Angela was loading dishes into the dishwasher, and Mattie asked if she needed some help.

"You sit and eat," Cole said. "I'll help Angie clean up."

As Mattie sat down beside Sophie, the child gave her one of her sweet smiles that always melted her heart. "See my horse."

"That's a nice one," Mattie said, settling into her chair, happy to be here with Cole's kids.

Sophie flipped a page on her pad. "And here's some flowers I'm gonna send to Mom. I talked to her on the phone tonight."

Mattie took the drawing Sophie was pushing toward her and examined it closely, knowing that's what the child wanted. "They're gorgeous, Sophie. How was your talk with your mom?"

"Good." Sophie grinned.

Mattie caressed a lock of Sophie's curly, soft hair as she handed back the pad, then turned her attention to her food. It boosted her energy, and she realized she'd been running on empty, not having eaten since her sandwich at lunch.

"Sophie, you need to be wrapping up your artwork so you can go upstairs to take a bath," Cole said, wiping his hands on a towel before hanging it up.

"Can Mattie read me a story?" Sophie asked.

Cole sighed. "No, Mattie and I need to talk about our plans for the morning. We're all tired and we have a big day ahead of us, so we need to get to bed early. Angie, can you help your sister get ready for bed? And can you make it an early night, too?"

"Ooo-kay," Angie said, glancing at Mattie before casting a sour look at her dad. "What are you doing in the morning?"

"I'm going up into the mountains on a job for the sheriff's posse. I think I mentioned earlier that I'd be gone before you woke up."

The frown on Angie's face and the way she shifted her eyes from her dad back to Mattie made Mattie think, *She knows. Or at least she suspects.* And with the trials the girl had gone through with her mother just yesterday, now was not the time to press the fact that her dad might be beginning another relationship with someone else. Cole needed to take care of his daughters tonight, because they were still hurting.

Mattie pushed back her chair and carried her plate to the sink. "You know what, Cole, I'm beat. I really need to get home and go to bed myself. It won't take but a few minutes for us to talk about what we need to, and then you can help Angie put Sophie to bed."

Cole opened his mouth to protest, but Mattie sent him a look and hurried to say good-night to the girls. "We can talk while I load up Robo," she said, before calling her dog to come and heading for the front door. As he followed, Cole told Sophie to go up and take her bath.

As soon as the door closed behind him, Mattie led the way down the porch steps, speaking softly. "Your kids need you tonight, Cole. They've been hurt, and I don't want to complicate things for them."

Cole placed his hand on the small of her back as they walked, and he bent his head toward her. "I just need to know if you're okay."

His touch felt reassuring. "I admit that it rattled me to learn that my past came up in a team meeting, but I can see how it happened."

Cole made a sound of agreement. "Evidently my family were talking about me in my absence tonight, and it's not fun. But you know what? Those people at the station are your family."

"Huh." Mattie huffed out a breath as she thought of Brody and how contentious their relationship had once been. Now he acted like a protective big brother. But the one thing that kept bothering her seemed to pop out of her mouth. "It's tough to think that Sheriff McCoy knew, and he didn't get me the help I needed as a child."

"Timber Creek doesn't have that kind of help for kids now, Mattie, much less twenty-five years ago."

He was right. The sheriff had probably done all he could do under the circumstances. "Yeah. He did get me into Mama T's foster home. I guess that helped more than anything."

While she loaded Robo into his compartment, Cole came around to the back of her car, where the view was somewhat sheltered from the house. After she closed the hatch, he took her in his arms. "I guess I need to know if everything's okay between us, even though it scares me that I might hear it's not."

The tension in her tired muscles melted as she leaned against him. "We're okay, Cole. I think I would've handled it the same way you did."

He released a sigh and held her in silence for a few moments. "I guess I'm going to have to tell the kids about us. Looks like Angie's starting to catch on."

She was glad he'd noticed, but telling them would make things official, and it felt like a big step. "Not tonight, Cole, unless she brings it up and you have to. You're all too tired, and you need to sleep before we head out tomorrow."

The sound of the front door opening, followed by Angie's voice, made them step away from each other. "Dad," Angie called. "Sophie wants you."

Cole leaned out from behind her SUV. "Tell her to get in bed and I'll be there in a few minutes."

After the door closed, he groaned. "I think Angie wants me more than Sophie does. I'm sorry, Mattie."

"Don't be." She kissed him softly on the lips before rounding her car and getting in. "I hope you get a good night's sleep. Brody and I will meet you up at the cattle guard."

They said good-night, and as she drove away, she thought about all the changes she'd made in her life over the past year. Before, she'd isolated herself most of the time, but now she could reach out to others. Now she had friends, friends she could even call family. And honestly, she wanted to be a part of Cole's family, to help care for these kids she'd grown to love. Maybe that wasn't too much to hope for.

TWENTY-THREE

Tuesday morning

Cole arose well before sunrise with a sick feeling in the pit of his stomach that wasn't wholly related to a short night's sleep. The idea of tracking a tiger made him nervous, and he hoped they could capture it without anyone getting hurt.

And if he was being honest with himself, a killer on the loose up in the high country frightened him more than just a little. This would be someone who'd killed two men, not just one. A good high-powered rifle could help this guy rack up another kill easily, and he feared not only for Mattie but for himself as well.

Last night after he and the kids had gone to bed, he'd lain awake thinking. During times like these, he was confronted with his own mortality. If something happened to him, who would raise the kids? Olivia wasn't in a place where she could do it by herself.

When he'd heard Jessie come home, he'd risen from bed to go downstairs to talk to her, to make her promise that she'd help Olivia raise the kids if something should happen to him before they were adults. Her promise had provided him with little comfort, but at least he'd finally been able to go to sleep.

Not wanting to awaken Jessie or the girls, he carried his boots and tiptoed downstairs in socked feet. Once in the kitchen, he flipped the switch to turn on the coffeemaker, which he'd set up before going to bed.

He'd also spent time during the night thinking about Mattie and how she fit into his life. Since his kids were dealing with the separation from their mother and the ongoing drama of trying to reunite, was it fair to thrust them into a situation where they would need to adjust to a new stepmother? But if he needed to wait, how could he deal with his growing desire to share his home and his spare time with the woman he loved? His was a world where he needed to get things done, and the quicker the better. Life didn't always match that pace, and he hoped he could find a balance in all this craziness called *family*.

Cole filled a thermos with coffee, grabbed a leftover burger he'd fixed the night before, and left the house to go to the clinic. Mountaineer, the one horse he owned himself, resided in a corral attached to a loafing shed just north of his office. Late yesterday afternoon, he'd brought in three other horses from his dad's ranch so that he could outfit the entire crew. It would take some time to saddle up and get the horses loaded into the trailer.

He paused at the tack room, an enclosed space at the end of the shed, and threw the switch on for the overhead yard light. A warm glow lit the area, making the horses mill around the corral. The early morning seemed darker than usual, and the chilly air told him a front had moved in during the night, changing the weather. Clouds covered the stars, and moist air touched his face.

Mountaineer met him at the gate, nosing his pockets gently for a bite of feed cake, a sweet mixture of grains pressed into the shape of a short cigar. He paused for a moment to smooth the gelding's neck in slow, firm strokes, taking comfort in his horsey scent. This guy didn't have a sly or dishonest bone in his body, and he was the one Cole would trust to carry Mattie. She feared horses, another residual left over from her time with Harold Cobb, but she'd come to an understanding with Mountaineer last month during their investigation up in the wilderness area, and the steady gelding would serve her well again today.

After placing a halter on the gentle giant, Cole looped the tie rope to the wooden pole fence and spent a few minutes catching the other horses. They circled the corral, trotting away from him, and Cole soothed them with his voice as he approached, halter in hand.

Duke, the bay gelding he'd brought from his dad's for himself, dodged away at the last minute, making Cole lure him in with a handful of cake until he could slip a rope over his neck and buckle on a halter. Then he caught Honey, a palomino mare that would work for Glenna, and Fancy, a black-and-white paint mare for Brody.

He opened the gate wide and led all four horses at once to the rail, where he tied them in a row. His fingers warmed as he whisked grit and loose hair away with a currycomb and smoothed the hair that would be under the saddle.

He moved from horse to horse like he was working an assembly line, putting on blankets, saddle pads, and then saddles. Leather creaked as he swung the heavy western saddles onto the backs of the tall animals before drawing up cinches. From his dad's tack room, he'd rustled up leather scabbards for carrying rifles, and he strapped those on last.

Cole first led Mountaineer to the open door of the trailer and then clucked his tongue to encourage the gelding to load. He stepped up into the darkened space without a fuss, and each horse followed until Cole had them all standing at a slant and tied to the same side. The door clanged when it shut, and he closed the latch firmly to make sure it would stay closed.

It was five o'clock when he pulled away from the clinic and drove down the lane. His headlights pierced the darkness and the windshield misted, making him flip on the wipers and scan the darkened sky. If it started to rain, it would ruin the whole plan, because rain would wash away the lion's scent.

Cole turned on the heater and reached for his coffee and burger so he could eat while he drove.

Despite his arriving fifteen minutes before the designated time, Mattie was already parked by the cattle guard. Brody exited the passenger's side of her SUV and Mattie the driver's side as Cole pulled in and parked his rig beside them. Both officers wore the brown Carhartt jackets favored by the Sheriff's Department, which offered some resistance to the damp weather.

"Morning." Cole greeting them both, while his eyes went to Mattie to check in on how she was doing. She gave him a thin smile, and although he could tell she looked worried, she didn't seem frightened. He hoped she was getting used to being on horseback.

Brody rounded the front of their vehicle. "It *is* morning, although this weather sucks, so I can't call it good. If it rains, we'll have to scrap the whole thing."

"This amount of moisture shouldn't interfere. If anything, it'll help us," Mattie said as she went to the back to unload Robo. He hopped out, tail waving, and beat a path toward Cole to say hello. Cole leaned down and patted the big dog's side.

Headlights appeared on the highway, and they all watched the oncoming vehicle slow and turn into the pasture. Mattie called Robo and bent to clip a leash on his collar.

Glenna Dalton parked and exited her truck, leaving her dog inside. "Hey," she called, lifting her hand in a small wave before turning to Mattie. "Is your dog going to help with the scent work?"

Mattie shook her head. "He's not trained for that. I'll keep him beside me after we get into the high country."

"Is he social?" Glenna gestured toward her truck with her thumb. "My dog's used to running with a pack, but he's an intact male. Can the two of them mingle without a fight?"

"Probably, but let's keep them both on a leash until we know for sure."

Glenna nodded and headed to the passenger's side of her truck. When she came back around, she led a Rhodesian ridgeback close by her side. Headlights made his burnished red coat shine, and Cole admired both his color and his athletic movement as the dog trotted around the front of the truck.

This boy was big, probably weighing in at eighty-five pounds, the upper range for a Rhodesian ridgeback male. The ridge of hair growing in the opposite direction along his spine for which the breed was named caught the light and stood out on his back. He wore an eager expression, and his black nose and dark muzzle contrasted with the red color of his coat. Cole decided he was a fine example of the breed standard.

"This is Moose." Glenna kept an eye on him as she brought him around. Moose seemed more interested in the humans than Robo, as he avoided eye contact with him, not overly aggressive and not fearful. Comfortable. This was typically the sign of a well-adjusted dog that hadn't suffered any bad experiences with others.

Cole glanced at Robo, standing at attention beside Mattie, alert and ready to guard if he needed to but still open and friendly.

"That's a good reaction so far," Mattie said. "Are you okay with dropping the leash and letting them smell each other? If we keep the leashes on, we can intervene if we need to."

"Sure."

Mattie gave Robo some obedience commands, which Cole thought were meant to remind him that she was alpha in their pack and he needed to listen to her. Finally she let go of the leash. "Go make friends," she told him.

The two dragged their leashes as they circled the enclosure made by the vehicles, darting in for a quick sniff of each other before trotting away to mark tires—a doggy pissing contest, but friendly and harmless.

"Time to unload the horses?" Cole asked Mattie.

"I think so. Is that all right with you, Glenna?"

Glenna had her eye on Moose, but she nodded agreement. "Looks like these two will run together without any fighting. They should settle in."

Cole suspected it was dawn, though the sunlight struggled to break through the cloud layer. He felt pressed to get started despite the darkness. He still needed to tie packs behind saddles and make sure everyone's gear was secure. If they were going to reach the high country before noon, they'd better get going.

★ ★ ★

Mattie had unclipped Robo's leash, and she let him lope ahead to sniff rabbit brush and then circle back to run beside her. When they reached the trees in the forest, she'd call him in to stay close.

Though being up so high on horseback still made her uneasy, she'd grown used to Mountaineer. Cole rode beside her, and she thought that as long as she paid attention to what she was doing, she should be okay. At least they had this gradual slope to navigate before reaching the high country. She considered it a warm-up.

By the time they arrived at the place where she'd found Wilson Nichol, the sun was shedding enough light for them to see. Robo alerted, and she wondered if he'd picked up the scent of the tiger or if he was reacting to the decaying blood on the grass. When he started to charge forward to go check it out, she called him back, and he came willingly enough. Glenna called Moose as well, so there was no competition for Robo to try to reach the source of the odor first.

When Glenna dismounted and opened the pack behind her saddle, her adept movements led Mattie to assume she'd had plenty of experience around horses and their gear. Glenna fished out a collar that jingled and clanged as she held it up and shook it. "Moose is silent when he's tracking. He wears this so I can keep up with him when we hit the forest."

Mattie found it fascinating that Moose took on a more businesslike attitude when he wore his special collar. *Just like Robo.* "You can tell Moose has tracked before."

"Oh yeah." Glenna also strapped an e-collar on Moose while she spoke. "We trained five lion dogs to hunt in a pack for our cougar project. Moose got lots of experience."

"How does that work? Robo tangled with a cougar last fall and got a gash in his skin for his trouble."

"There's something about these dogs that must be passed on in their DNA. They're driven to corner the lions, but they rarely move in close enough to attack. They were used for big-game hunting in Africa back in the nineteenth and early-twentieth century. Not so much today."

"What did you do once you found the cougars?"

"The dogs would typically run them to ground or up a tree. We darted, weighed, and measured them while they were sedated, and then recovered them and set them free."

Mattie asked the question that concerned her. "What are the chances we can sedate and relocate this tiger?"

Glenna frowned. "It will depend on whether or not Moose can tree it. That's the easiest way to get to these big cats without anyone getting hurt. I read last night that tigers will run from humans if they can, but they'll fight if they're cornered. We'll just have to see how close we can get. If necessary, we'll have to kill it."

Glenna called Moose and led him over to the tiger prints. After he sniffed the area, his demeanor shifted, and he trotted around with excitement. Glenna patted his side and chattered about getting ready to hunt, elevating his prey drive in the same way Mattie did with Robo before a search. Finally, she sent him off with a gesture and the command she must use for tracking cougars: "Hunt it up. Go find a lion."

Moose took off toward the layer of foothills that fronted the distant peaks, loping along with occasional sniff checks on the ground. The damp morning had apparently enhanced the tiger's scent, as Mattie had thought it would.

When Robo dipped his head to sniff the track, Mattie noticed his hackles rise. He probably remembered the scent and had cataloged the growl they'd heard inside that smart brain of his. Her dog was a quick study, and he'd already locked in this scent and was ready to follow the track; it didn't matter that he'd never been trained to do this kind of work.

"Let's go," Glenna said, mounting her horse. "Don't let Moose get too far ahead."

Glenna and Brody kneed their horses forward at a lope. Mattie's anxiety surged when Mountaineer began to follow at a teeth-jarring trot, and she clutched the saddle horn with both hands, almost dropping the reins.

She was thinking she couldn't do this when Cole rode up next to her, providing instruction in a quiet, steady voice. "Keep your heels down and tighten your grip with your legs. Just a little bit."

Mountaineer's gait smoothed out into a rocking-chair-like canter.

"There," Cole said. "Now try to keep your back straight and relax your hips in the saddle."

Mattie began to hope she could manage to ride with the others. Once they caught up to the dogs, Duke slowed and Mountaineer automatically matched his pace. This time she was ready for the rough trot, and they alternated between a trot and a canter as they followed behind the dogs, moving upslope. Within a mile they came to a fence, and Mattie called Robo back. She didn't want him to try to duck under the bottom strand and get hooked by the barbs.

Robo looked disappointed, but when she told him to heel, he stayed by Mountaineer's side. Grateful for their countless hours of obedience training, Mattie rode toward where Glenna and Moose waited on the near side of the fence.

"This is the far end of the BLM," Glenna called to Cole. "Do you know where we can find a gate?"

"Wait a minute. I thought we might run into fencing, so I brought a pair of wire nippers. We'll have to repair fence later, but this will be all right for today."

Cole dismounted, took the wire snips from his saddlebag, and strode to the fence. He bent to cut the bottom strand but hesitated as he reached for the second one. "See this," he said. "Hair."

A tuft of short, tawny-colored hair was caught in one of the barbs. Glenna dismounted to examine it. "There's an orange cast to it," she said.

Though Mattie had hoped following the tiger would lead them to Tyler Redman and his hunting party, this bit of hair caught in a barb cast a different light. It made the tiger more real. She wanted more than ever to find it alive and keep it that way.

Cole cut the fence, and Brody dismounted to help, pulling the sharply barbed wire back so the horses could pass through the gap. Mattie waited for Cole to swing back into the saddle, and they fell in line at the end as they started the climb through the foothills.

The trail Moose followed took him into an arroyo about six feet deep and the same distance wide, and though Glenna rode Honey down into it to stay with her dog, the others remained on the bank. Piñon, ponderosa pine, and juniper sprang from the rocky soil around them, and Mattie kept Robo from trailing down into the lower ground. If the tiger attacked, it would most likely come from above.

Shod hooves clicked against stone as they continued upslope. After a half hour, Moose left the arroyo and headed up into the forest, where lodgepole pine and spruce grew sparse at first but soon thickened, reducing visibility in all directions. The ground underfoot became rough as the incline steepened. Mattie grabbed the saddle horn as Mountaineer lurched up the side of a draw.

Moose led them into the wide mouth of a canyon filled with pockets of aspen amid the evergreens. Rock shards rolled from under the horses' hooves as they churned their way upward. Gradually the canyon narrowed, and the horses had to pick their way around boulders. As the terrain grew more and more rugged, Glenna called more often for Moose to wait.

The trail led them to a narrow path, pinned against the canyon wall on one side and thickets of thorny currant bush on the other. An eerie feeling of being watched crept over Mattie, and she scanned the top of the canyon wall. A breeze fanned her cheeks, telling her that at least they would be downwind from the tiger if they should overtake it in this narrow passage. That might prevent it from sensing their presence and attacking from above.

A deep growl came from behind. Mountaineer tucked his tail and hopped forward, making Mattie grab the horn to stay on. Once he stopped up against the rump of Brody's black-and-white paint, Mattie turned in the saddle to look over her shoulder at Cole. He reined to reverse direction, eyes searching the canyon rim.

The growl escalated to the snarling rumble Mattie remembered only too well. Moose bayed, booming sounds that echoed off canyon walls. He rushed past Mountaineer's legs, making him spook. Barely able to keep her seat on the lunging horse, Mattie tried to calm him. Thank goodness he was wedged in on the narrow path and unable to bolt.

The horses jostled, crowding each other. The snarl intensified to a full-throated roar, one that sent chills down her spine.

"Can you see it?" Glenna shouted from up ahead.

Robo stayed beside her, his fur bristled. Mountaineer settled enough that she could scan the top of the canyon wall.

And then she saw it.

Teeth gleamed as the huge tiger loomed over them on the canyon's rim, crouched and poised to leap. The creature was so magnificent, it stole Mattie's breath. Rifles scraped out of their scabbards as Brody and Cole pulled them free. Mattie realized with horror that they might not have a choice. For their own survival, they might need to shoot this superb beast, a disastrous end to their mission to save it.

A gunshot echoed from a distance. Impossible to locate, but it sounded like it came from up above. The tiger whirled and disappeared behind the canyon rim. Moose continued to bay and tried to scale the wall, falling back to the path time and again until Glenna called him off. Robo stopped barking and stood guard beside Mattie, bristled and growling.

"What in hell?" Brody shouted as he struggled to control his horse.

While the horses settled, Cole made eye contact with Mattie, his gaze stunned. She knew how he felt. Their target's sudden appearance had staggered her as well.

"We're going to need a different plan," Glenna said, cool as creek water.

TWENTY-FOUR

Mattie realized she was trembling. "I need to get off this horse," she said to Cole.

He swung down to help her, but she'd already slipped from the saddle. As soon as her feet touched firm ground, she got a grip on her shudders and turned to stroke Mountaineer's neck, trying to soothe him. At the same time, she settled Robo with her voice, telling him to cease his growling while she assured him he was a good boy.

"This is a challenge," Brody said, resting his rifle crossways against the pommel of his saddle. "We've found our tiger and our hunting party at the same time."

"How do you think they're tracking it?" Cole asked.

"I don't know," Glenna responded in a quiet voice. "I thought I saw a collar on its neck. Did anyone else?"

Mattie had to admit she hadn't. She'd been too rattled and distracted by trying to stay on Mountaineer.

"They could have a GPS locator on it," Glenna said. "Like the one I use on Moose."

The two different purposes posed an awful contrast: one to protect an animal, the other to kill it. Mattie wanted more than ever to find the members of Tyler's hunting party and arrest them all.

Glenna dismounted to huddle with Mattie and Cole on the narrow trail, and they kept their eyes moving along the canyon rim. "Where did that shot come from?"

"Good question," Cole said. "It sounded like it came from behind us, farther back in the direction we came from but up above."

"We've got to get out of this canyon," Brody said. "We're sitting ducks down here."

"True," Cole said. "For the tiger anyway. But whoever shot that rifle might not know we're in the area. Our approach would have been shielded from sight unless someone scouted along the canyon's edge."

Mattie wanted to get up above so Robo could find the trail of whoever had shot that rifle. And the sooner the better. "What's the fastest way out of here?"

Cole frowned. "I don't know this area well enough to say what's up ahead. It's best to go downhill and find a place where we can ride up."

"Let's go," Brody said. "I want to get out of this trap and up to a place where we can see."

After remounting, they headed downhill, with Brody in the lead setting a fast pace, and the horses seemed eager to be going toward home. Mattie scanned the rim as she clung to the saddle horn, lurching with Mountaineer when he tucked his haunches and slid down the steeper parts of the trail. She'd much rather have been on foot.

As the canyon opened up, she searched for a break in the wall and soon spotted a chute choked with brush, but it afforded an incline that she knew she could scale. She pointed it out to the others. "Robo and I can head up there. I want to get onto the trail of that gunman."

"No, we stick together," Brody said.

Mattie tried to convince him. "Our suspect in a double homicide is in that party, Brody. Once we get to them, we can arrest them all for illegal hunting activity and sort it out later. I'm better off on foot in this kind of terrain. Besides, if we stay on horseback, they'll hear the four of us coming a mile away."

"I'll go with her," Cole said, eyeing Mattie with concern.

"As soon as we get out of this canyon, we'll decide on a plan." Brody reined his horse back down the trail. "But for now, we stick together."

Mattie disagreed with his decision and chafed at the fact that he was the one in charge. She kept her eye on the left side of the canyon, and another quarter mile down the trail, she spotted a gap in the wall that looked promising.

Brody saw it too, and picked up the pace. The gap turned out to be the mouth of a dry streambed that looked steep but passable. "We'll try to go up here."

"Lean forward on the uphill," Cole reminded her as she nudged Mountaineer forward. "Heels down and squeeze your legs tight."

Pebbles and stones rattled and rolled down the incline as each rider entered the dry bed. The horses tucked their hind legs under themselves as they strained and heaved up the fifty-foot incline. The herbal scent of sweet sage being crushed under their hooves infiltrated the air.

Mattie clung to the saddle, feeling Mountaineer move beneath her, and she admired the power harnessed in the body of this animal, one so willing to do whatever she asked of him. Even though she'd once feared being on top of him, she seemed to be getting the hang of it.

When she gained the top of the rim, a view of the mountainside opened up to an expanse of evergreen forest, dotted with boulders and rugged outcroppings—perfect cat country. She pulled a set of binoculars from her pack and used them to scan the hillside. Mist covered the high crags, concealing anything that might be hidden.

The last one to reach the rim, Glenna pulled up beside them and dismounted to grab Moose by the collar. "Let's take Moose to the rim where we spotted the tiger and set him on the trail from there."

Mattie knew Robo's strengths far better than anyone, and she knew he could find human scent left by the shooter. She looked at Brody. "When we see which way the tiger went after he left the rim, I need to take Robo across country from there, so he can find the shooter's trail."

"Let's split up, two and two," Glenna said. "We'll have a better chance of taking that tiger alive if we find whoever's hunting him."

Mattie could tell Glenna's focus was on saving the tiger, and that was good; Mattie wanted it taken alive, too. But above all, she wanted to catch the person who'd killed Nate Fletcher and Wilson Nichol, and splitting up made sense for her plan as well. "Chances are the four of us are going to end up back together anyway."

"Who's the best shooter?" Glenna asked. "I've never tagged a cougar with a dart. Someone else handled that job."

"Brody's the sharpshooter in our department," Mattie said.

Brody eyed Cole. He looked like he was thinking it over. "Can you keep up with Cobb if she takes to the ground?"

"I think so."

Mattie knew Cole had stepped up his fitness program a few months ago to include running the foothills around his house. He wouldn't slow her down. "We can stay together."

"Okay, you and Cole go after the shooter," Brody said to Mattie. "We'll track the tiger. Stay in touch." He tapped his pocket where he'd put his cell phone.

Glenna got back on Honey and chattered to Moose about finding the cat, taking him with her as she reined uphill. Mattie urged Mountaineer forward, and Cole rode up beside her. They dodged between trees and rocks as they trotted upslope, and Cole called out to the others: "That tiger is going to go up high if it's being chased. Watch your backs when you ride under anything."

Within a quarter mile, Moose charged forward, leaving Glenna's side to circle around an area at the edge of the canyon rim. He bayed a few times, obviously excited by the freshness of the cat's scent. The Rhodesian ridgeback paused only long enough to vacuum up the scent, then headed uphill, nose to the ground.

"Brody, we're going to split off here," Mattie shouted, reining Mountaineer away from the edge of the canyon rim.

Brody lifted his hand in acknowledgment as he nudged his horse into a trot to follow Glenna and Moose.

"Come, Robo. Let's go find a bad guy." Robo fell in beside her as she set a diagonal course away from the rim and downhill, keeping one eye on the ground for tracks while taking quick glances to scan the tops of boulders and promontories.

Cole rode close behind. "The shooter is probably on horseback instead of on foot. Look for horseshoe prints."

Robo sped forward and came across the track first. He circled around, sniffing as if he didn't know whether to go uphill or down, and they hurried to catch up with him. The open-ended ovals of horseshoe prints could be seen plainly in the coarse soil.

Cole dismounted to check the prints. "Only one horse, headed uphill."

Mattie slipped off Mountaineer and reached to get Robo's search harness out of her pack. "I need to be on the ground with Robo, Cole. That's what he's used to."

Cole took her reins. "I'll stay on horseback and lead Mountaineer. I'm not leaving him tied to a tree out here, not with a tiger on the loose."

Mattie buckled the harness on Robo and gave it a quick tug to settle it into place. She let him lap water from her canteen out of her hand and began the chatter that he loved. Unable to contain his excitement, he performed a pirouette on his hind legs while she patted his back. "Come on, let's find a bad guy."

With a toss of his head, Robo hit the trail, following the horseshoe prints uphill. The prints disappeared for a long stretch in the stony soil, but when they reappeared, it assured Mattie that Robo had kept them on the right track. Her body warmed as she jogged after him up steep grades, and her breath came in uneven cycles. She was used to running the foothills every morning, but this steep mountainside challenged her lungs.

The track led into a dense part of the forest, and she heard Cole unsheathe his rifle from about ten paces behind her.

A few seconds later, Robo bristled. What lay ahead? Human or tiger?

Mattie came to a sudden stop, her heart pounding in her ears. She kept her voice barely above a whisper. "Robo, wait."

He stopped and turned to look at her, his mouth open in a pant.

Cole swung out of the saddle and was beside her in one quick stride, rifle in hand. "What is it?" he murmured.

"Something ahead. Look at Robo's back."

Cole swept his gaze past Robo uphill and then back to the horses. "The horses aren't afraid. We're downwind. I don't think it's the tiger."

She followed his reasoning and agreed. "Must be the shooter, and I think he's close. Could you stay here with the horses? I'll scout on ahead with Robo."

Cole dropped the reins of both horses so they trailed the ground. "They'll ground-tie unless something spooks them. And they'll be able to get away if the tiger comes. I'll back you." He held his rifle ready in both hands, his face set with determination.

Mattie was used to trailing fugitives, and she knew the danger of stumbling into an ambush; however, she wasn't used to putting Cole in harm's way. She didn't like it one bit. Even though she'd caught her breath, her chest tightened with anxiety.

She wished she could argue or order him to stay back, but she knew there wasn't time and he wouldn't listen. Robo pressed against her legs as if trying to drive her forward. His prey was near, and she couldn't put him on hold any longer. She used a whisper, but it was every bit as intense as a shout. "Go ahead, Robo. Find the bad guy."

Robo raised his nose and sprang forward at a lope, air-scenting the person they were following, which told Mattie he must be near. She surged after him, pine boughs whipping past, their needles pricking through her shirt to sting her skin. When she caught up to Robo, she whispered for him to wait so that he would slow his pace. The hair on his back stood on end, and the hair on her neck prickled.

She grabbed Robo's harness but allowed him to lead her through the trees and bushes. In the distance, she heard a roar that could only be coming from the tiger. A shot fired, very close and upwind. Mattie flinched. *Are they firing at us?*

No bullets zinged past. Mattie looked over her shoulder to check on Cole. Rifle at the ready, he was only a few paces behind her. She held Robo at heel with her left hand as they crept forward.

Through the trees, she spotted the edge of a ridge. They'd been coming up a hogback, and it looked like the ground dropped off in about fifty yards. Stealing through the trees, she scanned the edge until she spotted the shooter. Forty yards away, he stood on top of the ledge with his back toward her, sweeping the terrain in front of him with a pair of binoculars, his rifle held loosely at his side.

He'd fired the gun within the last few minutes, and she counted on the blast dampening his hearing. She released Robo's collar, withdrew her Glock, and sprinted forward, holding it in a two-handed grip out front. She covered the last twenty yards in an instant, Robo beside her.

"Freeze! Timber Creek County Sheriff! Do not move!"

The man whirled. It was Flint Thornton.

"Robo, guard!" Mattie pinned him with her Glock while Robo snarled at her side, white teeth gleaming. "Drop your weapon, Flint! Drop it!"

A collage of astonishment, frustration, and then fear chased across Flint's face. He raised the hand that held the binoculars into the air and slowly bent forward to drop his rifle onto the ground. As he straightened, he raised both hands toward the sky.

TWENTY-FIVE

"Don't move or this dog will attack. Do you understand?"

Flint nodded, eyeing Robo and then Mattie as she approached, gun extended. She moved close enough to kick the rifle away and then followed through with a few extra shoves until she could safely bend to pick it up. Only then did she glance at Cole, who stood with his rifle sighted on Flint.

She backed up to be near Robo, carrying Flint's rifle with her but keeping her handgun trained on him. The last thing she wanted was for Cole to be placed in a position where he had to shoot a young man he knew.

"Do you have any other weapons, Flint?"

He stood still, moving nothing but his eyes as they shifted between her and Robo and back. "No."

She pointed to a large pine about six feet from him. "Move slowly. Put your hands up against that tree. If you try to touch me, this dog will attack. Robo, guard."

Robo hovered, his toenails digging into the earth as if ready to launch. Mattie patted Flint down, extracting a small pocketknife from his jeans pocket before she finished.

"I forgot I had that," Flint murmured when she showed him the knife.

She didn't argue with him, since she suspected he probably had forgotten—a pocketknife was standard gear for most farmers and ranchers. She pulled his cell phone from one of his shirt pockets.

"All right, Flint, you can turn around and talk to us now." Mattie glanced at her dog, who looked more than eager to get a chance to bite. "Out, Robo."

Robo looked disappointed and adjusted his fierce stance only one degree. Flint turned to face her, his hands raised.

"You can lower your hands, but keep them where I can see them. Don't make any sudden movements." Mattie gestured toward Robo. "He still has his eye on you."

The hands came down slowly an inch at a time.

"What in the hell are you doing out here?" Mattie asked.

Flint shook his head and studied the ground.

"We've seen the tiger. We know you're hunting it."

He looked up at her, his face showing his concern.

"Why are you shooting at it?" Mattie asked.

"I'm not."

"Well, someone is, and my dog led us right to you."

"I'm just shooting into the air."

Mattie narrowed her eyes as she studied him, considering what he'd said. Was this how Wilson Nichol had been killed? A stray shot into the air? "What's the purpose of firing into the air? Those bullets come down somewhere, you know."

Flint shook his head and lowered his gaze, his lips tight.

"What's going on, Flint? There are other law enforcement officers out here, and we need to know what we're getting into. Where are Tyler and his hunting party?"

He eyed Robo, his jaw clenched.

Cole spoke up. "Flint, your dad isn't going to be happy with whatever you're hiding. It might go easier for you at home if you help us straighten this out and keep someone from getting hurt."

Flint's clenched teeth told Mattie he wasn't going to talk, and she didn't have time to waste. She took out her cell phone and called Brody.

He connected immediately. "What's up, Cobb?"

Mattie explained the situation. "He's not talking, but I think he's trying to herd the tiger toward Tyler's group. Be careful. Where are you now?"

"We're about a mile farther uphill from where we left you."

"I can use Flint's cell phone to call Tyler and tell him to call off the hunt."

Brody paused, evidently weighing the pros and cons. Mattie had considered those herself, but much as she'd like to catch the hunters red-handed, it was too dangerous for them all to be in an area where a stray bullet could hit any one of them—not to mention the poor tiger. If they could get the hunters to stand down, they had a chance of keeping the animal alive.

Brody finally answered. "Probably a good idea to call him. Cuts down on the chance of collateral damage."

"I'll call you back." Mattie disconnected her phone, and then she tapped and swiped the screen on Flint's cell phone until she found a number for Tyler Redman. She and Flint locked eyes while she listened to the phone ring and ring. "Why isn't he answering, Flint?"

Flint shrugged.

Mattie continued to listen to the ringing while her temper rose. "So you're willing to take the rap for this one, huh? We've got two murders and all kinds of wildlife violations here that we can slap you with. You're willing to take the heat?"

The message sounded in her ear, a friendly Tyler Redman telling her to please leave a message. "Tyler, this is Deputy Cobb with the Sheriff's Department. Cease this tiger hunt at once. Do you understand? We need you to stand down. Don't shoot. There are people out here that you could hurt. Call me back at Flint Thornton's number. Now."

She looked at Cole as she disconnected. "Shall we tie him and leave him here while we ride on?"

Flint's face blanched. "You can't leave me tied up with that tiger in the woods."

"Cooperate, then," Cole said.

Again, Flint clammed up.

Mattie sent Brody a quick text that she'd been unable to reach Tyler and then strode up close to Flint, pulling her cuffs from her utility belt. "Place your hands together."

Flint glowered but did as he was told.

Mattie snapped on the cuffs. "Where's your horse?"

He shrugged and nodded off to the right, where she glimpsed his horse tied in a clump of spruce.

"Robo, out," she said, calling off her dog before gesturing toward Flint's horse. "Start walking."

★   ★   ★

It didn't take long for them to mount up, and Mattie led the way down and around the hogback before finding a game trail that she hoped would lead them close to Brody and Glenna. Cole led Flint's horse while the cowboy sat slumped in his saddle, looking defeated.

Thunder boomed and lightning streaked the sky. A crackling pop erupted when a bolt connected with a tree, close enough to make the hair stand up on the back of Mattie's neck.

She rode as fast as she dared, keeping Robo beside her and her ears tuned for either the tiger's roar or other riders in the forest. They rode along the top of a shallow ravine, where a stream trickled below. Soon a deep, resounding bay echoed down the ravine, and Mattie turned in the saddle to look at Cole. "Moose."

"He must have spotted the tiger."

Robo darted off, running down the side of the ravine toward the sound, making Mattie's heart jump into her throat. "Robo, wait! Come here to me."

She could tell he didn't want to, but her dog backtracked and waited at the top of the gulley until she caught up. Mattie nudged Mountaineer faster along the barely discernible game trail, dodging tree branches and crashing through foliage.

The bays created an auditory beacon to home in on. She called Brody to inform him they were coming, and his terse reply confirmed that they had sighted the tiger from a distance but had lost sight of Moose. "We can't hear him. Where are you?"

"Down in a gulley on the east side of the canyon." Mattie raised her face to the elements and felt the chill wind on her cheeks. "We're downwind from him, and the sound must carry down this ravine."

"We've got him on the GPS, and we're getting close."

"We'll try to meet you."

Despite the chilly temperature, adrenaline made her sweat. Mist hung in the air and raindrops splashed down from the lowering clouds. Mattie bent over the saddle horn, pushing Mountaineer upslope while the downpour thickened and saturated her shirt. Heavy drops diminished the sound of Moose barking, forcing her to depend on Robo's sharper hearing. She allowed him to take the lead.

Rain blew into her face, blurring her vision. She pushed Mountaineer hard to keep up with Robo. The terrain flattened and trees whipped past as the gelding picked up speed. Mattie hoped the rain would slow down the hunters and someone in her party could reach the tiger before Tyler and his group found it. Hoofbeats from Cole's horse kept pace behind her.

Mattie followed close enough to see Robo travel upslope and break from the forest into a clearing. She called for him to wait, and he hovered at the edge of the trees. The rain lessened, and she spotted Brody and Glenna streaking into the small clearing off to her left. She reined Mountaineer in their direction and pressed him into a gallop.

They'd entered another stand of pine when a low-pitched, snarling growl rumbled through the forest, making the horses slow. Mattie pulled Mountaineer to a halt, slipped off, and dropped the reins to leave him while she hit the ground running. Robo had outdistanced her, and she shouted at him to wait while she closed the gap.

Up ahead, Brody and Glenna dismounted—Brody with his AR-15 slung across his back and the dart projector in his hands. Her boots thudded on the rocky soil as she ran.

The rain ceased as suddenly as it had begun, affording Mattie a view of a promontory that rose above the trees—a view that rattled her bones. Poised on top of a chimneylike rock, the tiger crouched, snarling and growling, the fur at its neck bristled around a brown collar. Its sharp teeth gleamed as it opened its mouth wide to roar at Moose, who continued to bay while he traversed the base of the rocky column. The sight of the majestic tiger stirred Mattie's heart even as it roused a primal fear in her gut.

Breathing hard, Glenna and Brody joined her. Mattie glanced behind to check on Cole. He'd stayed back about fifty feet, still holding on to Flint's horse and tussling with both their mounts as they became more and more spooked by the tiger.

"If I dart it, it'll probably fall," Brody said, squinting into the mist.

"What is that, maybe thirty feet?" Glenna asked.

"Around that," Brody said. "Maybe fifteen to where it widens at the base."

Concern creased Glenna's face. "He's most likely to roll once he hits the wider part, which will soften his landing. We don't have much choice. Let's do it."

Brody arched a brow. "Once we get it sedated, we'll have to keep it that way."

"I know! I've got the supplies we need. We'll build a travois and haul it out of here. We'll do whatever it takes to get it to safety. Go ahead, shoot it."

Brody raised the projector and was drawing a bead on the tiger when a gunshot echoed off the side of the mountain. The big cat roared and leaped from its perch, a bright scarlet patch blossoming on its shoulder. It lit on its feet where the base widened, covered by rocky shale. As soon as its paws hit the ground, it stumbled and its front quarters crumpled. The tiger slid to a halt, grinding its chin into the shale.

Barking, Robo charged toward the tiger, and Mattie screamed for him to come back. She ran after him, grabbing his collar when he hesitated. She clung to it and dragged him with her as she scooted backward away from the rocks.

Moose scrambled out of the tiger's path as it slid, snarling and hissing, down the shale to the base. Brody fired the projector, landing a hit. The dart embedded in the tiger's haunch.

The whooshing sound the dart gun made when its carbon dioxide cartridge released gave Mattie a chill. The last time she'd heard that noise, the dart that was fired had embedded in *her* back. It had been only a month ago—not enough time to dull the memory of the pain from when that dart hit.

Its hind leg and right foreleg dragging, the tiger tried to run. It gradually slowed, and its haunches sank to the ground. It pulled itself forward with the claws of one front paw, snarling as it dragged itself, its head wobbling back and forth. Finally its head bobbed and then flopped forward, and the tiger lay still and limp. Still holding on to Robo, Mattie didn't know if the tiger was dead from the gunshot wound or sedated by the dart.

Moose edged forward, nose outstretched as if to sniff the tiger, but Glenna called him off and told him to stay. She and Brody eased up close to examine the big cat.

"It's breathing," Glenna called over her shoulder.

Mattie turned toward Cole. He'd dismounted but was still holding the reins of Flint's horse. Telling Robo to heel, she sprinted back to him and took charge of the prisoner. Cole grabbed a pack from the back of his saddle and rushed over to the tiger.

As Mattie watched Cole bend over the beautiful, exotic creature that had been transported to this unfamiliar mountain wilderness to be chased down, stalked, and killed, a fury like no other filled her belly.

Since Brody and Glenna had been unable to hear Moose barking, maybe the hunters had been in the same boat. Furthermore, the tiger had been perched up high while she and the others had been at the bottom of the promontory. Maybe Tyler hadn't received her phone message and the hunters hadn't seen them.

There was a killer in that hunting party—and she didn't believe it to be Flint. But one thing she knew for certain. If the person who'd shot that tiger didn't show up soon to claim his prize, she planned go after them all and hunt *him* down.

★ ★ ★

Cole placed his hand on the tiger's chest, and its body felt warm and lax beneath his fingers. Its heartbeat thumped slow and steady, telling him the cat had been sedated, not killed. "Let's roll him so that I can see that shoulder," he murmured to Brody. "Be ready to jump back if he starts to come out of the sedative. Stay clear of those claws."

Glenna dumped her backpack behind the tiger and helped roll the heavy beast. "This tiger was so worked up before it went down, the sedation might not last as long."

Cole moved in beside her to examine the shoulder. "How long can we count on it with a cat?"

"You can never count on it, but if we stay quiet and avoid stimulation, we might get up to four hours." Glenna opened her pack and took out a long strip of torn cloth, which she started wrapping around the tiger's eyes.

Reducing visual stimulation. That's a good idea, Cole thought. Blood oozed from the wound on the tiger's shoulder. "Trying for a heart shot and missed. Looks like it missed major arteries, which is lucky as hell. But no telling what that bullet did to this shoulder."

Cole palpated the shoulder gently, feeling a huge amount of abnormal play from destroyed soft tissue as well as the crackling of shattered bone.

He had to consider euthanasia, because he never wanted an animal to suffer unnecessarily. He rocked back on his heels to lock eyes with Glenna. "This is bad. Without an X-ray, I don't even know if it can be repaired, but I do know that I'm not the vet who should tackle it. We need a wildlife specialist, and we're certainly not in a situation where we can do anything for it out here."

"Ever since we determined this was a tiger, I've been thinking. Under the circumstances, this cat is never going to be released back into the wild anyway. It's headed for a zoo. I've talked to the folks at Cheyenne Mountain Zoo in Colorado Springs already, and they'll take it. I'll have a team meet me down at my truck, and we can transport it from there. Maybe only have to sedate it one or two more times."

The job would be hard to carry out, but a zoo tiger that was fed and cared for could survive with a bum leg. He decided this cat deserved the opportunity. "I'll stabilize the shoulder and stop the bleeding, and we'll give it a try."

He reached into his pack for gauze and bandages and got to work.

"I'll go look for some limbs that are strong enough to build a damn travois," Brody muttered, slinging his rifle strap over his shoulder as he turned to hurry away.

TWENTY-SIX

Mattie kept one eye on Flint while she watched the others work feverishly to save the beautiful cat. She admired Glenna's dedication to the wild creature as well as the quiet and gentle skill Cole used when he handled injured animals. Or injured people, too, for that matter. *He must have a large capacity for love in that heart of his.*

Flint looked like a whipped puppy.

"Get down from the horse and sit on this log," Mattie told him as she pointed to a fallen tree trunk.

With his hands still cuffed in front, Flint swung down nimbly from the saddle, both hands on the horn. He sat where she'd told him to, looking down at the ground.

Mattie figured the tiger hunt was not this hired man's brainchild. She hadn't been able to spend enough time to break him down earlier and make him talk, but they would all be better off if she could bring him over to their side. She felt the pressure of passing time, expecting the hunters to reach the clearing at any minute. If they saw what was happening here, they would scatter and the person responsible for a double homicide might avoid capture. She suspected Zach. He best matched their evidence, and he had connections with both Nate and Tyler.

She wanted to work on Flint some more. The hard line hadn't done it, so she decided to try the soft touch.

"Did you see that tiger up on that rock fighting for its life?" she murmured as if to herself. "What a shame."

Flint's Adam's apple rose and lowered as he swallowed.

"It's a gorgeous creature. Now it will probably be maimed for the rest of its life. If it lives."

She could have been mistaken, but she thought she saw him wince.

"I wonder what Nate Fletcher was thinking. This had to be all his idea, didn't it?"

Flint gave an almost imperceptible headshake, as if he wanted to say no but just couldn't bring himself to do it.

Mattie had been thinking of the information shared by Nate's parents—the part about how Kasey was asking him to do things he didn't want to. In light of what she knew now, she was certain these alleged "things" hadn't involved Nate and Kasey's private life, as his mother suspected. It must have involved this tiger hunt.

"Flint, did you have an ax to grind with Nate?"

His eyes widened, startled. "No, ma'am. I worked for Nate the past couple years, and I learned a lot from him. I have nothing but respect for him."

"All right. But the way I figure it, someone tied up with this tiger hunt must have killed Nate." She figured a bit of deception might help in this instance. "I still wonder if it could've been you."

A look of pain that had to have also been physical consumed Flint's face. "I didn't kill Nate. I've never killed anyone."

"Not even Wilson? I think he got wrapped up in this fiasco somehow and suffered the consequences for it. What do you think?"

Flint was wagging his head as he avoided eye contact and studied the ground.

"Flint, I'm gonna be honest with you. I believe you're not the ringleader of this circus, but you're the one I have sitting here in cuffs. Now, I plan to go after the other players in a few minutes, so I don't have much time to sit and chat. But you've got to realize that when it comes to the law, a bird in the hand is worth two in the bush. We've definitely got you for the wild-life charges, and we'll be looking at you hard for the murder of two men. Is that the way you want this to go down?"

Flint raised his face and stared at her with haunted eyes.

"If you truly respect Nate, you'll help us catch his killer." As Flint continued to stare at her, Mattie sensed he was on the edge of spilling something. Cole had mentioned his father before, and she decided to play that card again. "If you help us out here, I'll make sure your dad knows you did the right thing."

His eyes welled. "I was just trying to help Miss Lillian and Mr. Doyle."

Help Lillian and Doyle? What did he mean? How were Lillian and Doyle involved? "How would this tiger hunt help the Redmans?"

"It's not right, them losing their home. The bank shouldn't have the right to take it from them." He shrugged and lowered his face, as if embarrassed about his tears, or perhaps about sharing what he knew.

"What's this about a bank?"

"The Redman Ranch is in foreclosure."

They'd known about Nate and Kasey's debt, and the strain on Lillian and Doyle, but this was the first they'd heard of foreclosure. No one had mentioned it before, not even Kasey. And of course she would know about it.

Mattie began putting the pieces together. Nate and Kasey had borrowed money from Lillian and Doyle to set up Nate's outfitting business, and according to Tom and Helen Fletcher, Nate needed to pay that back now. Kasey seemed eager to collect Nate's insurance money, even though she denied being pressured by her parents. Her deceptiveness during that part of the interview made sense now.

Nate's death benefit would probably save the Redman Ranch and more. Was Kasey responsible for his murder instead of Zach? Or did this new piece to the puzzle give Lillian a motive for killing her son-in-law?

Mattie had figured the killer was on the loose here in the mountains. But maybe that person was waiting back home on the Redman Ranch. "Tell me what you know about how Nate was killed. Quick. We don't have much time."

Flint raised his head to look her in the eye. "I don't know anything about Nate's death or who killed him. And that's the God's honest truth."

"How about Wilson Nichol?"

"Same. I was setting up supplies for this trip when Wilson was killed. I don't know anything."

Well, she would bet her next paycheck that Flint knew something about Nate's trafficking business. "Then tell me what you know about this tiger. Who planned the hunt?"

Flint looked sincere. "Nate did. He brought it in the van. In a cage."

She'd already guessed that. "How did he get lined up with a tiger?"

"Nate said a guy out of California sold it to him, brought in from Mexico."

Glenna's theory was checking out, but how would Nate ever make this kind of contact in the first place? "I don't get it. How did Nate connect with someone selling a tiger?"

Flint's shoulders hitched forward. "Some guy he met in Vegas at a casino."

"You have a name?"

"No. Nate only told me about it last week, because he was bringing the tiger in. I guess it all started a few months ago, moving drugs and animal parts from California to Nebraska, where another guy picked them up. That guy would drive the stuff out east to sell. Nate said he was trying to make money to pay back the Redmans, and he had to do it. He didn't want to."

"Was Wilson Nichol involved in this business?"

"Not that I know of. And I bet he wasn't." Flint winced and rubbed the back of his neck. "Nate didn't care too much for Wilson, him having history with Kasey and all."

In Timber Creek, everyone seemed to know everyone else's business, and Mattie wanted to mine what Flint knew about the Redmans. "What about Tyler? Was he involved?"

"No, ma'am. Tyler came on this hunt because Kasey asked him to. But he was pressuring Nate for the money to pay back his mom and dad, I do know that." Flint dropped his chin to his chest. "I shoulda done something about this hunt. I shoulda told somebody. I knew this wasn't right."

"You're telling me now, and I appreciate it. I'll make sure your dad knows you did the right thing and told the truth." Mattie eyed Flint, wondering how much further she could push him. "Do you have a way to get in touch with Tyler?"

Flint straightened. "If you'll give me back my phone, I can find out where he is and tell him to come on down to get this tiger."

"But he didn't answer when I called him earlier."

"He's not carrying the cell phone with that number. They're all carrying throwaways."

Mattie pulled his phone from her pocket and swiped to his contact list. "Do you have their numbers programmed here?"

"Yeah. Under Z. ZT, ZZ, and ZB. For Tyler, Zach, and Ben."

He reached his cuffed hands toward her to take the phone, but she held it and swiped down the list herself. She opened the details under each listing to check the phone numbers, looking for the number she'd memorized from that last incoming call made to Wilson Nichol.

And there it was under ZZ. *Wilson's last call came from the phone assigned to Zach Irving.*

★   ★   ★

Carrying Cole's rifle slung across her back, Mattie ran through the forest, Robo setting the pace in front of her. She'd struck a course uphill and stayed away from game trails, keeping within the shelter of evergreens whenever she could. She watched her footing, working hard to step between the ankle-turning stones, while keeping an eye on Robo's back.

"Let's find the bad guy," she murmured to Robo, knowing he would smell the riders coming long before she would hear them.

The rain had ceased and blue sky appeared in patches, the afternoon sun peeking through clouds to create shafts of light that stretched from the heavens to the earth. The twittering birds had fallen silent, as if they knew people with malicious intent were passing through. When the hair on Robo's back bristled, she felt gooseflesh prickle her shoulders.

She spoke quietly to her dog. "Robo, here. Heel."

She crouched behind a ponderosa pine, one arm around Robo, while she waited. His tongue lolled in a pant, and her dog studied the uphill terrain, making her follow his gaze. She strained to see through the trees.

Robo's ears pricked, and he ceased panting for several seconds while he cocked his head to locate the sound. Mattie tucked a strand of loose hair behind her ear and listened with all her might. Then she heard the distant sounds as they approached—the click of shod hooves against stone, the jingle of curb chain on bridles, someone whistling a tune. *Whistling!*

She unslung the rifle from her back and held it across her knees as she hunkered behind the heavy pine boughs. She exchanged several deep breaths, drawing out the exhalation while she worked to slow her heartbeat and fill her chest with oxygen to feed her muscles for when she needed to run again.

Robo tensed under her arm, and she glimpsed the movement of riders flashing in and out of the trees as they made their way downhill. "Easy. Wait," she whispered, moving one hand to her dog's collar.

Within a few more minutes, she could make out features and faces. No surprises here. Tyler Redman led the way on a stout red gelding, while Ben Underwood and Zach Irving followed behind on their own mounts.

She spotted the whistler. Irving rode with his lips puckered, emitting the light tune "A-hunting We Will Go."

Mattie whispered to Robo to stay quiet and then held her breath as the horses inched past about fifty feet from her position, their hind legs tucked under to keep their footing as they half slid and half stumbled down the steep slope. Though the shot had probably come from about a half mile away as the crow flies, there had been much more ground territory to cover to reach the tiger's last stand.

These men were armed with powerful rifles that had scopes, and one of them, namely Zach Irving, was a murderer. After they passed, she waited until they'd gone another fifty feet downhill, and then she and Robo fell in behind them. She crept from tree to tree, keeping Robo at heel and following the group at a distance.

She knew they'd reached the checkpoint when she heard Brody's shout. "Halt! Don't move! Timber Creek County Sheriff. Don't move!"

With a burst of speed, Mattie sprang forward, carrying the rifle as she ran. She reached the game trail in a few strides, her feet churning down the steep, rocky slope. She scanned the hillside, looking for cover. Spotting a boulder off to her right, she headed for it, telling Robo to come with her.

The three riders bunched. Zach reined his horse hard, pivoted into a turn, and headed back uphill.

"Halt!" Mattie shouted and stepped out to show herself. "We've got you covered. Hands up where I can see them!"

Robo stood beside her, his muscles quivering, his toenails digging into the ground. Ready.

She aimed her rifle at Zach Irving. "Halt! Zach! I've got you in my sights!"

He pulled his horse to a sliding stop and bailed off. Landing on his feet, he tugged hard on his mount's reins and positioned it between him and Mattie. He swatted it on the rump, sending it in her direction while he used the cover to take off into the trees. He dodged around a boulder and disappeared.

"Robo, take him!"

Robo shot forward, vanishing behind the cover of the evergreens.

Mattie flew after her dog. When she rounded the boulder, she glimpsed Robo, a black shadow streaking through the forest, silent and lethal. She pushed herself hard, her boots smacking against rocks and fallen tree branches. Robo, growling and snarling, disappeared into a draw.

Mattie reached the top of it and spilled down the side, losing her footing and her rifle as she tumbled on the loose stones. She slid to the bottom, where Robo had Zach pinned by one leg. Zach hollered and roared, kicking Robo in the head with his other boot.

Her dog refused to let go. Zach struggled to sit while lifting a short limb like a club. Mattie shouted for him to stop, got to her feet, and launched herself at the man at the same time that Robo released his leg and went for his arm. Robo had been trained to always go for the arm that held a weapon, and that's exactly what he was doing.

Just as Mattie landed on the man's chest, Robo's mighty jaws clamped down on Zach's forearm, making him scream and drop the limb. He'd released his foul breath in a loud *humph* when Mattie dive-bombed him, and the odor of alcohol made her stomach lurch.

Robo tugged backward, dragging Zach out as much as he could, since Mattie's weight anchored him to the ground. Still the man fought. Knowing that Brody would be busy with the others and this takedown was up to her and her partner alone, Mattie drove her knee into his crotch and went for his other fist at the same time.

When she landed the knee strike, Zach groaned and drew up his legs in the classical pose of groin protection. Mattie threw her entire weight on his free arm and pinned it to the ground. Robo's growls filled the draw as he took advantage of the fact that Mattie no longer weighed down their captive. He dragged him along the rocky ground, bouncing the man's head off a rock as they went.

Zach lay stunned, faceup, Robo on one arm and Mattie on the other. She pressed her advantage and shouted into his face. "Don't move! Stay still and the dog will let go!"

She felt the fight go out of him and swiftly reached for the cuffs she'd taken off Flint earlier. She clicked one onto the wrist she was holding. "Robo, out! Guard!"

Robo dropped Zach's arm, saliva dripping from his mouth onto Zach as he backed away maybe one whole inch. He loomed over their captive, his black lip elevated in a snarl, exposing his sharp canines.

"On your stomach! Don't reach for me or this dog will bite your face!"

Zach rolled to his stomach, turning his face away from Robo, while Mattie grabbed his free wrist and snapped the other cuff on it. She stood, her legs shaking with the adrenaline rush. "Robo, out!"

After Robo backed off, keeping his eyes pinned on their captive, she forced herself to settle. She took a few deep breaths and found a voice that sounded much more calm than she felt. "Do you have anything sharp in your pockets? Weapons? Needles?"

Zach grunted. "You have no right to do this to me."

Mattie patted him down, tipping him from one side to the other as she searched his front pockets. She found only a cell phone. She opened the screen to the call history and found the outgoing call to Wilson's phone, just as she'd suspected she would.

Zach lay still under Robo's guard until Mattie told her dog to back away.

"Okay, Zach, you can sit up now."

With his hands cuffed behind, he struggled to sit. He glared at her with baleful eyes.

"Tell me what you know about Wilson Nichol's death," she said.

"Go to hell!"

If I was in his shoes and just got a knee in the nuts, I wouldn't want to talk to me either. She grabbed the collar of his jacket. "Stand up."

After helping him to his feet, she pointed toward the steep side of the rocky ravine. "We've got some climbing to do to get out of this draw."

Robo hustled to Zach's side so he could escort their captive up the incline.

TWENTY-SEVEN

Robo escorted Zach Irving out of the draw while Mattie followed. Her dog held his head high and waved his tail, so proud to be completing this last duty of fugitive apprehension. Life seemed so simple for Robo: rest and relax when you can, take pleasure in a job well done. He didn't lie awake at night wondering if he'd done the right thing. She loved him for it.

While they walked to where Brody was waiting with his two captives, Mattie hoped a little time would give Zach Irving a cooling-off period. She still wanted to question him about his connection to Wilson Nichol's murder and see if she could uncover a link to Nate Fletcher's. Even though the evidence pointed to him as the killer in both homicides, his motive remained murky.

Why would Zach kill Nate Fletcher right before a hunting trip he'd paid good money for? And if Wilson Nichol had presented a business deal to Zach that would benefit them both, why would he kill Wilson? The puzzle pieces seemed misshapen and didn't quite fit.

Brody studied her as she approached, and she gave him a thumbs-up to let him know all was well. Tyler and Ben Underwood sat on a log, their hands cuffed in front. Under his billed cap, Tyler was red in the face, his eyebrows gathered into a pained expression. If Flint's information had been correct, Mattie guessed that Tyler regretted ever agreeing to lead this tiger hunt for Kasey. If so, maybe she could get *him* to talk.

On the other hand, Ben sat with his shoulders back, observing everything around him with an air of confidence. His face still wore that friendly mask she'd begun to associate with him. He would be one cool customer in a poker game. She remembered how the two had acted when she'd first met them—Ben had acted open and friendly, while Zach had been shut down and nervous. At the time, both had been guilty of preparing to participate in illegal wildlife activity. But had one or both of them already committed Nate's murder? Was Ben just better at hiding it?

Her cell phone pinged with an incoming text, and she took it out of her pocket to check. It was from Stella, and it read, Z. IRVING WAS IN COURTHOUSE MONDAY AM ASKING ABOUT TAX STATUS OF REDMAN RANCH. TAXES ARE DELINQUENT. WILSON NICHOL WENT THERE GETTING THE SAME INFO THREE WEEKS AGO.

That was interesting. It not only confirmed what Flint had said earlier about foreclosure but indicated that both Wilson and Zach knew the ranch was floundering, too. She slipped her cell phone back into her pocket.

Zach's horse was nowhere in sight, but Brody and his two prisoners mounted up and began a slow plod downhill to join the others. Mattie and Zach followed behind on foot.

Robo was still escorting Zach on his left side, and Mattie moved up to walk on his right. "I have something I'm curious about, Mr. Irving."

"I won't talk to you about this hunt without the advice of an attorney," he said, closing his lips in a thin line.

"I'd like to talk to you about a completely different subject."

He sent her a sidelong glance. "What's that?"

"What's your interest in the Redman Ranch?"

He jutted out his chin. "I heard it's a nice piece of property that the owners might want to sell."

But as far as she knew, the owners weren't at all interested in selling the land. "Are you looking to move here, Mr. Irving?"

"Hardly." He smirked. "I'm a residential real estate developer. Nothing illegal about that."

"Agreed, but I'm wondering how you learned about this particular property."

"Wilson Nichol contacted me about it. I decided to come to Timber Creek to see it." He threw Mattie a hard look. "That's why I came here."

She wanted to keep him talking, so she didn't mention the illegal game issues.

"What exactly did Mr. Nichol tell you about the Redman property?"

He shrugged. "He thought I might be interested in subdividing the property to sell for building sites. He was pretty excited about its potential, and I told him I'd see if the project would be feasible."

"And when did you speak with Tyler Redman about it?" Mattie asked, testing a theory.

He shook his head. "I didn't speak with Tyler. Wilson said he didn't want me to discuss it with the family yet."

That was odd. Wouldn't a developer speak to the landowners first? "Why not?"

"He said the family was having some financial problems and he didn't want to get their hopes up until he knew if I was interested in the project."

Something seemed shady about the way Wilson and Zach had been going about it. "I see. So did you discuss it with Tyler after Mr. Nichol's death?"

"Actually, I didn't. I need to run a feasibility study and talk to my partners back home before approaching Tyler. If we decide not to go forward, there's no reason to share the project details with him now."

This still sounded backwards to her. "I'd think you'd want to involve the landowners prior to doing the work of a study. What if they don't want to sell? You would have done all that work for nothing."

Zach grimaced. "Wouldn't be the first time. Besides, from what I understand, the land will be for sale one way or another."

Mattie figured she already knew what he was talking about, but she wanted to determine how much Zach knew. "How so?"

"Wilson said the land would be for sale either by owner or through a bank foreclosure."

Mattie started to get a sick feeling. Zach had confirmed her suspicion—Wilson Nichol, a friend of the Redman family, had been acting on his own, circling the land along with the bankers, like buzzards waiting to pick it off.

Why would Wilson instigate a plan to subdivide the property without involving the family? Did he hope to offer them a way out of their financial problems, or did he hope to make money off their misfortune? The answer might have died with him, but Mattie would have bet her monthly wage on the latter.

She pressed on. "To your knowledge, are any of the other Redman family members aware of you discussing the possibility of subdivision with Mr. Nichol?"

"I've never discussed the project with anyone but Wilson. I don't know who he might have involved."

The fact remained that Zach Irving's burner phone had called Wilson Nichol prior to his murder. "Why did you call Wilson Nichol late Sunday afternoon?"

Zach's eyes widened, and he shook his head. "I didn't call Wilson this weekend. Our last conversation was Friday, and that was in person, right after he showed us the ranch property."

His surprise seems genuine. "By us, you mean you and Mr. Underwood?"

"Right."

She decided to pursue more information in a roundabout way. "Where did you get the cell phone you had on you?"

"That's not my phone." He shrugged as if answering her question was of no matter to him. "Eve Redman gave me that phone yesterday."

Eve? Kasey's sister?

Yesterday meant she'd given Zach the phone on Monday, not Sunday when Wilson had been killed. Did that mean Eve had

had the phones in her possession on Sunday afternoon? Did it mean she'd been the one to call Wilson? Mattie's scalp prickled.

"She handed them out to all of us," Zach went on. "One to me, one to Ben, and one to Tyler. She said she'd programmed the numbers and showed us how to contact each other." Though he kept walking, Zach turned his head to look at her fully. "Eve's up here, you know. Back at the camp."

Was this his way of diverting suspicion, or was he just being honest? Given the way he'd opened up while talking about the potential real estate transaction, Mattie believed he was telling her the truth. Her pulse quickening, she fell back a few steps so she could observe him while she considered this new information.

Eve had passed the GSR test the night of Nate's murder, but a good jacket, gloves, and a shower would have done the trick. And Eve was a tall, slender girl; her shoe size would probably match the prints left at Wilson's crime scene. Was it possible that she'd killed Wilson? After all, she'd seemed hostile toward him when Mattie had observed her at the ranch.

But then what about Nate? What would be Eve's motive to kill her own brother-in-law?

Kasey's passionate statement to Stella that none of the kids would ever consider selling the ranch—it was their home, their heritage—resonated with Mattie. Eve probably felt the same way toward the ranch as her sister. Nate's gambling and inability to pay back the Redmans had jeopardized their home and their livelihood. And Wilson had plotted to take that away as well.

As they breached the last rise and could look down at the scene where Cole and Glenna were working on the tiger, Mattie knew what she was going to have to do. She needed to find that campsite and apprehend Eve Redman so that the girl could be interrogated for the murders of Nate Fletcher and Wilson Nichol.

And unlike Robo, she would have no satisfaction at all when the job was completed.

TWENTY-EIGHT

By the time Mattie reached the others, Brody had made his two men dismount and they were huddled together on a log a short distance away from where Glenna, Cole, and Flint were still working on the tiger. Robo escorted Zach over to join them while she checked in with Brody. Then she pulled Tyler aside for a private conversation.

"Tyler, was this fiasco your doing?" she asked, fully aware that it was not but hoping to put him on the defensive.

"No!" His denial was adamant. "This was all Nate's idea."

She'd hoped challenging him with her question would start him talking. "So how did you get involved?"

"Kasey asked me to do this." Tyler started off all blustery, but quickly fizzled as he realized he'd just implicated his sister. "She didn't plan it either, but Nate had already collected money from these yahoos, and she couldn't afford to refund it."

Mattie pulled the cell phone she'd confiscated from Zach out of her pocket and held it up. "Did you set up these cell phones so you could all communicate with each other?"

He stared at the phone for a moment, and she could see his wheels turning, trying to figure out if she was trying to trap him in a crime.

She reassured him. "There's no crime connected with providing these cell phones for the group, Tyler. It's a simple question. Are you the one who prepared the phones?"

He shook his head. "No. Eve did that."

"Did she have the phones this Sunday before you came up here on Monday?"

"As far as I know." His eyes widened slightly, and Mattie thought he might be thinking about his sister. "Eve had nothing to do with this, but she came up to help cook and take care of camp. We left her there this morning because she didn't want to come with us. She was upset. Said she didn't have the stomach for what was going on."

Didn't have the stomach to hunt down the tiger, but what about killing two men in cold blood? "Why did she come on this trip, then?"

"To help Kasey." Tyler's tone was impatient. "Maybe you don't get it, but we're a family. We help each other when times are tough."

That dig about family hurt, even though Tyler would know nothing about her or her history. "And times have been tough for your parents lately, haven't they? What do you know about Wilson Nichol asking these guys to take a look at buying your parents' ranch?"

Tyler scowled, and she realized it was more in anger than in surprise. "Wilson wanted to offer Mom and Dad a way out, but I told him to forget it. We're working on a way to pay off the bank. We're going to find a way to save the ranch."

Like Nate's life insurance policy? "How?"

"Selling the calf crop early, for one thing. And Eve is looking into wind technology to see if we could set up windmills on our land. We have plenty of space, and lots of wind blows through that valley."

"Does Eve know about this deal that Wilson was working on?"

Tyler took on a pained expression. "Yeah, she was with me vaccinating calves when Wilson came out to talk to me about it. I've never seen her so mad. She told him to get his nose out of our business."

Everything he said was leading to Eve. Mattie just wanted to pinpoint one more thing. She held up Zach's phone again. "Could Kasey have had these cell phones on Sunday?"

He shrugged. "I don't think so. Kasey has been out of it since Nate. She asked us to take over."

Not one hundred percent definitive, but enough to point a finger in Eve's direction. "So Eve is up at your campsite waiting for you to come back. Can you call her?"

Tyler shook his head. "There's no cell phone service up that high. I don't think she even brought a phone with her."

Mattie pointed at the log where the others were sitting. "Go ahead and sit back down."

"Someone needs to go up and let her know what's going on before sundown," Tyler said with concern. "She'll be worried and start looking for us. I can take you there."

Mattie didn't like the sound of that. Tyler wasn't in the clear yet, and the last thing she wanted was to be up in the high country with a brother and sister who might have plotted the murder of two men. "Go ahead and sit down," she repeated, and made sure he followed through before going to talk with Brody.

★ ★ ★

Cole had stabilized the tiger's shoulder with bandage and tape, doing the best he could for damage control. After raising the blindfold, he tapped the cat's eyelid. A little twitchy. He injected another small dose of BAM into the buffalo cap on the IV he'd placed earlier in the foreleg beneath the injured shoulder. If this tiger came out from under the sedative, he would be less likely to use his damaged leg to swipe with those dangerous claws.

Glenna shook out a large wildlife net and spread it on the ground alongside the cat. "Let's wrap him in this first. Then I have a light tarp we can use to secure him."

While squatting at the head and shoulders of the limp animal to pick it up, Cole noticed the sharp teeth inside the slack jaw and hoped the sedative held long enough to recover him at the zoo, where personnel would know how to handle him. On the count of three, he and Glenna lifted the cat and lowered him onto the net, where they trussed him like a Thanksgiving turkey.

Cole glanced at Flint. "How's that travois coming along?"

Flint had woven rope between two poles to make a hammock-like sling.

"Almost done. Just tying off the last rope."

With the net securely in place, Cole and Glenna made short work of wrapping the tiger inside the lightweight canvas tarp. His limp tongue protruded from his mouth, and Cole moistened it with water from his canteen. Flint brought over the travois, and the three of them started the process of loading the bundled tiger onto the hammock.

"Do we have a horse that will pull this?" Flint asked. "I mean, this tiger's asleep, but the horses are still going to be afraid of it."

"One of mine will do it." Cole had already thought of that, and Mountaineer was his top pick. The horse was steady and had previous experience hauling logs and firewood from the forest. He would do the job. Unfortunately, that left Mattie without a mount, but Duke was stout enough to carry the two of them.

Cole headed toward where he'd tied the horses. One of the Redman geldings had come running downhill without a rider earlier and had crowded in among them. After releasing Mountaineer's tie rope, Cole secured the other gelding into the open spot.

Mountaineer gave the tiger a walleyed look while Cole led him past. He sidestepped as Flint and Glenna lifted the poles on the travois, but Cole coaxed him to stand still while they pulled the contraption forward and anchored it to the saddle. They were ready to go.

This method of sedation meant they needed to get this tiger off the mountain ASAP. They didn't have time to wait. Cole looked to see what was going on with Mattie and Brody, who were wrapping up their conversation. He caught her eye, and she walked off to the side, nodding for him to join her and Robo. He handed Mountaineer's reins to Flint and followed.

She stopped a short distance from the others. "You're ready to go?"

He nodded. On close inspection, he could see the scratches on her face and dirt on her clothes, but he knew she'd brush him off if he mentioned it, so he held his tongue about that. "I had to use Mountaineer, but Duke can carry the two of us."

"We're not going with you, Cole."

Her words surprised him. "Aren't we all going down together?"

Mattie met his gaze. "Eve Redman is still up at their camp. We need to get her and bring her in, too."

Cole glanced at the three prisoners, cuffed and sitting on logs or leaning against boulders. "Are you all going?"

"We don't know yet. Brody called the sheriff for backup."

Cole didn't like the idea of splitting off from Mattie to leave her in the wilderness, but she wouldn't be alone, and he had to move that tiger. Mountaineer began to paw the ground, punctuating Cole's feeling of urgency. He needed to get this show on the road.

"I'm going to take Flint with me. I need his help, and it's best not to leave him with these other guys," he said, taking Mattie's hand. "Call me when you get back to town."

She squeezed his before releasing it, her eyes dark and serious. "I will. Be careful with that big cat."

As she turned to stride toward Brody and the captives, Cole had the feeling he didn't know the complete picture. But he couldn't do anything about it. He headed back to take charge of

Mountaineer while sending a message to the powers that be to keep her safe. *Because heaven knows, this woman I love and her dog are the first ones to rush into harm's way when they're needed.*

★ ★ ★

Mattie watched Cole's departure with an empty feeling, but she pushed it aside to go retrieve her backpack. Brody had already told her he wasn't going to let her go after Eve Redman alone, so she'd have to wait until others arrived from town.

She wanted to take care of her partner while she waited. Robo had covered a lot of territory since his last meal, which had been well before sunrise, and he was beginning to look in need of food. She took out two collapsible bowls from her pack, splashed water into one, and poured a generous portion of his kibble into the other before sinking to the ground to sit cross-legged beside him. She nibbled an energy bar while he ate.

Robo scooped up a large mouthful, scattering nuggets as he chomped, staring into her eyes and waving his tail. Propping her head with one hand, elbow to knee, she stroked the glossy black fur on his back.

After finishing his food, Robo lapped half a bowl of water and then gave himself a mighty shake. She stroked his fine head, hugged him, and rose from the ground to approach Brody, who'd just ended a cell phone call.

"How much longer before help arrives?"

"The sheriff's hustling up horses and manpower, but he's run into problems. He suggested we take these guys down lower, and they'll meet us on the road to take them in. Then we can come back here to go after Eve."

Mattie considered it, but the sun would be setting in a few hours, and they didn't have time. "Can you handle these three by yourself?"

Brody gave her a scornful look. "Of course."

"Right," she said, lifting a palm in apology. "If you wait here with these guys, Robo and I can go get Eve, and then we'll all go down together."

Brody lifted a brow. "How do you propose to find this campsite?"

Robo had been trained to backtrack a captured fugitive to find evidence that had been dumped or hidden along the way. "Robo can follow Zach Irving's scent trail all the way to the campsite."

Brody huffed, shaking his head. "For God's sake, Cobb, why don't you just send the damn dog up there by himself to bring her in?"

Mattie could tell he was weakening, and she gave him a thin smile. "That's what I'm doing, but I might as well go along and provide backup for him. Two officers, Brody—that's within protocol. We're a team, we can do it. Besides, the sun will be going down in a few hours. We only have this little window of time."

Brody studied her while he thought it over, and Mattie made her face bland and unconcerned. It worried her some to know there was no cell phone service where she was headed, and that a woman suspected of killing two men would be at the end of the track. But someone needed to bring in Eve, and she had no doubt she and her partner could accomplish the job.

"All right," Brody said. "But check in by cell phone as you go."

"I will," Mattie said, hitching up her backpack and hooking the straps over her shoulders. And she would—she would check in for as long as she could, before she climbed out of range for cell phone service.

TWENTY-NINE

To ensure that Robo backtracked the right man, Mattie led him over to Zach and told him to "scent this," his cue to pick up the scent of the person or object she indicated. Zach glowered at her and protested, but he didn't have a leg to stand on. Cops might need a warrant to collect DNA from a person, but there was no law on the book to inhibit a K-9 officer from taking in someone's scent.

Tyler didn't show any concern about what she was doing, and in fact he seemed relieved that Mattie was going to go get his sister. He seemed to have no clue that Eve was now their number-one suspect in a double homicide. From the way he'd reacted when she'd discussed the phone with him, she believed he knew nothing about it being used to contact Wilson Nichol. At this point, he seemed most interested in someone finding Eve before nightfall so she wouldn't strike off from the camp alone to search for the hunting party.

Robo set a fast pace away from the group and trotted uphill, heading toward the point where they had apprehended the hunters. Clouds flirted with the sun, casting dappled shadows on the forest and lowering the temperature. The damp soil and foliage retained scent, giving Robo the best conditions possible for his task.

He kept his head lowered, moving along at a pace that Mattie could match easily, and she followed him this way for over an hour. Mattie checked in with Brody halfway through, giving him a description of the direction they'd come and the landmarks around them.

In turn, Brody updated her on Cole and Glenna's progress. "They reached the edge of the BLM. Glenna has arranged for another wildlife manager to meet her in a van equipped with a cage. She'll go on with them to Colorado Springs."

"And the tiger's still sedated?"

"They're having no problems. He's wrapped up snug as a bug in the proverbial rug. Cole thinks they'll make it."

What a relief. "I'll check back later," she told Brody before disconnecting.

As the forest closed around her, the track became more and more clear to the human eye. They were on a game trail that wound through the pine and allowed little deviation from it through the thick overgrowth. Horseshoe prints and churned-up soil in steep passages marked where the riders had come down the mountain, and soon Mattie reached a small clearing.

Robo led her to a point where she could see for miles. Mist swirled around crags like ghosts, and she imagined this was the outlook that had given Zach Irving his shot. She couldn't see the group of men below, but she knew they would be there, hidden by the trees.

Mattie took out her cell phone and noted she had two short bars. One last check-in was probably all she could do. She dialed Brody, and even as he answered, she could hear the small cuts in his voice that told her reception was spotty.

"Ask Tyler how far the camp is from where they shot the tiger," she told him.

"What . . . say, Cobb?"

She could decipher his question but decided reception was too poor to try to hold a conversation. "I'm okay, Brody, but I'm about to lose cell phone service," she said. "Do you copy?"

"Damn . . . come back . . ."

The broken signal was still clear enough for her to get the message, but she had no intention of turning back now. "Can't hear you. I'm at the point where I think they shot the tiger. We're heading uphill. I'll check in when I can."

Mattie disconnected the call, set Robo's nose back down on the track with a hand gesture, and told him to search. He continued across country on the game trail, traversing the steep grade at a diagonal. She had a feeling they didn't have much farther to go, and she began to worry about the girl at the end of her journey. Robo had met Eve before at Kasey's house and considered her a friend, which most likely meant he wouldn't sense her as a threat.

If Eve sets up an ambush, there'll be no raised hackles to warn me.

Still, Mattie studied Robo's body language as closely as ever. Any change might indicate the presence of another human. Soon the sound of rushing water filtered through the trees, telling her there was a stream ahead. People usually pitched campsites around water, and Mattie strained to see, hoping to spot tents or wood smoke.

Robo led her to the edge of a small meadow, and she told him to wait. She scanned the area filled with rich grass, spotting the creek that ran through it. This would be the perfect place for camping with horses, but there was no sign of a campsite or a human. She told Robo to search and followed him into the damp grass, where she could see the smashed and bent stems that the horses had trodden on earlier.

After crossing the meadow and entering the tree line, Robo raised his head and sniffed the air. The skin on Mattie's shoulders crawled, and she placed her hand on his search harness to slow him down. He put his nose back to the ground, leading her forward, and soon she caught a whiff of what Robo had been sampling in the air. Smoke.

She grasped Robo's harness to stop him. Pulling him off the track, she whispered, "Good boy," petting him while she paused behind a tree and scanned the way ahead. Evergreens blocked her view for the most part, but if she stayed on course, it looked like she would come to a rise. Beyond that she glimpsed a sheer rock cliff face that towered around fifty feet above the treetops.

She hoped to stay hidden until she came to the campsite. She whispered to Robo to heel and crept upslope, moving from one pine to another for shelter. As she went, she loosened the strap on her holster that secured her sidearm, even though she intended to use it only as a last resort.

At the top of the rise, she peered around a dense spruce tree and spotted the campsite about fifty yards below in a small clearing near a grove of aspen. Three orange dome tents had been pitched near a stream, and farther beyond three horses stood resting on a picket line strung between the aspens' white trunks. No sign of Eve.

Robo brushed against her as he stretched his neck to peer around the boughs of the spruce. Mattie glanced at him to get a read—head up, panting, looking ahead. But no hackles. He stopped panting to sniff the air. No change in his body language.

A campfire flickered within a rock fire circle. It had been fed and banked recently, so Eve had to be near. Maybe she was inside one of the tents.

Staying under cover, Mattie slipped closer until she was about twenty yards away. One of the horses tossed its head and nickered, making Mattie's stomach drop. If Eve was inside a tent, that might bring her out.

What are the chances she's armed? Guns would be plentiful in a hunting party, but if Eve was an animal lover, she might not carry a weapon. And as long as she remained out of sight, it would be impossible to tell.

A boulder up ahead offered protection. Mattie held on to Robo and crept up behind it, making sure he was covered. She peered around its edge and called, "Hello."

No movement inside the tents. No answer.

Had Eve taken a walk? Left camp for a few minutes? If so, she could be anywhere. Mattie scanned the area at her back, searching for a flash of movement.

The tent flaps were tied back, but the bug screens were zipped into place, which at this distance interfered with seeing inside them.

"Eve," she called out. Still no answer.

Telling Robo to stay, Mattie moved into the camp with a few swift strides. Within seconds, she peered inside each tent and cleared the area. Eve was nowhere in sight.

Damp clothing hung by the fire, and Mattie quickly spotted a woman's T-shirt. She called Robo and told him to scent. She patted his side and held him close, murmuring sweet nothings and encouragement before gesturing toward the ground near the fire. "Okay, buddy, let's find Eve. Search."

Zach Irving's scent had to be around this campsite as well as Eve's, and here she was, asking Robo to switch the search from one person to the other. Would he be able to do it?

Robo lowered his nose and circled the fire, sniffing in all directions before choosing a scent trail that led out of camp toward the creek. He passed boot prints in the wet soil on the creek bank that appeared to be the size and shape of those left at Wilson's crime scene. No time now, but in her mind, Mattie flagged them as evidence to be taken later.

When Robo started up a sheer incline that appeared to lead to the top of the cliff, Mattie's gut tightened. This had every hallmark of an ambush. What if Eve had seen them coming? Like the tiger, she could have gone to the high ground to strike from above.

She told Robo to wait. "Eve," she called. "Eve, it's Mattie Cobb. I know you're here."

Thunder rumbled, but the nearby forest lay still. Mattie shivered. This was what she hated most. It wasn't so much that danger awaited her—she could face that. She feared losing Robo. If a bullet killed him, it would kill her, too.

The way ahead was more like rock climbing than hiking, too steep to clip on his leash. She had to let him go out front. She told him to search, murmuring, "Easy, easy," to keep him as close as she could. A cold breeze came from behind, chilling the sweat under her shirt.

Expecting a gunshot to ring out at any time, Mattie clung to the rocks, climbing on all fours as she followed Robo. He hopped from one place to another until he reached a ledge near the top. There, Mattie told him to wait. Her legs shaking, she eased up to peek over the edge.

Nothing but a flat expanse of stone and scrubby pine. After telling Robo to stay, she pulled herself slowly to the top and crouched. Flat rock ran across the top of the cliff, littered with boulders and monoliths where someone could hide. Exposed and vulnerable, she squatted at the edge and crawled over to take cover behind a boulder. When she called Robo, he scurried up and over to where she could grasp his harness and pull him in with her behind the rock.

Now what? There weren't that many places to go up here except off the edge of the cliff face. And that led to a seventy-foot free fall. Eve had to be near. As she huddled beside Robo, he swiped her cheek with his tongue and then tried to see around the boulder. "Stay here," she whispered, hugging him close and loving that warm touch of reassurance.

"Eve," she called. "It's Mattie Cobb. I want to talk to you."

A gunshot cracked, echoing across the cliff. A bullet pinged off a boulder to her left, spraying rock shards in its wake.

Mattie grabbed Robo and held on tight as he tried to lunge from cover. In his training, gunshots meant *Go! Find the shooter! Take him down!* But here, with the edge of the cliff so near, it would be a death mission. Using a quiet but intense voice, she urged him to sit and stay.

"Go back," Eve shouted. "I don't want to shoot you. Or your dog."

With both hands holding Robo, Mattie couldn't even draw her service weapon; but Eve didn't need to know that. "Good," she called. "Because I don't want to shoot you either."

"I know why you're here."

It was hard to tell, but Mattie thought she heard a sob at the end of Eve's statement. Maybe a light touch would be best to neutralize the situation. "We found the hunting party. Tyler said you'd be up here. We didn't want you to worry, so I came to get you. There's no need to be afraid. Put the gun down."

"I'm not afraid. But I'm not going with you."

A scuttling sound followed by rocks clattering came from within yards. Mattie peered around the edge of her boulder, and the sight took her breath away. Eve crouched farther along the edge of the cliff, a pistol in her hand. Thunder boomed overhead and lightning cracked, its crooked slash striking the forest directly behind Eve. She held the gun low, pointed at the ground, and she was looking over the edge as if gauging the sheer drop.

Mattie rose a few inches, showing her face. "Eve, what are you doing? Come away from the cliff."

Eve waved the gun in her direction. "Stay back. There's no reason for you to die today."

Eve's cheeks were tear-stained, her expression desperate. A pulse of fear surged through Mattie, more for the girl's life than for her own. "Eve," she said, "come away from the edge. There's no reason for *you* to die today either."

Pointing the gun at Mattie, Eve shook her head, sobbing quietly. "I know why you came to get me."

Robo had obeyed her command to stay, but he felt like a spring coiled beneath her hands. Releasing him was not an option. Even if the girl didn't shoot, his takedown would push both him and Eve over the edge. "Eve, just put down your gun. Let's talk."

Eve used her free hand to brush tears from her cheeks. "I *am* sorry I did it. Tell my mom and dad that, okay? I just thought, well . . ."

As Eve's voice trailed off, she glanced down and edged to within inches of the brink. Mattie's only option was to keep her talking. "Did what, Eve?"

"You know. That's the reason you came after me."

Robo crouched and struggled forward enough to peer around their boulder, sending Mattie's heartbeat into overdrive. "Stay," Mattie told him again, grasping his harness and then showing Eve her empty hand. "I don't have a gun on you, Eve. Put yours down so that Robo doesn't try to take it from you. If he gets away from me, he'll knock both of you off the cliff."

"I don't want to hurt him."

"I know. But he's trained to protect. Please, just put down the gun."

Eve hesitated. "Don't come any closer or I'll jump."

"I understand. If you put down the gun, we'll both stay where we are."

Much to Mattie's relief, Eve knelt and placed the gun on the ground. Some of Robo's tension melted away, and Mattie allowed him to move forward enough to watch Eve before telling him to lie down and stay. Now, if she could just keep the girl from jumping to her death.

"He's a good dog," Eve said, watching Robo with sorrowful eyes. "I saw you coming."

"I figured you did." Mattie kept one hand on Robo's harness and the other where Eve could see it, feeling like she dared not move an inch.

"I didn't know it would hurt Kasey so much." Eve touched her chest over her heart. "Killing Nate."

It seemed like Eve wanted to confess, and Mattie was afraid it was because she planned to kill herself. *Keep her talking.* "Why did that surprise you?"

"They fought all the time. A few months ago, Kasey wanted to divorce him. Then, after he was dead, she put him on a pedestal."

Now that the gun was out of the girl's hand, Robo had settled, and Mattie felt she could concentrate fully on Eve. "That's often the case."

Eve knelt at the overhang, her shoulders slumped. "Tell Kasey I'm sorry I hurt her."

"You need to tell Kasey yourself."

Eve winced. "But I'm not sorry Nate's gone. He's been nothing but trouble for Mom and Dad."

"What do you mean?"

"He's the reason the ranch is failing. At least his insurance money can save it now. Kasey had nothing to do with his death . . . tell that to the investigators. There's nothing to keep them from paying her."

Mattie doubted Nate was the sole reason for the Redmans' financial problems, and she wondered if, under these circumstances, the insurance company would contest the benefit payout. But she didn't want to bring that up, and the longer she could keep Eve from jumping, the better the chance she would change her mind. "How did you know about the insurance policy, Eve?"

"I heard Kasey tell Mom they planned to borrow money on it to pay them back, but it wasn't enough to save the ranch. Besides, Kasey was crying her heart out about Nate running up their credit card bills, too. He was causing more trouble than he was worth." Eve scooted closer to the edge as she wept. Thunder cracked overhead, and huge raindrops splashed down, splattering on the rocks. "Dad loves our home. He grew up there. I couldn't stand by and let the bank take it away from him. Not after everything he's been through lately."

Mattie hoped the girl's father would be the key to changing her mind. "Just think how heartbroken your dad would be if he lost you, Eve. Don't put him through that."

Eve rocked back and forth, hands fisted against her thighs. "He'll suffer no matter what I do. I've made such a mess of things. Everyone will be better off if I'm dead."

"These are your parents you're talking about, Eve. Losing you is the worst thing that could happen to them." Mattie judged the distance between them to be about twenty feet. Too far for her to be able to grab Eve and hold on, when it would take only a split second for the girl to lean to the side and fall. "Don't make your parents suffer the death of their youngest child."

"It wasn't just Nate; it was Wilson, too." Eve stared at Mattie as if looking right through her. "I tried to pin it on him, but I screwed that up."

Though the rainfall drenched Mattie within seconds, the dead look in Eve's eyes chilled her more than the storm. Maybe if she tried to align herself with Eve in some way, it would help. "Why did you want to set Wilson up, Eve? Help me understand."

"He wanted to cheat Dad out of the ranch. Prey on my parents when they were down and try to get them to sell their home. The only home my dad's ever known." A spark of anger seemed to put some life back into her eyes. "Tyler and I told him to back off, but he said he planned to talk to Mom. I thought if I could send him to prison for Nate's murder, that would get him out of our way."

"How did you try to pin it on Wilson, Eve?"

"I took his gun from his car when he came out to see Tyler at the ranch, and I planted it in the ditch beside Nate's van before I set it on fire. I also left the Molotov cocktail supplies outside his office. I thought my plan was going to work, but then it all started falling apart."

Mattie projected her voice over the clatter of the rain. "What do you mean?"

"Wilson called Tyler and accused him of stealing his gun to shoot Nate. It made Tyler so mad. Of course he denied it. Tyler didn't know I was the one who took that stupid gun." Eve hung her head, shaking it woefully. "It scared me. I figured it was just a matter of time until Wilson pointed the finger at me. Or worse yet, he'd point it at Tyler. I wanted to make Wilson's death look like a suicide, but I botched it."

Mattie figured the girl wasn't used to planning a murder, and she didn't seem to be thinking clearly. "What do you mean, botched it?"

Eve's mouth tightened with scorn. "I called Wilson, told him to come up to see the tiger. When he got there, he was all excited. Brought his binoculars. But then I panicked and shot him in the chest instead of the head. Nobody shoots themselves in the chest. I planned to put *that* gun in his hand, but ended up keeping it instead." Eve gestured toward the gun she'd put down on the rock.

"Where did you get this gun, Eve?"

"I've had it since I was in high school. Dad taught me how to shoot, and I used it for target practice."

Mattie's mind went in two different directions. One, they now had a murder weapon to match to the slug Robo had found at Wilson's crime scene. And two, how could she talk this girl off the ledge?

"I'm curious, Eve. Why did you burn Nate's van?"

"I didn't want the stuff he'd been doing to fall back on Kasey. She had nothing to do with his crap."

"What stuff?"

Eve shook her head and glanced away before answering. "Bringing in that tiger to hunt. Running drugs and God only knows what else across country for months."

The breaking of eye contact was enough to make Mattie believe Eve knew about all the trafficking activity, and if she knew, then Mattie believed Kasey knew about it as well. But now wasn't the time to bring it up.

"Eve, listen to me, okay? What I'm going to say is very important. Everything you've done has been to try to help your parents. I can tell how much you love them. But if you kill yourself, it would be the worst thing you could ever do to them."

Eve straightened, staring at Mattie with strained eyes, reddened from crying, her blond hair plastered to her head in the rain.

This seemed to be the only statement that brought Eve out of herself, and Mattie decided to press the point. "Parents love their kids more than they love property. Your mom has faced tough times this year. Don't give her something she can't bear. And I've seen the way your dad looks at you. He loves you dearly. Don't hurt him, Eve. Don't make him endure that kind of pain on top of what he's suffered this past year."

Eve bowed her head and sobbed, covering her face in her hands. Cautiously, Mattie rose from behind the boulder. "Let me take you to them, Eve. Let's go to your parents."

Eve extended her hand, and Mattie took that as permission. She hurried forward and knelt close enough to gather Eve into her arms and snatch her away from the ledge. As the girl sagged against her, Mattie held her and rocked backward, scooting away from Eve's gun.

They sat that way in the driving rain while Eve wept for what seemed like a very long time, huddled together on the hard stone. *The things we do for love*, Mattie thought as she gently rocked the sobbing girl back and forth.

She wanted to assure Eve that everything was going to be all right, but nothing would ever be the same for her again. Eve loved her parents and her home, but her reasoning had been driven by anger and hate.

Eve had lost everything, trading her blessings for a life in prison.

THIRTY

It was dusk by the time Mattie and Eve arrived at the spot where Brody waited with the captives. On their hike down the mountain, Eve had at first chattered, like she was driven to talk. She told Mattie about her hopes and dreams for the ranch, how she wanted to use her education to help turn it around so it could support not only her parents but also their three kids. Mattie let her talk, even though it became painful to hear. If only the girl had stuck to legal means for producing income rather than criminal ones. It was a relief when Eve apparently talked herself out and fell silent.

Robo stayed close to Mattie as they traveled downhill, but he was not averse to the occasional petting from Eve. His presence seemed to be a comfort to the girl, and she called him to her whenever they paused to rest. His work was done, so Mattie allowed it, because she found herself feeling sorry for Eve even though she told herself not to. After all, the girl had confessed to a double murder. Truthfully, she felt sorry for the entire family. Eve was completely right about one point: she'd made a mess of things.

At the station, Stella and McCoy took Eve into an interrogation room to get her statement while Mattie took Robo back to her office to feed him. The three hunters and Flint had been booked into jail to await charges, which would be sorted out once Glenna returned from Colorado Springs. Mattie wondered if Glenna would go easy on Flint in exchange for his help and testimony.

After Robo ate his fill and bedded down on his cushion, Mattie sat at her computer and wrote her own report of what had happened on the mountain. It was late by the time she finished and Stella entered the room to find her. Robo was curled up on his cushion, lightly snoring.

"Does he always snore like that?" Stella asked as she settled into a chair she pulled up from Johnson's desk.

"Sometimes," Mattie said. "He's really tired tonight."

"I bet." Stella studied her. "You look like you've had better days yourself."

Mattie brushed her cheek, touching the scratches and the sore spot on her cheekbone. She hadn't checked a mirror yet, but she figured she was sporting a few bruises. "How did the statement go?"

Stella sighed. "She waived her right to an attorney and confessed to both murders."

There were a few details Mattie still wanted to know. "I assume Kasey and Nate were using a trip to Nebraska as a cover story with the family when really he was up in the BLM releasing that tiger, right?"

"Yep." Stella released a heavy sigh. "I took the bait on that one the night we met Kasey."

Mattie admitted that she had taken the bait, too, and she felt Stella's frustration. "So how did Eve get Nate out to the county road where she killed him?"

"She tried hard not to implicate Kasey, but when I told her we already knew Kasey had been involved with the tiger hunt, she opened up enough to tell me that Kasey confided to her that she and Nate had been fighting last week. Evidently Nate wanted out and threatened to not go through with the hunt. Eve decided to take matters into her own hands. She called him, told him her car had broken down, asked him to pick her up, and that's when she shot him."

It sounded cold-blooded, but Eve's story had indicated feelings of resentment and anger; she had seized the opportunity and acted on it. "What about the gloves? Why a pair of men's gloves?"

"She grabbed a random pair. She doesn't know if they're Tyler's or her dad's."

"DNA will tell us that. I guess it doesn't matter as much now, but can we find the glove that matches the one we have?"

"She says she burned the matching glove in their trash barrel. We'll have to go out and see if any of it's left. She was pretty tearful through the interview, but when she realized we'd found the glove, she really poured on the waterworks. It tore her up to think she'd accidentally planted evidence to implicate her dad or her brother."

"Yeah, but her DNA will be inside that glove, too." Mattie shared a little bit of what worried her. "When you compare her intentions with the crime scenes, you can see she was disorganized. It makes me wonder about her reasoning and what kind of stress she's been under during the past months."

Stella rubbed the back of her neck. "Sheriff McCoy called her parents and has allowed them to see her. They were devastated, as you can imagine, but they say they're going to hire an attorney. I suppose that's something that will be sorted out by someone other than us. It's our job to have the evidence and statements in line when they're needed. We've already got a warrant to retrieve clothing and her boots, cell phone and records, a cast of tire prints from her car, and anything else we can find to back up her statement. Sheriff McCoy and I will head out there now to execute it."

"Do you need my help?"

"No, you've done enough today. You need to go home."

After Stella left, Mattie texted Cole to tell him she was getting ready to leave work. He replied right away: DO YOU WANT TO MEET AT YOUR PLACE OR MINE?

After this long, hard day, the one thing she wanted was to feel his arms around her. She knew he didn't like leaving the kids alone at night, so she told him she would come over. It was shortly after midnight when she parked at the edge of his yard.

He opened the front door and strode down the sidewalk, meeting her at her car door as she stepped down from the driver's seat. He took her in his arms to hold her close, and she felt like she'd come home.

But the closeness made her think of his friend. "How's Garrett?"

"A little better. The doctor thinks it's possible his vision will clear with time. He'll probably come home in a day or two."

The thought of Garrett and Leslie at home together after such a scare made her teary. "That's such a relief. And what about the tiger?"

"He's stable. He came out from under the anesthesia without problems and is resting quietly in a secure area at the zoo. The bullet caused a lot of damage, but they cleaned it up and decided to leave the leg until they see if the shoulder heals. Maybe he'll get by without having to lose it."

"I hope so."

"Me too." Cole put his hand under her chin and tilted her head back to examine her face in the moonlight. "Did you get those scratches tended to?"

"I washed them. It's nothing."

"I guess I'll get used to you mixing it up with the bad guys someday."

Cole bent his head, and Mattie welcomed his kiss. The kiss was deep and long and it took her breath away, but it no longer felt confusing; instead it left her with a warm sense that she was loved. There were no more secrets to hide from him, and still . . . he loved her.

After the kiss, Cole spoke quietly against her lips. "I love you, Mattie."

With her lips against his, she was finally able to say it, though in a whisper. "I love you too."

"You don't know how happy it makes me to hear you say that."

She shrugged inside his embrace, not sure what to say. "I guess I'm a slow learner."

Robo barked from inside the Explorer.

A short chuckle rumbled in Cole's chest beneath her ear. "I don't even want to know how I stack up against him in your affections." He paused for a moment. "Did you eat dinner?"

"No, but I'm not hungry."

"Too tired."

"No, it's been an eventful day. We solved both our homicides, but there's not much to celebrate."

"Let's get Robo out of the back and go inside where we can talk."

Mattie leaned in and released the door latch at the front of Robo's cage. He bailed through, jumping down to the ground to circle Cole's feet, his tail wagging. Cole thumped his side, told him what a good dog he was, and then took Mattie's hand to lead her up the sidewalk to the porch. Robo darted in front.

Belle and Bruno greeted them at the door with exuberance, and it took a few minutes to get the dogs sorted. Cole led the way to the kitchen. "Did Robo eat?"

"I fed him at the station."

"How about some hot chocolate for you? Does that sound good?"

"Actually, it does."

It took a while for Mattie to summarize everything that had happened after Cole left with the tiger.

When she told him about Eve's confession, he made a sound of exasperation. "What a shame."

Grim faced, he handed her a cup of steaming hot cocoa. "So will Kasey be arrested?"

"We have no evidence against her yet, but we'll investigate her on suspicion of drug and wildlife trafficking. Even though both she and Eve will deny it."

"And Tyler's in jail, on hold pending the wildlife charges?"

"Along with Flint, Ben Underwood, and Zach Irving."

"Poor Lillian and Doyle." Cole shook his head, staring at the floor for a moment while he absently sipped his chocolate. "Let's go sit in the living room where it's more comfortable."

He led her to a seat beside him on the sofa, placing his arm on top of the cushion at her back. With the warm cup between both hands, she nestled against him while Bruno and Belle went to their dog beds. Robo lingered at Mattie's feet, but with a bit of encouragement, he went to the extra cushion, circled a couple of times before plopping down, and opened his mouth in a squeaky yawn with a great deal of pink tongue curling against his sharp canines.

"That's good, Robo," Mattie said. "Time to sleep." He placed his head between his paws and heaved a sigh.

"It's hard to believe Eve Redman could get that desperate," Cole said. "I mean, that ranch is special to the Redmans, but to go to the extreme to kill for it?"

"I think there's more to that family dynamic than we know at this point. Eve holds a lot of anger and resentment against Nate and perhaps some misplaced blame for the fore-closure. I think their inability to make ends meet has more to do with the kids growing up. Foreclosure doesn't happen overnight, and they'd already sent Tyler and Kasey to college. Now Eve. I think the family needed more income than they could generate."

"Not to mention that cattle prices have been down the past few years. Family-owned farms and ranches struggle to compete with agricultural corporations. Sometimes I worry about my own parents in today's times."

They sat and sipped their chocolate for a few minutes while Mattie thought about Cole's family, his parents' connection to the land, and the different choices for careers their children had made. "What will happen to your parents' ranch when your dad needs to retire?"

"We never talked about it, but they might already be thinking about what they would do. I suppose their land could be the only retirement investment they have. I really don't know."

"Would you want to start working on the ranch?"

She could feel Cole cringe beside her. "It tears me up to think about my parents selling their land, but I wouldn't want to go into ranching. I'm happy being a vet."

"How about Jessie?"

"I think she's happy with her life in Denver and her career as an attorney, but if she wants to take up ranching, I hope she'll say." Cole remained silent for a minute before sharing his thoughts. "Ranching is a hard way of life. You battle the elements to raise your livestock and your crops, and you tend to your animals and plants three hundred and sixty-five days a year. You work outside during rain, sleet, and snow to give your animals food, water, and shelter, and you don't even know what a family vacation is. Your income fluctuates depending on the agricultural markets, and you never know when things are going to tank. But the lifestyle gets under your skin and into your bloodstream. You love the land and your animals, and you want to pass it on to your family."

Mattie nodded and leaned her head against Cole's arm. They sat while she digested Cole's words, and she assumed that, like her, he was thinking of how they applied to Doyle and

Lillian. And even to their daughter Eve, now in jail facing a prison sentence. After several minutes, she spoke. "I guess I should go home and clean up so that I can get some sleep. Back to work for both of us again in the morning, right?"

Cole tightened his arm around her. "You must be stiff and sore. Do you want to soak in the tub here?"

Mattie tipped her face so that she could study his. He leaned down and kissed her, a kiss that was tender and full of promise. It had been a long time since Mattie had known such intimacy. She hated for the kiss to end.

Cole lifted his lips to speak. "No strings attached on the offer of the tub, but I want you to stay the night. I'm in this relationship for the long haul, and I want what's best for you. Your decision won't change my love, one way or the other."

Her heartbeat quickened. "The kids?"

"The kids and Jessie are staying with my parents tonight."

Mattie touched his cheek, and he turned into her palm to press his lips against it. "I say yes."

Without another word, Cole stood and took her hand to lead her up the staircase.

★ ★ ★

For the life of her, Mattie couldn't sleep. She rose on one elbow to study Cole's face by the light of the moon shining through the open curtain. His features were relaxed in sleep, his lips parted slightly.

His bedroom window was closed, something she couldn't stand, but she didn't want to awaken him by opening it. Noiselessly, she slipped from between the sheets, put on a clean T-shirt he'd laid out for her, picked up her cell phone from the bedside table, and padded down the stairs with bare feet. Immediately alert, Robo and Bruno lifted their heads when she entered the den.

"Go back to sleep, you two. It's just me," she murmured as she sank onto the couch, picking up the chocolate fleece throw from the back and covering herself with it. She leaned into the couch pillows and considered going home, but decided against it. She didn't want Cole to misunderstand.

Her sleeplessness had nothing to do with Cole; it was her problem. He'd been perfect—tender, decent, and loving. What passed between them might not have meant a change in their relationship for him, but now she loved him more than ever. And the excitement of being with him had resulted in a restlessness she couldn't define.

On one hand, she'd never felt such joy in her life; on the other, she'd never been this terrified.

What if she didn't know how to handle this heady love she felt for Cole and his kids? What if she messed up? What if she lost him? She supposed these were questions she'd need to talk over with her shrink.

She didn't want to think about the Redman case anymore, and her mind needed a distraction from her relationship with Cole. Since she hadn't had time to check her email all day, she decided to pass the time looking at it. Maybe she would grow drowsy enough to fall asleep on the couch.

An email from the ancestry database she'd submitted her DNA to was buried in the middle of her incoming list. It took her by surprise, even though she'd expected to hear from them for days. She squinted at it while she hovered her finger over the screen, afraid of what it might say. Had they drawn a blank while searching for family matches for her?

She tapped the screen and took in the email at a glance, scrolling to the end for results. Her heart tripped as she went back to read it more carefully.

Cole charged down the stairs, headed for the kitchen. "Mattie!"

"I'm in here, Cole." Clutching her cell phone, she stood and met him at the doorway.

He swept her into his arms. "You were gone. I thought you'd left."

"No, I just couldn't sleep." She squeezed out of his grip far enough to lift her cell phone to where he could read it. "Look. I heard about my DNA."

Still holding her with one arm, Cole took the phone, manipulating the screen with his thumb. "They've found a match! An immediate family member. A sibling?"

"That's what it looks like."

"How in the world? A full sibling. Older or younger?"

"It doesn't say. I have to email them to find out."

All three dogs, Belle included, jumped up from their beds to gather at their feet, frolicking with each other in excitement as they soaked up their humans' mood.

Mattie pressed her hands against Cole's chest and leaned back so she could see his face. "I have a brother or sister."

"And maybe they'll know something about your mom."

Her heart was full to overflowing, and Mattie couldn't speak. She hugged Cole as hard as she could, hoping to convey how thrilled she was that he was here to share this glorious news with her. And how much hope she held in her heart for the future.

Acknowledgments

To the readers of the Timber Creek K-9 Mysteries, thank you so much for your interest in the series and for sharing your time with me. I appreciate that you allow me to take you on a journey to Timber Creek each year.

Thank you to the professionals who gave their time and knowledge to assist with this story's procedural content: Lieutenant Glenn J. Wilson (Ret.); Nancy Howard, District Wildlife Manager (retired); and Charles Mizushima, DVM. Any misinterpretations or fictional enhancements of the information they provided are mine alone.

As always, I'm deeply grateful for my publishing team. Huge thanks to my agent, Terrie Wolf of AKA Literary Management, for her constant support; to publicist Maryglenn McCombs for helping me spread the news about the series; to my editor, Nike Power, for helping me find this mystery within the manuscript; to copyeditor Rachel Keith for her attention to detail; and to publisher Matt Martz, marketing and editorial assistant Ashley Di Dio, assistant editor Jenny Chen, and the talented staff at Crooked Lane Books for supporting this series.

A special thank you to readers Scott Graham, author of the National Parks Mysteries; Kathleen Donnelly; and Susan Hemphill for their help with early drafts.

Love and gratitude to friends and family who've encouraged me along the way; to my husband, Charlie, for help with planning and plotting; and to my daughters, Sarah and Beth, and son-in-law, Adam, for their input and love. You all mean the world to me!